*The
Jeweled
Daughter*

RANDOM HOUSE 🏠 NEW YORK

Anne Maybury

The Jeweled Daughter

The
Jeweled
Daughter

I

THE LATE SEPTEMBER SUNLIGHT, shafting between the tall buildings, lit up the Hong Kong waterfront. I was in my favorite city in my favorite month of the year. And yet, as we left the wide streets and drove inland, crossing the island, I felt that only the car was at peace with itself.

Few people were rich enough to use a car like a Rolls in these teeming, overcrowded streets, but Viscountess Theodora Paradine saw herself royally and, as with queens, her way through cities was regal.

The hood of the great car nosed out of the city, past the university and out around the hills toward Aberdeen, the fishing town where the junks, the homes of the fishing people, nestled flank to flank on the edge of the South China Sea.

I knew by the set of the chauffeur's back that he had resented Theodora's cutting remark about a smear on the polished door of the car. But like all those who worked for her, Ah Lee-ming put up with her trivial, lacerating complaints because she paid him so well.

Theodora herself was more restless than usual. Her thin, bejeweled hands kept jerking and weaving, and her cold, water-light eyes continually swiveled around toward me, as if, now that the moment of confrontation with a stranger was near, she was as nervous as I.

I watched the light play on one of her rings—a ruby set with sapphires, for which only two months ago I had bid at Christie's auction sale in London.

Theodora had said, "I want that ring, Sarah. I hear that Templemayer is after it for an unknown client. Well, just outbid him. I have an old score to settle with that man, so I don't mind how high you go."

I was twenty-six years old, small and dark, and although a qualified gemologist, not even remotely up among the great experts like Templemayer. The fact that I outbid him was not due to my brilliance or my experience. It was merely that I had had my orders and I had obeyed them and, bidding outrageously, won for Theodora

Paradine the ring which had once belonged to the last Tsarina of Russia.

That triumph had produced a newspaper article about me. My photograph, taken at my worktable in my studio, showed my hair wildly untidy; the topaz ring with the curved gold shoulders which I had designed for myself was very much in evidence.

"Sarah Brent," the article had explained, "is a young gemologist with a brilliant future. She has already won the De Beers Award for the most promising newcomer to her profession and the Handsworth Prize for design. She has also made a study of jade and has become an expert. Born in Hong Kong, where her father was in government service, she had, as she puts it, 'been brought up with jade on my doorstep.' She is married to the orthopedic surgeon Marius Brent. Our congratulations to this most attractive and clever young woman."

But that young woman was at the moment pressed back in a corner of Theodora's custom-built Rolls, cushioned in cream upholstery and trying to reassure herself that three people in a powerful car would be safe from any possible attack out on the lonely hills beyond the town.

By my side, Theodora's cream Thai silk suit rustled as she crossed her long legs. I wondered if behind the cool arrogance that was her natural manner she was perhaps regretting the impulse of driving to meet a man in an isolated place, with only his word on the telephone that he had a valuable jade to sell. I wondered, too, if she really believed him when he had told her that he was a cripple and housebound.

I rubbed my arms and felt gooseflesh. The only warm things about me on that autumn afternoon were the pale orange of my dress and the golden glow of my ring.

I had worked for Theodora for nearly two years, long enough to know that if she wanted something—a jewel, a house or a man—her money would get it for her. Inherited wealth from her American father, Bernard Creech, poured in from the silver mines in South America, the phosphates in Florida, the platinum in Alaska. The freely flowing cash was a toy with which Theodora played unendingly —spending, spending . . . "I want, therefore I must have" was the litany of this too-rich woman.

Heaven only knew what she could be leading us into at the end of the journey we were taking across Hong Kong Island, and I was very aware that her blind willfulness to acquire what she wanted had, in the past, led her on equally foolhardy adventures. Once she had personally flown her private plane into a war-torn Middle East because the expert who then represented her refused to go. She had returned to America in triumph, bearing a rare golden Panagia—an icon in the form of a pendant.

I tried to check my alarm about our present mission by shutting my eyes and thinking of things a long way away. But so dominant was Theodora's personality that what I saw with my mind's eye was connected with her. I saw, like paintings on a lavish backdrop, her four homes, and played with the question of which I would choose if it could become mine. I leaned my head back against the high upholstery of the car and saw them, one by one.

Her father's mansion on the East Side of New York—vast and formal, the ground floor turned into a grand suite of offices from which her empire was ruled. The house just off Park Lane in London, an early Georgian gem, with a walled garden full of her favorite flower, the white madonna lily, which she so seldom saw because she was so rarely in England. Her third home was the white terraced Villa Salamander near Antibes. ("I could have bought a château in the Loire, my dear, but it wouldn't have been so accessible for my friends, and they all come to Antibes at some time or other. Salamander is so lovely. I want you to come out some time. I need your advice on some *basse-taille* enameled snuffboxes I have out there. I inherited them from my grandmother.")

I went to Antibes because she insisted, but refused to value the boxes for her, explaining that I was no expert on enamels. It was while I was there that I realized the complications of so large a fortune for a person like Theodora, who could not leave the business side to her directors and her managers but was always on the telephone, summoning someone, commanding someone.

Her fourth house, the Pavilion of Apricots here in Hong Kong, had been purchased only very recently.

"I wouldn't say you are being the most amusing of companions this afternoon, Sarah." Her voice came fretfully through my wandering thoughts.

"I'm nervous," I said, "and you are too."

She swung toward me, affronted. The sun caught the glittering scroll brooch she wore, which was said to have been originally one of the diamond shoe buckles of the eighteenth-century Duke of Burgundy. Though she was dressed beautifully in current fashion, by Saint Laurent and Givenchy, Theodora Paradine's jewelry often made her a kind of showcase for history.

"My dear Sarah, *I'm* not nervous. Why should I be?"

"Because the whole affair is suspect."

She was still not used to my frankness, since those who surrounded her seldom gave it. "I told the man that I was not bringing a large sum of money with me. Also, he's in a wheelchair and that's why he couldn't come to me. Besides, I have two people to protect me." She glanced at the chauffeur's back. "Although it's a good thing he *is* a cripple, because I doubt if Ah Lee-ming could protect me against a brutal fighter. But nothing is going to happen to us. The money, in cash, is at the house, and not a single Hong Kong dollar is going to be brought here unless you think the jade is worth it."

"This man knows your name, knows you are a collector. He must know, too, that you have lovely jewelry. That brooch you're wearing . . . those rings . . . To him, those would represent a fortune. He may be in a wheelchair, but he could have someone with him. And it's possible he is using this jade as a bait just to get you into the hills."

"For a few pieces of jewelry?"

"Men have attacked for less."

"There are three of us."

"And how do you know there won't be three of them to meet us—and all armed, at that?"

Theodora laughed. "Oh, Sarah, I thought you had more courage."

I said, stirred to impatience, "It's a matter of being realistic."

"Then change your ideas, because you're coming all the way. There'll be no waiting for me in the car. You're the expert and I'm relying on you to see that this jade is what the man says it is—always presuming, of course, that you would know."

It was an insolent afterthought, although I doubted it was deliberate. Theodora had never learned to temper her spoken word in consideration of the feelings of others.

I sat, quiet but unrelaxed, remembering Felix Revillon, the man to whom I had been apprenticed after qualifying as a gemologist. He had said, "You have chosen a profession which is peppered with rich women coveting the Koh-i-noor diamond or Charlemagne's sapphire. You won't have an easy time satisfying them with less. You'll need patience and tact."

I had needed both, and never more so than when I began to work for Theodora Paradine.

I watched her as she leaned forward, looking ahead. I guessed her to be past forty, a woman beautifully preserved and yet with a face on which, for all the expert beauty treatment, were etched the first faint lines set there by an inner hardness and total ambition.

I had read so much about her. *Vogue* ran an article on the Villa

Salamander at Antibes, with a magnificent colored photograph of Theodora in white silk seated on a crimson sofa. *House Beautiful* had featured her London home—very small, very elegant. All the "glossies" had, at one time or another, described her, invariably calling her "the beautiful Viscountess Theodora Paradine."

That was lip service paid to a rich woman. In actual fact she was somewhat plain, but she contrived to defeat her lack of good looks by being deliberately unique—something which, rich as she was, she could do magnificently.

No one could be under any illusion that her bright mahogany hair was natural or that the curves of her wide lips were not accentuated by make-up. Her nose was her most beautiful feature, the straight Grecian line running smoothly from forehead to tip.

Unlike my own family—my father and I had remained close after my mother's death—the Creeches seemed to be a family supremely disinterested in one another. Or it could be that her relatives were either rich enough not to curry favor with her or so poor that she had shrugged them off.

Two husbands had given her titles. The first, the Marquis de Tasman, had been killed hunting in the Amazon. Her second husband was Count Viktor Paradine, who had returned after the divorce to his mother's Austrian castle, where he was living very comfortably on the fat allowance Theodora had settled on him.

"I had to get free of him," she told me once in an expansive mood. "He liked to play practical jokes. He still does. I believe he gives his guests trick eggs for breakfast." Her tone was harsh with disdain.

The third husband was Oliver Farache, whose family home was a small but beautiful Elizabethan house in Wiltshire. In order to pay for the upkeep, his father took in paying weekend guests, and such was the charm of the house, the food and the wine that the family made an excellent living out of it.

When Theodora told me the name of her third husband, I said, "Of course. Cadence Manor is their family home. I've been there."

She had cut me short, not interested in what I had to say. "Oliver was the nicest of the three of my husbands, Sarah. But I don't use his name. I enjoyed my titles, and so I chose to revert to the Paradine name when I left Oliver. Nobody can stop me—after all, Viktor Paradine has never married again. He daren't—or I stop his lovely money. His English father is dead and there is no male heir. The title is more or less defunct. But I enjoy it. It's an entrée to so much, for the Paradines are linked with some of the great families of Europe."

I wondered if any of her so-called friends really felt anything for

Theodora. Gushing friendship could so easily be bought from those who looked ahead to a time, when dead, Theodora Paradine might leave behind a golden will. In the meantime they enjoyed the rich hospitality of her homes and the patronage of her name.

She had once said to me, in a torrent of rage, that the only people she could trust were her servants. Luckily, there were plenty of them.

Everyone—even the bravest and the strongest—has an Achilles heel. After two years of working for Theodora, I knew hers. She hated to be alone. She kept a permanent staff in all her homes, and when she traveled from house to house she took with her Célie, her personal maid, and a young girl who worked in New York as assistant to her social secretary. Unkind people said that she chose Janet Shield because she was efficient and had no idea how to make the best of her homely appearance and Theodora wanted no competition from someone more attractive than herself.

Janet had recently been taken ill and was recuperating in Boston from an appendix operation. Here in Hong Kong, Célie was coping as best she could with Theodora's mail with the help of two small, pretty and intelligent Cantonese girls who worked out of an office in Connaught Road.

Husbandless and childless, Theodora had to find another way to carry her name forward, to attain some kind of immortality. This was what she was working for obsessively, and this was what I was helping her do.

Each of her beautiful houses was a museum in which she displayed her rare possessions—the paintings, the bronzes, the icons and the jades which she had sent experts across the world to buy for her. The beauty of each object was only of secondary importance to her, their acquisition easy, since she had such vast wealth. The grand plan, the marvelous dream, was that when she died these houses would be permanent showplaces for her collections. The Theodora Paradine Museums would carry her name through to future generations.

On the spring day two years ago when Theodora had summoned me to her London house, I was quite certain that all she would want was a valuation for some piece of jewelry. Nothing prepared me for the initial shock as I walked into the paneled drawing room. Theodora, seated in a Louis Quinze chair, as upright and forbidding as a Victorian duchess, first looked at my hands. "You are married."

"Yes."

"Your husband wouldn't object to your traveling abroad for me— that is, of course, if I decide that you are sufficiently qualified to work for me?"

"Oh, Marius, my husband, has his own absorbing career."

She gave me another dubious look.

"You're very young. Are you tough enough for the competitive, unsentimental game of outbidding experts?"

I stood silently, making no comment because I had no idea what she was talking about.

"Turn around," she said. "Look in that mirror!"

I looked.

"You're so small, aren't you?"

I bit back a retort that I wasn't being interviewed for a modeling job.

"But I've often found that small people are assertive," she said. "That's what is needed when you're dealing in a tough market. And I hear good reports of your designs."

"Thank you."

"Sit down. I have work for you."

I sat in a chair that faced a mirrored panel, so that I had to see myself unless I turned so that my back was half to this imperious woman.

So this is you, Sarah Brent, seeing yourself in a stranger's looking glass. Hair brown and swept back into short swirls around my neck; eyes caught in the light from the window, blue-green. Small and slim and wearing a russet dress.

"There is a pendant," said Theodora Paradine, tapping a catalog she held in her lap, "which is up for sale. I want you to bid for it." She opened the thick, glossy book and turned it toward me. "You see?"

The photograph on the page looked like a hen's egg that had been painted green and decorated with crimson and gold. But I read the description below and held my breath in alarm.

I was looking at the great Gioconda emerald, which had belonged to the Hapsburgs at the time of their power in Europe. Staring at the picture of the famous jewel, I found Theodora Paradine's challenge terrifying and irresistible. In a kind of dream I heard myself say that of course I would go with her to see the emerald. I didn't dare think further than that . . .

That night I told Marius. He had said enthusiastically, "You really are moving among the 'greats,' aren't you, Sarah? I'm delighted. Good luck. Just one piece of advice though. Keep your head."

"Of course," I had said. That pendant had been my very first triumph.

Suddenly Theodora's voice, coming from beside me in the car, startled me back to the present. "Now, remember, Sarah. When we get to the place where this man lives, we must bargain. These people expect it."

"Bargain?" I had turned bemused eyes on her.

"The jade. The jade . . ." she nearly shouted at me. "Really, Sarah, where *were* your thoughts?"

"Back at our very first meeting in London," I said, "when you broke it to me that I was to bid for the Gioconda stone."

"Ah, yes. You did well then. I hope you'll be just as successful with this jade we are to see."

I held on to my secret thought. I had done well because there had been no limit to what Theodora would pay for the Hapsburg emerald. Inwardly, while I had made my bids at the sale, I had felt almost sick with nerves. I had had the same feeling recently when I had bid for the Tsarina's ring.

I was nervous now, but this was a fear of something unknown. I stared ahead of me at the tall concrete apartment blocks of Aberdeen, and the junks clustered around the large restaurant boats with their long terraces and peaked roofs. The junk people—the sea peasants—were milling around the waterfront.

A child got in the way of the car, laughing at us.

"Why don't they teach their children discipline?" Theodora said impatiently.

I wondered what discipline Theodora had known as a child. And then I said, "There's a challenge about defying danger. I think the little girl felt that way."

The hills beyond the village were very green and very quiet. I wondered where the crippled stranger, Ch'i Pai-shih, awaited us. And I shivered.

II

THIS JOURNEY we were taking was the result of a telephone call early that morning. Theodora had swept into her drawing room, where I was checking some bronzes for a new valuation.

"I have just had a call from a man who has a jade he wants to sell," she said. "He tells me it's from the Sung period and says it's rare. I'm inclined to believe he's speaking the truth. So I want it. *Jade* . . ." She stressed the word for my benefit, knowing how irresistible it was to me.

"Who is this man?"

Her shoulders twitched—a characteristic gesture when she was irritated at being questioned. "I don't know. All I *do* know is that if this jade is what he says it is, then I must have it. Anyway, I intend to see it. He lives beyond Aberdeen, in a hut in the hills."

"You usually buy from reputable dealers," I protested.

"Oh, don't worry. I shall take you along with me to see that he doesn't cheat me."

"Someone rings you up out of the blue and tells you that he has a valuable jade for sale? If he's genuine, why doesn't he come here?"

"My dear Sarah, I make efforts when I want something. And you must know by now that valuable art pieces are sometimes found in unexpected places."

"But not in shacks on lonely hillsides—"

"You know perfectly well that thousands of Chinese poured into Hong Kong at the time of the Uprising. Some of them have probably brought treasures that have been in their families for centuries, and are now selling them one by one as they need the money."

"He wouldn't wait," I protested, "until all he can afford to live in is a hillside hut before he sells something valuable, however much it might break his heart to get rid of the jade. Stark hunger doesn't bow to family sentiment, and he must have known hunger before he reached this stage of living!"

"I intend to see that jade," she had said. "And we have to watch out for a man at one of the end stalls holding up a blue umbrella. He will tell us how to find the place."

The car swung violently around an old Chinese weaving across the road on a bicycle. I watched him turn and grin at us, showing one bright gold tooth. That tooth could be his entire wealth, his careful savings there in his mouth where no one could steal it from him. And he looked so happy.

I glanced at Theodora. I wasn't a sentimentalist, believing that simple poverty brought happiness. But neither did great wealth. It was fine to collect beautiful things—I would have liked to be able to own some rare jade myself—but there is no response in a jeweled medallion or a lapis lazuli vase. Only human contact can warm and support and satisfy. Theodora surely needed that, as I did . . . I did . . . I checked my thoughts. Even so, behind the thought, the name was in my mind, in my heart and in those terrible longings that were, for those who loved, unending.

Marius . . . Marius, whom I had married on a blazing, joyful impulse, and who had left me. Marius, who was also on the island . . .

I forced myself to stop thinking of him, and instead wondered about the jade Theodora was to be offered by this unknown man. White jade or lavender, kingfisher blue or cinnabar red—I loved them all. But however beautiful and rare the pieces I might handle, none would ever be as precious to me as the translucent emerald-green jade which had been known only for about two hundred years and was in fact not a native of China, but of Upper Burma, the rare and lovely *fei ts'ui*.

The car slid between the apartment blocks and the vast village of junks and yachts. At one time the people who had their permanent homes on the boats were called the "egg people" because they paid their taxes in eggs. How changed was my world of Hong King since Father first came to live there . . .

We came to a row of stalls, most of them shaded by p'engs, the straw awnings stretched on bamboo poles.

"Now"—Theodora gathered up her purse—"now for finding this man. At least he told me his name."

"Ch'i Pai-shih," I said. "But to give a name means nothing."

"I choose to see it as identification." My suspicion annoyed her.

Ah Lee-ming stopped the car and was opening the door for Theodora. Immediately the reek of drying fish swept toward us, and from the boats came a cacophony of barking dogs.

"What a teeming place this is," she said, shuddering. "How can these people live without privacy?"

"They don't have much choice; besides, it's the way they like it. The Chinese love families, their own and everyone else's."

She made no further comment, but turned to Ah Lee-ming. "Are you sure this is the place?"

"There is the man holding up a blue umbrella. See, Mistress Lady, he is looking our way."

"Stay by the car," Theodora told her chauffeur, "or this mob of children will be scrambling all over it. But watch us and see where we go. Do you understand? We don't know the man we are going to see. So, if we are longer than half an hour, you must get that man by the ginger stall and find us."

Ah Lee-ming nodded that he understood, and Theodora swept up to the old Chinese and ducked her head to the face under the umbrella. "We are looking for someone called Ch'i Pai-shih. Will you tell us where we can find him?"

The man gave a series of short, funny little nods like a mandarin doll I had been given as a child. "He lives up that road." He stuck out a long, thin finger and pointed to an almost invisible path up the nearest hillside. "You go past the trees and more trees, and then you'll find a hut with a piece of green cloth on a bush. That is Ch'i Pai-shih's place."

The path led through clusters of camphor trees. The way was rough where boulders broke out of the long, wild grasses. Bracken, burnished by the sun and the dryness of the past few weeks, stung our legs.

It was the first time I had ever seen Theodora walking other than on paved streets. I knew that, city-bred as she was, she hated every step of that uneven track, and that the glory of the scene below us, which grew more lovely at every turn of the path, meant nothing to her. In the distance the island was like a shimmering shell in a setting of blue-velvet water. My father used to say that Hong Kong held an eternal love affair with the sea.

We brushed past a clump of gordonias and for a moment all my qualms as to what might lie ahead vanished as I looked and marveled at the golden bush.

"How lovely it is."

"Yes," said Theodora, barely glancing at it, and pointed. "Look, there's the place. That brown hut up there. Can't you see something green hanging from a bush?"

The track was so well marked, I was certain that groups of refugees had settled there after the Chinese revolution, building their shacks and their lean-tos. These must have been well cleared when the government rehoused the families in tall apartment blocks, for all that remained were bare, trodden-down patches of earth among the wild banana and the straggling bamboo.

But climbing by Theodora's side, I felt growing alarm, and when a little sea eagle swooped above us, I started back as if a shot had been fired at me. Only a few steps further on, I slipped on a boulder made treacherous by the fallen seeds of the flame-of-the-forest tree.

Theodora said impatiently, "Oh, do look where you are going!"

"When I was a little girl and Father used to take me walking in these hills," I said, "he told me a lovely story about how the Chinese in the old days would fix small pipes to the pinion feathers of pigeons, so that when they flew, they made music."

"How charming," she said without interest. "Ah, now you can see the actual hut, and it *is* just a hut"—there was the faintest hint of doubt in her voice—"almost hidden in those trees."

I looked behind me, down to the road. Ah Lee-ming was standing, watching us. I raised my hand to him and saw the answering lift of his arm. I felt just a little safer as I followed Theodora past the scrub where Ch'i Pai-shih's sentinel green cloth drooped listlessly in the tranquil afternoon.

In spite of the spoiled earth where the lean-tos had been, the flowers still grew, the lady slipper orchids and the bauhinias smelling like limes. Orioles and parakeets winged above us, cautious and curious about these strangers who walked on the lonely hill.

Theodora was already at the open door of the hut, calling, "Mr. Ch'i? Are you there? Is *anyone* there?"

He appeared in the doorway at her third call. I guessed from his rather tall stature—which was obvious, even in the wheelchair—that he came originally from North China, where the people were taller and paler than the Cantonese. He was probably about thirty, though his emaciated look made his age difficult to judge. There was a long white scar cutting into the left side of his face. The wheelchair in which he sat was so battered that I felt it might collapse if anyone less fragile than Ch'i Pai-shih sat in it.

He swiveled the chair aside for us to enter, and I heard Theodora catch her breath in distaste at the stuffiness of the dim, ill-furnished room.

"If you will sit down—madame," he said hesitantly, as if not knowing how to address this illustrious American with the splendid European title.

Theodora looked about her and scorned the dilapidated cane chair. "We have very little time. You told me you had a jade to sell."

"That is correct." He spoke with careful enunciation. "It is a very valuable piece, very genuine."

"You will allow my assistant to verify that," she snapped.

I peered around the dark room. "But you must be at least half a mile from a telephone in the village," I began. "How did you—"

Theodora cut me short, her voice impatient. "This is Mrs. Brent and she is an expert on jade. You will show me this piece you have?" How Ch'i had managed to telephone her was his concern. Her curiosity concerned a possible purchase.

He had wheeled his chair to a stained and broken cabinet, which had probably been retrieved from some rubbish dump and brought to the hut. I watched the thin wrists reach forward and pull out a drawer. He picked up a small parcel and held it out to Theodora.

She waved toward me. "Take a good look, Sarah," she said.

I unwrapped the piece of red-and-blue-striped cloth. Inside lay an elaborately carved girdle of oblongs of white jade linked together with thick golden rings. Holding it in my hands, I knew immediately that this was no fake. Just as connoisseurs of ivory could tell whether a piece was genuine or had been soaked in tea to give an aging color, so I knew by experience and instinct that this was genuine and ancient jade.

To the casual buyer, very little significance might be placed on the actual dynasty; the value was in the work itself. But to the art historian or to a rich collector like Theodora, dates were important. I went to the door and examined the jade under my magnifying glass. So often the only way of dating a jade carved before the eighteenth century was by its type. This carving had been worked by the old method, with a small lap wheel and abrasives. The crippled man sitting patiently in the room behind me had shown us a ceremonial belt which had been used by the Sung or Ming emperors when officiating at the altars in their temples.

Pure-white jade was said not to exist, but the piece I held was discolored only with age. I felt that it must once have been almost perfect white.

Each oblong piece was carved with one of the Signs of the Zodiac in a typically Chinese manner of using animals to symbolize the hour, the month or the year. The dragon, the hare, the tiger, the fox, the rat and the pig were still clearly marked, and on the gold links were engraved narcissus, the flower the Persians had brought to a Sung emperor centuries ago. The buckle was a dragon's head.

White jade girdles like the one I held had been used to officiate at the Altar of the Moon; yellow jade was used for the ceremony at the

Altar of the Earth. It was almost impossible for me accurately to date the belt without much deeper study, but I knew at once that it was of great value.

The sun was warm on my back as I stood—as I had so often done when I held an old jade piece—feeling myself borne back through the ages, to the old jade markets of Peking. In my upturned palms lay one element of a thousand years of ceremony and ritual, of Dragon emperors and lovely concubines.

"*Sarah . . .*" I pivoted around to face an exasperated and impatient Theodora.

Ch'i was behind her, his face lifted and anxious. "It was always in our family, you understand."

"But this piece surely has a history?" I said. "How did your family come by it?"

He shook his head. "To us it is precious. That is all."

Theodora had no time for sentiment. "What is it worth?" she demanded.

I shook my head. "I would have to—"

"*Parlez en français,*" she cut in.

I glanced at Ch'i, whose expression was puzzled.

It was impossible to make a rough estimate. The prices of art treasures—and particularly of Chinese objects—had risen phenomenally. This ancient and almost perfect piece of rare white jade might possibly fetch twenty or thirty thousand pounds, or even more, if sold in one of the great auction rooms.

Before I could speak, Ch'i said, "One hundred thousand dollars . . . Hong Kong dollars."

He had obviously misunderstood my expression of utter disbelief in the undervaluing of the jade, for he added, pleading, "It is a lovely piece. So rare."

I said in French to Theodora, "It is worth far more than he is asking."

"And that is something you can forget," she retorted in bad French. "You could be making a mistake." Then she added in English, "I am still not convinced that it might not be a very clever fake."

I felt my blood quicken. "Then you must get someone else to value it. I have told you what I honestly think."

"All right. All right." Her voice was raised, and I knew that she was afraid I would say too much and that Ch'i would realize he was asking too little. She turned to the Chinese, "If that's what you're asking."

"I am, madame."

She seized my arm and dragged me aside. "Sarah, you have no doubts about that piece? You are certain that it's genuine?"

"Yes. And very valuable."

"So I have a bargain."

"If you give him only one hundred thousand Hong Kong dollars, the equivalent to roughly, ten thousand English pounds, yes, you have."

A slow smile spread over her face. "Then that's fine."

"Is it? I wonder."

"What do you mean?"

A gust of light wind blew the piece of green cloth set up for our guidance. The bamboos that almost screened the hut rustled above us. Behind, in the shadow of the sagging doorway, Ch'i waited.

"I can't believe this man would not have sold the jade before he reached this state of abject poverty. So . . ."

"Go on. Go on."

"I think it must be stolen."

"That's not our concern—and besides, we have no proof."

I shook my head, looking away from her over the steep hillside to the jumble of junks and sampans clustered in the typhoon shelter below. "No," I agreed, "we haven't."

"Then don't you think it's a very rash suggestion? There are many families rich in their own country who had to leave everything but what they could carry in their arms, and escape. Ch'i's family might very possibly have been wealthy in China—you can tell he's well educated, he speaks excellent English. But now he has been reduced to selling their last prized possessions." She left me and went inside the hut to speak to Ch'i.

I wandered further down the hillside and watched the red ants scuttle over the boulders and the little sudden wind tease the long grass. I didn't want to hear any more haggling. I had done my job, valued the jade, and now it was up to Theodora. I stood watching in the distance a great cruise ship resting like a child's toy on the water. Beyond lay Kowloon and the New Territories, a world of rice paddies that was once known as the Emperors' Rice Bowl.

"It's settled." Theodora joined me. "You tell me the jade is worth far more than I'm paying. So I have agreed on the price. Of course, I tried to bargain, but he got very agitated. I've arranged that you'll come back with the money and collect the jade this evening, Sarah." She turned again to Ch'i. "My chauffeur will come with my assistant. He will act as guard."

Ch'i said, "There will be no need. The lady will not be harmed."

But as he spoke his eyes looked beyond us, roving the hills. Then he turned back into the hut and rewrapped the jade in the striped cloth, returning it to the drawer.

I noticed that the lock was broken, but then he wouldn't leave this room, so the jade would be guarded. He might even have a gun hidden somewhere.

"Come, Sarah, we must get back."

"You will bring the money in used notes," Ch'i called. "Small notes . . ."

"No," I said quickly.

"*Yes*." Affronted at my answering for her, Theodora swung around to me. "I said yes."

I was almost out of hearing, walking away from her down the hill, leaving her to follow me.

We saw no one as we left the shelter of the bamboos and made our way over the boulders and mounds of tough grass back to the car. I had learned that whenever Theodora had been successful in buying a treasure for her collection, she would lapse into long silences. Unkind acquaintances said it was because in spite of her vast wealth, it hurt her to part with large sums of money. But I knew it would hurt her far more to be denied what she wanted.

III

I HAD LEFT SCHOOL with two qualifications that had proved useful in the career I chose. I had studied languages and was proficient in French and Italian. I had also specialized in natural history, which involved visiting museums and studying minerals, and I came to love the color and the look and the feel of stones.

I studied jewelry design at the Royal College of Art in London and became a qualified gemologist. I believed that before I could design and set jewels, I must understand gold, that magical metal that retains its glitter, like Tutankhamun's death mask, even after thirty-four centuries. But while I was searching for a place to work as an apprentice, my mother died in Hong Kong of a particularly virulent form of influenza. I had had to return to the island to take over the running of the home there until someone could be found who would look after my father. It was then that my serious interest in jade began. For a few months, until I found Nam Tsao, the wonderful Cantonese woman who became my father's devoted housekeeper, I set out to learn all I could about the many and varied kinds of jade. When my father seemed settled with Nam Tsao, I returned to London.

My greatest stroke of good fortune was that I was accepted into the workshops of Felix Revillon, the elderly eccentric who was one of the greatest names in the world of jewelry. I remained with him for two years, learning not only the marvels of taming gold into the shapes I wanted, but also the subtleties of precious stones. I had learned the techniques before I had been able to qualify as a gemologist. Felix taught me the magic.

My real success began when I won the De Beers Award. I was an aspiring unknown competing with seasoned designers and I had no money for precious stones or gold. But since the designs for this award were judged at the sketch stage, the lack of expensive materials did not matter. I won. And after that I entered pieces at exhibitions of modern jewelry in London, Paris and Milan. Then, through Felix's intervention, famous jewelry firms became sufficiently interested in my work to ask me to submit designs for customers. It was exciting and I loved it, and in spite of tempting offers from various people, I remained free-lance. I worked near the river in Chelsea in a small studio which my grandfather's modest legacy had allowed me to buy.

When I started on my own, Felix had given me, as a celebration gift, models of the two golden eagles of Byzantium. They stood on a shelf, and if ever I was dispirited because a design I had taken a great deal of trouble over was not approved, I would look at those eagles. Patience and effort and initial mistakes must have gone into the originals of those as into most of the very great works of art. The thought cheered me whenever a design of mine failed. Who was I to think that everything I did was absolutely right and deserved unqualified approval?

When I was Felix's apprentice, I sometimes went with him to the great auctions, treading gently, cautiously, feeling my way in a world that half fascinated, half terrified me.

I sat in at sales and watched the way in which the bidding was carried out. The rooms would always quiver with tension, though the faces of the men and women were often like masks. Things of tremendous value were sold by only a small gesture that, to my uninitiated eyes, was barely perceptible.

"You see?" Felix had said after a few of these enlightening excursions into Christie's and Sotheby's. "The agents usually win. If *you* want to succeed, then your only weapon at the moment, my sweet, is stacks of good hard cash. You'll take years to be tough enough to meet these people on their shrewd level—if you ever do."

He was right, of course. But the gods seemed to be smiling on me all ways. First there was Marius.

We had met one another in an odd and casual way. I had been to the dental clinic and as I came out of one surgery, Marius came out of another. He shot me an amused look as we went into the elevator together.

"It doesn't hurt to have teeth filled these days, does it?"

I had said, "No," and then made some comment about wishing the gadgets a dentist used were prettier.

Marius had said, "Deck them with daffodils."

We had both laughed. It was spring, we were strangers, and we walked together through Hyde Park.

We became engaged a few weeks later, and eighteen months after our marriage, Viscountess Paradine sent for me to work for her. It seemed at the time that the gods had smiled on me again. I knew Theodora's name, I knew of her enormous wealth.

The seasoned buyers at the sales I went to in order to buy for her were aware that I had only the weapon of cash against them, and I knew that they waited for my fall. Sooner or later that would happen if only because of Theodora's arrogant and demanding temperament. But in the meantime, the great jewel and jade sales of the world were open to me.

I knew perfectly well that I had not been chosen to work for Theodora because I was considered a phenomenon. I was certainly not that. But I *was* conscientious and competent, and she knew it.

In their time, almost all the great experts had worked for her. With each one, the pattern was the same. There would be arrogant anger on Theodora's part and icy insults from the experts. In the end, infuriated by her hints—or even sometimes her open accusations—that she was being cheated, they would refuse to work for her. She would suspect them of using inferior gold when they redesigned one of her beautiful pieces of jewelry, or of double-dealing at a sale.

Theodora had told me of the times when she had been quite certain that the expert who was bidding for her at a sale was pushing the price up or bidding against her for another secret buyer. I didn't believe her, but I had learned that to try to argue with her was tantamount to experiencing a white-hot rage.

In a way, her tragedy was that she had never had to come up against life. She'd had an adoring father, and after he died his immense fortune had shielded her against "the slings and arrows." Shakespeare's words were true in the case of Theodora. Fortune was, for her, utterly outrageous in the material sense. But in the ways of the heart and the mind, the sensitiveness that warmed others, fortune had been miserly. She was caged in ice, and though she hated men, she needed them for her vanity's sake.

I had never forgotten the words of the great jewel expert, Templemayer, when I had made that bid recently for the Tsarina's ring: "Young lady, you have the ambition and the drive of the devil. But I can guess who sent you to bid. Good luck. That stone is magnificent, but you've paid far too much for it."

What mattered was that Theodora didn't think so.

So far as I was concerned, she soon learned that I would take no bullying and that if I felt "No" was the answer, I would say, "No," whether it angered her or not. As yet, I had never been given the full treatment of what had been called "Theodora's royal rages." But then, I wasn't a man to be hit out at, and so far I hadn't crossed her where her social ambitions were concerned. I was too far away from her world ever to do that.

On the other hand, I was ambitious and Theodora traded on that. She was quite certain that she was the golden ladder by which I hoped I would climb to great success—and in that she was right. My great disappointment was that she went to enormous lengths to avoid introducing me to her friends in America and Europe. She had no intention of recommending me to someone to whom she might lose a jewel she coveted.

Every two years I flew out to Hong Kong to visit my father and my friends on the island. I usually went in May and earlier that year I had made my usual plans. But when the news came through John Tarquin, a physician and a great mutual friend, that Marius had given up his post at the London hospital where he had worked since before our marriage, and had gone to Hong Kong, I canceled my flight.

It was one of those ironies that it was I who had first introduced him to the island. When we became engaged, I had taken him there to meet my father. Then a year later we had gone together a second time for a holiday. Now, so long after our separation, I learned that Marius was once again in Hong Kong.

When he told me about it, John Tarquin spoke angrily, seeming to take Marius's resignation from the hospital in London as a personal insult. "He has abandoned all he has worked for, turned his back on orthopedic surgery and gone to Hong Kong to study the unorthodox fringe methods of healing. It's sheer insanity. A man with Marius's potential to disregard years of training for a few wild ideas!"

"Wild?" I had asked.

"Well, damn it, acupuncture may possibly have something to be said for it, and there's some truth in this color therapy idea. But to abandon everything here is complete lunacy. Sarah, why the hell did you let him go?"

"We've been separated a long time, but even if we had been living together," I had said, "I couldn't have held him. And I doubt if I would have wanted to."

John had lifted his hands in despair. Marius's behavior was beyond his understanding. For me, it was not.

It had taken me a week after that conversation to decide that I would be wrong to let an emotion over a dead marriage affect my plans. I wanted to see my father and my friends and I was going to do just that. My brief marriage was over. Because it was such a small island, Marius and I would probably meet in Hong Kong, and when we did, we would be calm and civilized, smile and greet one another, and go our separate ways.

I booked my flight east that September.

Some months earlier—influenced, she told me at the time, by my glowing description of the place—Theodora had decided that she intended to take a house on the island.

"That is, of course, if I can find something I like well enough. I don't want a modern villa nor do I want a penthouse in a block. I need a place that is beautiful and permanent." Her voice had drifted into silence and her eyes had grown dreamy with the anticipation of this great new interest in her life. "I have so many Chinese art treasures and it would be wonderful if I could collect them in a fine house in Hong Kong—an *old* house, I think. I would make it another museum to my memory in future years."

She had flown out, found her house—her Pavilion of Apricots— and had collected together her scattered Chinese art treasures. With the aid of experts, the staff in her American and French houses crated the jades and the bronzes and the lacquer furniture and flew them out to her. I was given the task of arranging the dispatch of the treasures from her London house.

It had been a task that took me back painfully to that earlier time when Marius and I separated and the house we had lived in was sold. It was I who had to pack up our possessions, dividing them as I thought fair, since Marius took no interest in what happened to the furniture and the pictures we had chosen together with such joy.

In a letter I sent to Theodora giving her details of what I had done about her Chinese treasures, I mentioned that I would be going on holiday to Hong Kong in a few weeks' time and giving her the name of my hotel in case she wished to see me.

Her reply was typical.

HAVE CANCELED YOUR HOTEL STOP YOU ARE STAYING WITH ME STOP
    PARADINE

I decided immediately to write and thank her for her offered hospitality but to explain that, as it was my holiday, I felt it would be better to stay at a hotel. Before I had a chance, she telephoned.

Her suggestion was tempting. I was to fly out to Hong Kong at her expense and help her with some of the details of arranging the art treasures. She would also like me to search for one or two jades and advise her on some jewels she wanted reset. She would need me, she said, for three weeks, and for that she would pay me four hundred pounds.

I knew Theodora well enough to be guarded about that tempting offer. She was demanding and willful and I doubted if our close proximity would work. Theodora, however, was adamant.

"Oh, Sarah, don't make difficulties! You say you are coming out for a holiday. Well, you can take your holiday *after* you've worked for me. And if you want to go and see your father while you are with me, I won't stop you. I'm not inviting you to a prison, my dear, and the house is beautiful."

The money would be particularly useful to me at that moment because I was planning to extend my studio. And I could easily arrange to take a holiday and see my friends and sail and swim after the three weeks with Theodora.

So I came to the Pavilion of Apricots.

I had been watching, without really seeing, the road Ah Lee-ming was taking. And suddenly I realized that we were passing Hong Kong's newest hospital, St. Cecilia's, so named because the rich Chinese merchant who had endowed it had a great love for music, the patron saint of which was St. Cecilia.

The stark modern whiteness of the hospital in no way resembled the dark Gothic building in London where Marius had spent so much of his professional life. But I felt certain that he would gravitate toward this particular hospital because it was said to possess the most modern equipment in any hospital in the East. And scientific advances, either in experiments or technique, were like magnets to Marius.

I saw Marius too clearly—a tall man, not particularly good-looking but with deep Scandinavian blue eyes and rich, bright hair.

"There's no justice," I had once protested, pulling a comb through my own brown hair. "A man having copper hair that curls."

He had come behind me and folded his arms around me, resting his face on the crown of my head. "I like my girls with thick straight hair," he said. "I like my girls with blue-green eyes and warm mouths . . . No, not my 'girls' but my 'girl.' "

Our laughter over, we had made love. It had been that way for a time.

Marius came from a medical family. His father was a surgeon, his mother a doctor. Their relationship had been a marvelous success and I knew that this had colored his idea of what marriage should be like. During our time in London I had tried to make him understand that his parents were lucky—that their careers were similar and that neither had had demands that took them away from the other.

Marius and I had been married two years and then, eighteen months ago, we had parted. We had no children. The amazement of our friends when we separated proved that we had been successful in our game of pretense as a totally integrated couple. It was difficult for outsiders to understand the attraction that had seemed to promise fulfillment and had turned into emotional failure.

Although Marius had been pleased that someone as important as Theodora Paradine had chosen me to work for her, it was because of her increasing demands on my time that our marriage had broken up. He was proud of my success in the designing of jewelry, but Theodora missed nothing in the way of important sales in the countries of Europe. I was sent to Paris, to Rome, to Vienna—anywhere where there were reports of something she might want for her great collections.

I loved it. It was like drinking champagne after being used to sherry. The excitement went to my head.

Marius, coming home after a long day at the hospital or returning late at night after an emergency, would often find only good old Matty, our housekeeper, to greet him. "I don't much feel like coming home and kissing Matty as a substitute for kissing you. And I certainly don't want her in my bed. So do you think you could ask your avid millionairess to get someone else to fly here, there and everywhere buying for her?"

I had replied, "It's a wonderful chance for me, Marius. You must see—"

"What?"

"That I'm making a name for myself. You have to seize your opportunities. If you don't, life seldom gives you another chance."

"A chance for what? Marriage or a career?"

"I never pretended I was going to give it all up when we married. I can't spend my life just waiting for you to come home at all hours from the hospital. I must be occupied by something more than shopping and cooking."

"Of course. A wife without interests of her own isn't particularly attractive—at least not to me. But your work always used to be here in London with your designing. It's only this past few months, since you've started working for Theodora, that you've been away for days at a time chasing round the Continent."

"Because I'm more successful, the demands are greater. Theodora—"

"That's just what I'm saying. Theodora, once known as 'Florence,' I believe. The spoiled daughter of an American investment king, a lonely and avid woman."

"And also," I had retorted, "my chance to expand, to become someone in my own right. Marius, I *can't* just jog along through life. It isn't my way."

The first argument ended in an uneasy truce. After that, other arguments came quickly, and each time the endings were more angry. We seemed to lose the gift for graceful compromise. I kept assuring myself, and Marius, that once prospective buyers realized I was working for Theodora Paradine, they would come to me, and that eventually I wouldn't need her any more and would be able to choose my commissions and concentrate on designing. But that was something for the future. And in spite of the nerves that tore at me every time I entered a sale room, either in London or on the Continent, the curious magic of it was irresistible.

"Wait," I kept saying to Marius. "Please wait—"

"For what? For you to come to your senses? Sarah, my blind darling, life isn't long enough for such a wait."

So the break between us came as inexorably as a crack in a ceiling. Marius changed, became restless and moody. He was dissatisfied with his work at the hospital, impatient for a place where he could put into practice all the elements of what he believed to be advanced healing. He maintained, as many other medical men were doing, that there was more to medicine than what was being taught.

I would often look at his broad and strong hands and know that they would have tenderness when manipulating the deformed bones of those who suffered. Children under his care loved him and ceased to be afraid when he touched them. Romantically inclined adults whom he treated would declare that he had "spiritually healing hands." He didn't, but he did have a fine knowledge of the human body and an understanding, born of intense years of study, of how to straighten twisted limbs.

What Marius wanted, however, was to understand certain "fringes" of medicine. He had exclaimed more than once, in despair, "If only I had more time . . ."

Once, when I leaned over his shoulder, intrigued by an acupuncture chart of nerve centers he was examining, he had said, "No treatment should be given without the doctor's absolute control of the medium. That's why I need a long time to study this."

I also remembered what he had said when talking of the investigation into the healing properties of color. "Psychological medicine has proved it to be so," he had said. "And the Medical Research Council has a special division for it."

"Oh, darling," I had asked flippantly, "what is the color for love?"

But for Marius it was a serious subject.

Another of Marius's unorthodox interests was Tai Chi—called by the Chinese "the gentle art of keeping fit." This, again, Marius thought, had been too superficially investigated.

"If only we knew how to live in harmony inside ourselves," he had said.

Tragically enough, he and I did not know this was exactly what had defeated our own life together.

My desperate desire to succeed in my own work stemmed from my childhood. My father had tremendous charm and intelligence, but it was my mother who had the drive and the ambition. Ever since I could remember she had been an impatient and discontented woman. Her great grudge against life was that she had never had a career. After taking a history degree at University College, she had gone straight into marriage to my father and had flown out with him to Hong Kong where he had a government post. There she had been caught up in the social whirl that was the life of foreign residents' wives. Her frustrations at having only her home on which to expend her energies had embittered her. But in spite of her dissatisfaction, my mother had not allowed her marriage to fail as mine had. At the time she met my father, his life had been full of tremendous promise. He had a wonderful ear for languages and such great charm that the government of Hong Kong had begun sending him on missions to Taiwan, where, able to speak Mandarin, he would enjoy long conversations with the intelligentsia of the Nationalist Government. But he had never fulfilled his early promise, and when there were better posts vacant, he was often passed over for another man.

Perhaps I was like my mother in temperament. Perhaps the devil of ambition in me was like a snowball, gathering weight and momentum as it rolled along the years. I hoped not. I hoped so desperately that however successful I might be, I would never lose my humanity.

But Marius had left me, so I had failed.

And he? Had he played a part in that failure? Or was I entirely to blame? I was too near it all to judge. All I knew was that I wanted happiness and contentment as much as anyone else and I had reveled in the hours I had spent with Marius.

But then Theodora would send for me and the demon whisper

would come again. In Paris a fine black opal was to be auctioned. Or there was a jade screen from the Summer Palace in Peking that had mysteriously appeared on the market and was being offered in Rome.

"No," I would think. "Oh, no . . . not another foreign commission!"

But my demon gave me another push and off I would go.

The marvel of finding myself capable of holding my own among the dealers and also the growing demand for my jewelry designs acted on me like a drug. Perhaps my success had come to me too early. Perhaps I used my restless drive as a psychological support.

The break between Marius and me came one evening when I arrived back in London after three days in Rome, where I had been trying to buy a Renaissance pendant for Theodora and had lost it to an outrageously high bidder. I found Matty, our housekeeper, in tears.

"Mr. Brent has gone away, Madame. He said he would be in touch with you tonight."

"Gone where?"

"He . . . he . . . said . . . just that he was . . . g–going," she had sobbed.

Marius called me an hour later. "I've left you, Sarah. I don't much care for sitting at home after a hard day, talking to the walls."

"Marius, you can't. You can't just walk out . . ."

"Oh, but I have. I'll pay a generous sum into your banking account."

"Damn my banking account. I don't need your money."

"My sweet Sarah, you'll need a hell of a lot more when Theodora Paradine suddenly gets bored with you. I've a feeling you're just a pretty novelty at the moment. But for such as she, there's always a greener pasture. It's time you learned something about priorities. There are needs beyond those for another sapphire or a piece of old jade. People matter . . ." The line went dead.

I heard that he was staying with another surgeon friend in Harley Street, and I wrote asking if he wanted a divorce. His reply was succinct: "I'll let you know when I do."

It was the last message he sent me.

IV

SEATED BY MY SIDE in the great, smooth Rolls, Theodora must have seen my head turn to look at the new hospital and sensed that my thoughts might turn to Marius. Her voice, always a little harsh and peremptory, cut across my private world. "Oh, by the way, I'm sure it won't upset you to know that Marius is coming to my party tonight."

She must have invited him days before, but had said nothing. It couldn't be, I thought, that she had wanted to surprise me and that she had in her that spark of humanity that would have delighted in patching up a broken marriage. Her next words denied any such idea. "I've never discussed him with you, but I knew that sooner or later you'd have to meet; in a place like this, it is inevitable. I didn't tell you before because—well—there will be so many people at my party that you and Marius can avoid one another if you wish. He and I, by the way, have become"—the same, light laugh, the hesitation were not in the least deprecating—"very good friends. I understand him so well."

I wondered how much she had enjoyed that little speech and its wounding effect on me. Or perhaps she honestly believed that all feeling was dead between Marius and me; perhaps Marius had even inferred that to her.

She must have decided that this quiet moment in the car was as good as any to tell me that Marius would be among her guests that night. She had not previously shown the least interest in my private life, and when months ago I had mentioned that Marius and I had parted, she had merely shrugged her shoulders and said, "That's life, isn't it, Sarah? Trial and error . . ." and then had broken off to discuss a jewel sale that interested her.

Pressed back into my corner of the car, I faced the fact that on an island as small as Hong Kong, Theodora and Marius would be bound to meet, just as he and I would eventually. I knew, too, that without unkindness, but fascinated by the emotions and tensions of others, the people who had known me and now knew Theodora Paradine would be watching to see if Sarah and Marius Brent were making moves toward one another. Or toward divorce.

"Did you hear what I said?"

"Yes."

My voice must have sounded small and subdued, for she said quickly, "Oh, come! You've been separated for—how long is it, Sarah?—eighteen months, I believe you told me recently. I can't think a meeting now with Marius would upset you."

She obviously imagined that if I felt anything at all, it would be embarrassment and not hurt. I doubted if she had ever in her life known either the birth or the death of love.

I said quietly, "I won't be at your party, Theodora."

"Oh, you will. I'm relying on you to show my guests around. You must explain the importance of certain pieces—that Hsu Pei-hung painting and the new Ming porcelains. I want my visitors to realize just how important my art collection is. You must explain to them why these objects are of such value."

I answered her with rising anger. "I know very little about porcelain or paintings. If you want a reliable guide for your guests, then you must ask one of those experts to come along!"

She sat quietly for a moment. "If it's a matter of not having brought a suitable dress with you, then I'll lend you something. There's that Chinese gown Lilo made up from beautiful old silk I managed to find. There wasn't enough material and it's far too short for me. You're small and I'm sure it would fit." She waited, but I remained silent. "You remember it surely, Sarah. I showed it to you. And you told me that it must originally have been intended to be made up into a young girl's marriage gown, because it was embroidered with peonies, the Chinese wedding flower." There was a hint of malice in the small silence she let hang between us before she flung her final amused barb. "It would intrigue Marius, wouldn't it? He might think you were wearing it deliberately."

The car swung around a bend and I crouched in the corner of the car, saying furiously, "I am certain that Marius wouldn't even know what the Chinese marriage flower was. And please understand," I added, as I heard her soft laugh, "it's over between us. All of it. Over."

"That's what I thought. Then there's every reason for you to meet like two civilized people." She leaned over and patted my hand.

I made no further comment.

The car pulled up outside the high wall of the house. The air was filled with the spicy cooking smells from the little restaurant where a chunky cheap china God of Plenty sat in his corner by the door, smiling a welcome. Crowds jostled one another in the street; hawkers brushed past, carrying everything from melons to dried fish on the poles slung across their shoulders. The shops opposite the great wall where we had stopped were ancient leaning structures, gaudy with huge brush signs and washing slung across balconies.

The setting was a curious one for Theodora's marvelous house. But then it had been built nearly two hundred years ago by a rich Chinese who had copied it from drawings of an ancient Manchu palace. In those days this particular part of the city was relatively quiet and sparsely populated. That had been in the days before the Chinese had fled from the mainland revolution and built their tumble-down shanties on the hills of Hong Kong. Here, although the lean-tos were being swiftly demolished, the mass of people still thronged the streets.

For all the bustle and chaos outside, the palace wall made it into a kind of fortress which was a perfect setting for Theodora's Chinese collection. She could never have considered living on the fashionable Peak. For many months of the year it was wreathed in a damp mist, which, for all the modern innovations that might be used, would still play havoc with the delicate silk scrolls, the rare lacquer furniture and even the jades.

I loved the streets of Hong Kong. There was a buoyancy, a vitality about the crowds. But had anyone from the West less rich than Theodora lived in that particular area, I doubted if the élite of the city would ever have descended from the elegant heights of the Peak or their villas at Shek-O to visit the Pavilion. But a millionairess, and a viscountess at that, was an entirely different matter. Only fire, flood or plague would have prevented them from attending Theodora's parties. The cheerful poverty of the tottering houses outside were another world that could be ignored.

The old gateman, Ah Baht, opened the double door to us. He smiled, bending with a charming lost courtesy as Theodora swept through. We crossed the paved court under the willows and went through the first moon gate. The flame-of-the-forest drooped clusters of shining seeds over my head. Flowers were everywhere, coxcombs and early hibiscus in stone urns and long carved marble vats.

The second moon gate led to a court filled with yellow chrysanthemums and the last of the white lilies. Against the dark-red walls was the pinkish-white explosion of second-flowering bauhinias. Bulbuls, their black crests like burning coals in the sunlight, chased the swallows from one court to another. Between the trees I could see the buildings—five separate pavilions making up the lovely compound once called a palace and known now collectively as the Pavilion of Apricots.

By the archway into the third and main court was a tiny stone niche, and set in it was a bronze Dragon Spirit, fangs bared, spine curved and twisted as if ready to leap. I could only guess that it was there because the compound of pavilions and lovely linking courts was probably finished in one of the symbolic years, the Year of the Dragon. This last court was known as the Court of the Lotus because of the small pool where in summer the lotus flowers bloomed.

The pool was like a sheet of silver, the fan-tailed goldfish somnambulant. Only a dragonfly skimming across disturbed the smooth sheen with its fragile shadow. To the left of the pool was a small marble bridge leading to a teahouse with slender scarlet pillars and a gilded roof.

The main pavilion stood before us. Ancient Chinese houses were only one story high, because in the days of the dynasties it was considered unlucky to be looked down upon. But Theodora wanted a two-story house and had engaged a great French architect, flying him out to Hong Kong in her private plane. He was an expert on Chinese architecture and had built on a second floor to the palace, carefully keeping the style of architecture intact.

The original ridge-and-furrow roof was replaced on the higher floor and the graceful lines dipped and curved as if the wind were ruffling them. Birds fluttered all day in the crimson frescoed eaves.

Beyond the low walls that divided the courts were the small guest pavilions. One had been used originally by the rich Shanghai merchant who had built it as a place of entertainment.

Theodora kept the room completely empty except when she had guests. She had told me, when she first showed me round her compound, that she planned, when she gave large parties, to have small gilt chairs brought to the room and buffet tables around the walls. "With so many luxuries, Sarah, I'll stun my guests," she had laughed and added that she would also hire a band of Cantonese musicians.

This great room was called the Pavilion of the Sacred Mountain because hung on the walls were paintings depicting Hua Shan, a lonely and exquisite place in China familiar to me because of my father's marvelous stories about it and the myths that surround it.

The paintings were beautiful, and in each one the sacred mountain appeared, towering among the clouds, partly pine-covered. One was of a Taoist religious dance being performed among the crags, which were like turreted castles; another showed the lower slopes ablaze with tree peonies.

The furthest pavilion in the compound was where the servants lived. Theodora kept a permanent staff of six in Hong Kong. Her housekeeper, Ah Lin; her chef, Maurice; her gardener, Ah Tat; her gateman, Ah Baht; her chauffeur, Ah Lee-ming; and Lilo Kam, a beautiful Eurasian girl who acted as a seamstress and assistant maid under Célie.

The leaves of the trees—acacia, willow, mimosa—hung dappled shadows across us as we walked along the marble paths. The fragrance of incense seemed always to lie over the gardens and the house. I liked to imagine that after centuries of burning incense sticks in the palace's small private temple, the scent had been captured and held for all these years until we, the aliens, walked the exquisite courts.

As I drew near the main pavilion, I could hear the wind bells in the eaves. So light, so delicate, that just a stir of air could set them dancing.

Theodora was some distance ahead of me when Lilo Kam appeared and took her purse and the gloves she wore whenever she went out to protect her hands from the strong sunlight.

They both paused for a moment at the pavilion entrance and I saw Theodora point upward. I remembered how she had glanced up as we had left, saying that Ah Tat must be told to clean the elaborately carved keyless jade lock—quite useless but decorative—which hung over the door between the wind bells as a talisman to protect the house from evil spirits. She was probably giving Lilo orders to have this done.

Lilo was a beautiful girl, small and exquisitely formed, with the facial beauty so often seen in those who were half-English, half-Chinese. Her straight black hair was abundant and shining; her eyes tilted slightly and were quite large. Unlike most modern girls in Hong Kong, she always wore the cheongsam, and the slim tight dress with the high side slits suited her perfectly sculpted body and legs.

Lilo Kam's greatest value in the palace household was that she was an expert needlewoman. Probably she had been taught in one of the dress houses of Hong Kong where exquisite embroideries were still made by Chinese girls. Lilo could mend frayed linings and darn torn embroideries so that the damage was almost invisible.

Theodora had a genius for finding lovely old silks which most of us in Hong Kong assumed had long ago been snapped up by the rich earlier travelers from the West. An elaborate old lama priest's robe would be made by Lilo into a housecoat, or a bolt of lovely silk embroidered with birds and flowers would become in her skilled hands a simply cut dress, which, because Theodora was tall and slim, would not look overpatterned on her.

I had often thought about the people who had preserved those silks and brocades so carefully over the long years, only to sell them to a stranger in order to live. I felt sympathy for the Chinese families forced to give up treasures that had been in their possession for generations, but I doubted if any compassion crossed Theodora's heart as she tossed them money for their beloved heirlooms, their bronzes, their jades and their silks.

"Sarah . . ." Theodora's voice sounded clearly across the court. It came from behind the screen of massed crimson flowers where I had found Mister Wu, the white Pekingese who was another permanent member of the household.

"Hurry, Sarah, hurry!" Theodora called. "I've a great deal to do before the party tonight."

Only the beauty of the objects that stood around the great hall saved the whole effect from one of an *embarras de richesses*. Bronze temple candlesticks, bowls of Imperial green Ming, an opium couch piled with cushions of yellow brocade that might once have robed a priest—all these things seemed to be in their natural setting in the wide, well-proportioned hall.

The drawing room was enormous and had the traditional conical wishbone ceiling. The sun gilded the ancient wood of the latticed windows and the deep niches in the walls.

I had bought some of the art objects that stood there. The curious Earth Spirit from the T'ang dynasty had been bid for at Sotheby's in London. I had found the incense burner of blue lapis lazuli in a side street in Rome.

While I stood looking at these familiar treasures, Theodora had gone into the small inner room where she kept a collection of less valuable objects. She seemed to have forgotten that she had called me.

"When do you want me to collect the jade?" I asked.

"Oh, later. I don't keep a hundred thousand dollars—even Hong Kong dollars—in my purse. I'll call you."

I left her singing to herself softly, a thing I had never heard her do before.

V

THEODORA HAD SENT Ah Lin to fetch me from my room in the guest pavilion. She was lying on a chaise longue, and her maid, Célie, was padding about in the adjoining dressing room.

On a table by Theodora's side were two sealed envelopes and an open leather case. The brooch and earrings of diamonds and rubies lying on the velvet lining were familiar to me, since resetting them had been one of the first things I ever did for her. It was said that the jewels had been given by King Charles IX of France to his bride. Since then they had been recut and reset many times and must now be only a quarter of their original size. But they were still very splendid.

"I'm wearing the blue mandarin gown tonight," she said, "and these"—waving at the jewels—"but I'm not at all certain that I like the earrings. I think you'll have to work on some new design for me. They're too long and my face needs width. I'm telling you now so that you can think about it and draw a few ideas for me to see while you're here."

I would have liked to have said, "Please don't wear flashing jewels with the rich and glowing materials of Old China. The necklace and the ring belong to the West. You have fire opals and star sapphires; both would look sumptuous and more in keeping." But Theodora paid for flattery, not honesty, and as I could not give her the former, I remained silent.

There was a knock on the door. Célie opened it, and took a letter from Lilo.

"What's that?" Theodora demanded and held out her hand for it. Then with a sudden angry exclamation she flung the letter from her. "Damn these people. They cling to formalities as if life depended on them. They address me as Viscountess *Florence* Paradine. I am *not* Florence. How many times do I have to sign my name for it to sink into their conventional heads that I changed it years ago?"

"I'm sure your secretary reminded them."

"My secretary," she retorted, kicking off her scarlet slippers to reveal bare and beautiful feet, "as you know, is prolonging her holiday by playing at being ill and being cosseted by her doting mother."

"Janet *is* ill," I said. "You can't have a bit of your inside cut out and fly thousands of miles back to your job in two weeks. You've said yourself how conscientious she is."

"Well?" Whenever she knew she was wrong, Theodora changed the subject. "Well?" she asked again. "Do *you* like *your* name?"

I laughed. "I think there should be a legal form sent round to everyone reaching the age of sixteen, asking if they prefer to have their own chosen names registered."

"I was exactly sixteen when I changed mine," she said in triumph. "After all, Lady Cunard—my grandmother was a friend of hers—changed *her* name from Maud to Emerald. And then there was Lady Ellenborough, who had all those lovers. She was christened Jane and was called Aurora. Here"—she flicked her fingers at me—"give me that letter, Sarah, please. I suppose I'd better open it."

I gave it to her, saying, "It will be dark soon and I don't want to be near Ch'i's isolated shack with a lot of money after sunset. So I'll go now."

"Take Ah Lee-ming all the way with you. Let *him* carry the eighty thousand Hong Kong dollars."

"A hundred thousand," I said. "Just as you agreed."

She shook her shoulders in irritation, and handed me the two envelopes from her table. "Sixty thousand in one envelope and forty thousand in the other. Hand him one, and if he counts it and makes a fuss, you can give him the rest. But mind you bargain."

I didn't argue with her, but I knew that I would not bargain over the agreed price.

She continued giving instructions. "And, Sarah, let Ah Lee-ming have the money. If there is anyone lurking around who knows you are bringing it, they'll go for your purse rather than his pockets . . . Célie"—she raised her voice—"how often have I told you not to creep around like that, giving me shocks? For heaven's sake, what do you want?"

"Your dress, my lady. The sapphire brocade, did you say?"

"You know I did. And now leave me. I don't want to be disturbed by anyone or anything, do you understand that? I want to rest. Leave me."

I turned on my heel.

"Where are you going, Sarah?" Theodora demanded.

"To fetch your jade," I said and closed the door. I glanced through the small landing window as I walked down the galleried passage.

Everyone in the household, it seemed, was in the courts, moving as if they were in some ballet, backward and forward, setting up tables, hanging lanterns, carrying porcelain epergnes piled with caviar and canapés, covered with protective cheesecloth until the moment the guests would arrive.

The Chinese love large gatherings, and they flitted up and down the marble paths, chatting and laughing. To have a party meant that your master or mistress thought a great deal of your skill in preparing delicacies. The fact that it was the French chef Maurice who had created most of the dishes seemed unimportant to them.

The telephone bell began to ring as I reached the hall. Automatically I crossed to the lacquer table and lifted the receiver.

A man's voice asked, "Is Lady Paradine available?"

"I'm sorry. She asked not to be disturbed. Can I help?"

"Probably." The voice held laughter. "And don't tell me, let me guess. You are Sarah Brent. Am I right?"

"Yes. But I can't think—"

"It's quite obvious, really. The gossip columns reported that Theodora had a talented English jade expert staying with her. They called her Sarah Brent. Célie has a French accent; the rest of the servants are Chinese, and Theodora's secretary is away ill. So it must be she whom my once wife describes as being 'a real artist at jewelry design.'"

"That's where you have the advantage." I relaxed. The voice was charming and friendly. "I don't yet know who you are."

"Oliver Farache."

Theodora's third husband. "Oh, then perhaps . . ."

As I hesitated, he finished my sentence for me. "—she'd like to be disturbed if she knows I'm on the line? No, don't bother her. It's not important. Just give her a message, will you? I can come to her party, after all, tonight. So you and I will meet then."

The warmth of his voice encouraged me to an impulse. I said, "Oh, we've met already, although you wouldn't know."

"Have we?"

"I once spent a weekend at Cadence Manor."

"I hope the beds were comfortable."

"Mine was. And I enjoyed every moment of it. Everyone there seemed to."

"Yes," he said. "My father's idea of having weekend paying guests is working very well. People pay high prices to stay in a stately home." He laughed at the phrase. "And we're lucky in keeping our staff; they've all been with us for as long as I can remember. My brother is acting host for the next two months, that's why I could get away. I flew East to see Hong Kong and Theodora again. It's nice when you can remain friends with your ex-wife."

"Yes." Someone was hovering behind me. I saw Ah Lin. "It's all right," I said to her. "I've taken a message for Lady Paradine." Then I turned back to the telephone. "I'll tell Theodora that you'll be coming tonight."

"And meeting you. That's a date."

The line went dead before I could tell him that I wouldn't be there.

I went to my room to get my purse, recalling the time when three friends and I had gone for a weekend to Cadence Manor, one of the smallest of the British stately homes. I remembered that there had been about twelve guests at the Manor and that we were treated as if we were valued friends. The weather had been good, the food a gourmet's feast, the rooms steeped in history.

There was a ballroom that had become the paying guests' drawing room. The paneling had lily-of-the-valley coloring and on the walls in the hall and up the great stairway were portraits of earlier Farache men and women.

The family members took turns playing host, and when we were there Roger Farache, the eldest son, was in charge. I also caught sight of the head of the family, Sir Brandon Farache, and of Oliver, but too many people had paid their fees for a weekend for any of the family to remember me. The strongest impression I had had after my admiration for the elegance of the house, was admiration for the family's tremendous will to survive inflation and taxes that threatened to destroy their home and their history. For this reason they had become "professional" hosts, probably despite all their inclinations.

It was still daylight when I got into the car and stuffed the two envelopes containing the money into the secret compartment at the back of the passenger seat which Theodora used to conceal her jewel case.

Although I had seen Ch'i Pai-shih in his wheelchair, the fear that had begun as an intuition on our first visit had now deepened. It was still possible that the jade was an heirloom from some happier past in China, but though I clung to that thought, the fear persisted. In spite of it, I was now committed. I had the money, I was empowered to hand it over, and I would carry out my orders.

The road was winding, and I glanced back through the rear window, ever enchanted by the familiar view I would see. Hong Kong lay in the late sunlight, distance disguising the high-rise buildings so that they looked like blocks of gleaming alabaster set in the green and gray of the hills. I could see the puffy white clouds that concealed the mainland mountain of Tai Mo Shan, at whose feet Kowloon sprawled. I knew it all . . . the smaller islands linked by occasional boat services and the hospital helicopters that brought the sick to Hong Kong.

The perilous position of Hong Kong always seemed to me ironical. It rested with its scrubby hills scattered with orchids and yellow gordonia, a little island on whose doorstep lived eight hundred million Chinese.

It was my island and I could not believe it would ever change. It seemed an incredible fact that there might be so few years left of British rule. But in the last decade the atmosphere between Red China and Hong Kong had changed and become one of "live and let live." Perhaps in their way, each side needed the other.

My drifting thoughts came to a sudden halt. Again in the distance I saw the white outline of the new hospital. Immediately I forgot the crippled Ch'i, the jade, the money, Theodora. My mind was once more filled with Marius. I saw us both in the early days, before Theodora had decided that I was sufficiently experienced to travel to the international sale rooms in search of jewels and jade. I saw myself in that past, curled up in one of the big fireside chairs, listening to Marius talking of his work. He had begun to dream of a clinic of his own; one modern in design, progressive in intent. He had talked, leaning back in his chair, his eyes brilliant, telling me how he needed to work out his newly formulated ideas without the dragon of orthodoxy breathing prejudice like fire at him. "I know there is so much to learn and so much I want to put into practice. Maybe it's all an illusion and I'll fail. Maybe the old die-hards are right and I'm wrong. But at least I'll have tried."

And I, excited for him and loving him, had listened. But in the end perhaps we had both been blind—Marius caught up with his profession, I bewitched by my success with Theodora. We had been two people with vastly differing careers, each of us overstimulated by our own prospects and unable to give enough time to understanding the other. We had told ourselves we were "in love" without considering the consequences of our relationship.

Just before I left for Hong Kong, I made a nostalgic and foolish pilgrimage to the small house in London where we had lived. I stood outside the wrought-iron gate, looking at a house I could scarcely believe had ever been ours. Someone had painted the lovely old brick work a hideous blue and had stripped the creeper and wisteria from the walls. The uncurtained windows were not very clean and the flowers in the small front garden had been dead a long time.

Nothing of us was left. We had cast no shadows. No one who came to live in that house after we left would be haunted by the young ghosts of Marius and Sarah Brent, who had exchanged dreams and then lost each other. The house had become a changeling and I was glad that it was so.

I began to think again about the party that night. Working for Theodora didn't give her the right to control my leisure hours, and I had no intention of meeting Marius. I would go and spend the evening with Father. He would be delighted to see me and would show me all his latest snapshots—he had become an energetic amateur photographer. And I would remain with him until I thought the last of the guests had left. Either Father would drive me back to the Pavilion or I would take the car and return it to him early the following morning in time for him to go to the yacht club, which was where he spent most of his days.

The light was still hovering in the sky as Ah Lee-ming drew the Rolls to a stop near the track that led to Ch'i's hut.

I hesitated about taking the envelope from the secret compartment, and gave a doubtful look up at the hillside where clumps of trees could hide someone lying in wait for us. "I hope it's safe."

Ah Lee-ming grinned and reached to his belt and pulled out a curved knife. "It is a beautiful gift from First Uncle," he said. "I always carry it with me. With this, we are safe."

"It's a deadly looking weapon."

"With Mistress Lady wearing so much richness, there has to be protection, you understand. I protect her, but she does not know. And you will not tell her?"

"No," I promised, "I won't tell her."

"Then we will now go to the hut." He sighed with increased distaste.

Together, with the villainous knife for protection, we climbed the hill.

The door of the shack was wide open. Ch'i must have heard us, for he appeared immediately, his chair sliding and creaking across the floor.

"I believe you agreed on a price with Lady Paradine," I said.

"One hundred thousand Hong Kong dollars. Yes . . . yes . . ." He seemed nervous, as if he wanted us to be off his premises. His hand, with its thin wrist, reached out for the envelopes.

"The jade," I said. "Let me see the jade first."

"Of course." He spoke without offense, and wheeling his chair to the cabinet, opened the drawer and unfolded the piece of red-and-blue-striped cloth.

I lifted the jade from the folds and held it for a moment in my hands. The ancient stone was as warm as flesh and the animal carvings were clearly visible in the light that came in over my shoulder. It was indeed the jade I had seen earlier.

I nodded, and he held out his hands for it. Then he wrapped it in layers of thin Japanese rice paper and handed it carefully back to me. "Jade breaks. Jade breaks easily," he said.

"I know. I'll be very careful." I gave him the two envelopes. "There is the money. Do you want me to wait while you count it?"

"No. No, please. I trust you. I am satisfied. Thank you."

I hesitated, and looked over my shoulder at the seemingly deserted hill. "You're sure it's safe for you to have all that money here? After all, you are alone—"

"It is safe. Thank you, thank you," he said again. He ripped open the envelopes, flicked at the money and then folded the piece of striped cloth around the bundles of notes.

I bade him goodbye and Ah Lee-ming and I left.

As we made the steep, uneven journey back to the road, I saw a dark car approaching. It appeared to be cruising along, as if the driver were enjoying the scenery.

Then, while Ah Lee-ming unlocked the doors of the Rolls, the car came abreast of us and the driver, slowing down, met my eyes.

He was Chinese and I guessed him to be about forty. His hair was very black and his skin pale ivory. There was a quiet elegance about him and at the same time an alertness, as if in one glance he could see everything he wanted. And what he seemed most interested in was my face.

VI

I SAT IN THE CAR, holding an exceedingly valuable jade, increasingly uneasy as we came to the center of the city and traffic jams kept holding us up. Small cars drew alongside us and interested eyes peered in at the girl in the expensive Rolls. Beyond the stream of cars and carts, the doors of the tumble-down houses were open, for the Chinese did their cooking and cleaning in full view of passers-by.

I had no idea what made me look back when we turned into the street leading to Theodora's walled home. There was nothing out of the ordinary about the car behind us—there were many black Avenger cars in Hong Kong.

But in a flash of low sunlight streaking between two tall buildings, I saw the man's face and recognized it. I had been followed from Ch'i's hillside shack by the Chinese who had seemed so interested in me on the road beyond Aberdeen.

I sat as far back in my corner as I could. Then as Ah Lee-ming drew the big car to a stop outside the heavy door of the palace, the smaller car went quickly past, scattering a cyclist, a hawker selling melons and a yellow dog. Though the man at the wheel did not look my way, I felt quite certain that he was not behind me in that narrow road by chance.

Ah Baht met me at the open door to the main pavilion. Theodora had asked that I be sent straight to her when I returned. Ah Lin was in the hall, and her bright, narrow eyes lifted toward the staircase, nodding that Theodora was in her bedroom.

I hurried up the stairs with the parcel and knocked on her door.

"Come in . . . come in."

The door was only half closed. I pushed it open, said, "Oh . . ." and stopped dead.

The man who sat in the rosewood chair got up.

Theodora was laughing. "Sarah, this is my last husband—and my favorite. Oliver Farache. He just flew into town."

"Oh, she knows," he said and held out his hand to me. "We spoke on the telephone."

"Be on your guard." Theodora was in a radiant mood. "I've always said that he should have a disk pinned to his lapel—'Beware of the charmer.'"

Something stimulating in the atmosphere of the room inspired a memory. I quoted, returning their laughter: "'Is this that haughty, gallant, gay Lothario?'"

"You see?" Oliver said to Theodora. "Sarah even knows her classics, which is more than you ever did, my disgustingly rich, one-time wife. Society bred you, but culture forgot to take a hand in your development."

As Theodora waved him out of the room, still laughing, I thought that he was probably the only man who could speak to her like that. "Leave us," she was saying. "Give yourself a drink, and you'll find the American and English newspapers to amuse you. I'll see you later."

He said, passing me, "And I shall see *you* later, Sarah."

"At my party, yes." Theodora spoke for me.

As the door closed behind him the curious, intangible air of excitement that went with him was replaced by one of tension. "The jade, Sarah, show me the jade." Theodora's hand was out, fingers curved as if to grasp her new expensive treasure.

She took it from me, turning it over, feeling it as I had done, but without my expertise. In spite of all she owned, Theodora was extraordinarily ignorant about jade, though so far she had been lucky. All the pieces she had were genuine. One day, when she was tired of me, someone would come along who wouldn't be so honest.

"Well," she demanded, "what do you think?"

I told her what I knew about such jade belts, explaining the ceremonies at which they were worn.

"The Sung and Ming emperors had four girdles," I said. "White jade like this for the Moon ceremony, yellow for the Earth. And there were also red coral belts which they used for the ceremony at the Altar of the Sun and carved lapis lazuli when officiating in the Temple of Heaven."

But I could see that she was only vaguely attentive, and at last she said, "Put down what you've told me on one of the explanatory cards. Print it carefully, Sarah." Theodora handed the jade to me. "And take it to the drawing room. I'll be down in a few minutes."

Lilo was in the gallery outside Theodora's room, leaning idly against the wall as if waiting to be summoned. I gave her a half-smile as I passed and saw her eyes move to the belt in my hands. She looked intensely curious, and I knew that when both Theodora and I were out, she would search the rooms for whatever it was that had been newly acquired.

I had to wait only a few minutes before Theodora appeared. She was so tall and so slim that she was magnificent in the blue gown she had put on for her party. The jewels she had chosen glittered in her ears and at her throat. Her scent, which was specially made for her in France, enveloped her in an invisible cloud of sandalwood and jasmine. She swept past me, saying, "The jade is going straight into the strongroom."

She went behind the sixfold Coromandel screen and after a few moments I hear the click of the lock. "Come here, Sarah," she called and I joined her in the small, windowless room, guarded by the great steel door and combination lock, where Theodora kept her greatest treasures.

Many years ago the room had probably been a family shrine. At the far end was a stepped ebony dais where once a serene Buddha must have sat. Now bronze T'ang ritual vessels, a golden bowl, silver and jade were arranged on it. Underneath each object was a small white explanatory card.

I had been in the room before, and each time had felt regret that these priceless objects were hidden away from people who would appreciate their beauty. Theodora herself, I was certain, gained no enjoyment from them: her passion was to collect, not to love.

To me, the most moving thing in that room was an Imperial dragon robe sewn with pearls, now discolored, the delicate kingfisher design faded. It had once been the pride of some little Manchu princess. The gown lay in its glass case, carefully preserved from the light and air that would destroy it.

Some of Theodora's jewelry was in leather boxes on shelves. Wherever she went, the historic gems that she had bought traveled with her. She clung to these as people cling to a family.

She had unrolled a piece of black velvet, brushed it with her hand and then laid the jade belt on it, standing back to admire the effect.

"I like it," she said, "and I hope you're right about its original function, because what you print on the display card must be accurate."

"Oh, yes, it will be."

She waved her hand toward the door. "Then let's go."

"I'd rather like to take the jade to my room and study it properly."

"Not tonight. There's no time. You can have it tomorrow morning. And now, Sarah, you'd better hurry and dress."

"I'm going to see my father tonight," I called as she disappeared for a last look into the strongroom. "I'm afraid, as I said, I won't be at your party."

She came out and closed and secured the door before speaking. "If you want to see your father, you'll *have* to be at my party. He's coming, too."

"Father?" I asked incredulously.

"Oh," she said casually, "I called him tonight and he jumped at the chance. He enjoys parties, and I'm sure he would be most hurt if you weren't here. Then, of course, there's Marius . . ."

I turned and walked to the door.

"Sarah."

I waited.

"You are in my house and I think, therefore, you should be gracious when I include you in my social gatherings. Quite a number of people you know will be coming. It amuses me to mix my guests."

I could not answer politely. Instead I asked, "Don't you want to show the jade?"

"No," she said sharply, "and don't mention it to them."

"Of course not." I didn't remind her that I wouldn't be there to tell anyone.

I walked down the hall, running a finger lightly across the blackwood and scarlet lacquer furniture as I passed. It was most certainly Theodora's business whether she chose to show her rarest treasures to her acquaintances. Her business, not mine. I had bought the jade, and that was that. *But it was not,* said a demoniac intuitive voice inside me, *the end of the affair.*

I went out into the lantern-lit court where Ah Lin was supervising the arrangement of the buffet tables along the wall by the white bauhinias. Oliver Farache was nowhere to be seen. He had probably gone back to wherever he was staying to change into formal clothes.

The sun would drop quickly into the sea, but this was the moment before it disappeared. The swallows jockeyed for place in the frescoed eaves, and the water in the lotus pool was like a sheet of gold in the lantern light. Only nature, however, was serene. The entire household was preparing for the party with bustle and scuttling feet.

I escaped to my room in the guest pavilion. Although the furniture was black lacquer, it was not in the least depressing—the Chinese knew how to make every color gay, tinting it with gold and pearl. A few charming Chinese *objets d'art* ornamented the chest and the tables. One particularly lovely piece was a butterfly cage of golden mesh. I thought of the brilliant fluttering wings that must once have been captive there, and infinitely preferred it empty. A gray jade vase held pink chrysanthemums.

I slid out of my dress and shoes and lay on the bed, arms behind my head, staring at the delicate carving of the latticed windows. I wished I had the jade girdle with me and that I could examine it in peace. It was probably nervousness that made it difficult for me to give a final judgment when anyone was watching me. I liked to be on my own, to get the "feel" of a piece—move it around, examine it in every possible light. But Theodora had the girdle and Ch'i had the money and I could forget about it.

The guest pavilion was near the outer wall and so I could hear through my open window the dim sounds of footsteps in wooden shoes, the cling of bicycle bells and the click of the mah-jongg pieces from the little restaurant next door.

I therefore didn't realize at first that the soft knocking came from outside my door. Lilo entered when I called. She carried over her arm the peony-patterned white gauze dress which Theodora had mentioned to me, dangling the thought of it as an inducement for me to go to her party.

Lilo was never overtly rude, but her manner to me implied: "You are only one of us, after all. A paid servant of a very rich American."

Aloud, she said, "Mistress Lady says you should wear this dress tonight."

"Please thank her and tell her that I can't be at her party. I have already explained that I'm going out."

Lilo laid the dress on the bed, picking at the peony pattern with a tawny finger. "Mistress Lady will be angry if you do not go."

"I'll explain to her again," I said. "Thank you, Lilo."

She waited a moment, watching me. "Are you staying long?"

"No. I have my home in England. I'm here to help Lady Paradine and then I shall have a holiday before going back."

"Sometime, I'll go to England . . . and New York . . . and California."

I watched this girl, talking of her golden dreams. "Or perhaps I'll stay here," she went on. "They say I look like Fay Mi."

I was vaguely aware that Fay Mi was one of the most famous of all Oriental film stars. But I had never seen her or her films, so I had no idea if they resembled one another. "You are very beautiful, Lilo," I said.

She sauntered to the mirror and looked at herself. "I think if I go to Movie Town in the New Territories, they'll like me."

Everyone in Hong Kong knew of the great Run Run Shaw, the head of the studios that made films for distribution all over the Orient. He was a kind of father figure to the many beautiful girls who lived in the apartments which he provided for his stars and in the dormitories for the starlets.

Lilo was watching me. "If Mistress Lady doesn't take me to America with her, I'll go to the Studios. I'll *make* Mr. Shaw like me."

I had no doubt that with her beauty, she could impress almost anyone. About her acting ability, however, I knew nothing.

She moved back to the bed and again began stroking the dress. Then, as she looked across the room at me, I saw the longing in her eyes for the riches and the comfort which surrounded her and yet of which she was no part. As she left the room I wondered where she came from and what her life had been like before she came to Theodora's Manchu palace.

The lovely white dress on the bed drew me like a magnet. I had no intention of going to the party and meeting Marius there, but I couldn't resist trying the dress on. I slid it over my head, zipped it up and stood in front of the tall mirror in the lacquer frame.

Although the dress was too short for Theodora, it swept the ground around me in layers of gauze, seeming as fragile as cobwebs and yet in reality lasting and resilient. The peony pattern ranged over it in splashes of rich pink. The Chinese wedding flower and my favorite . . . Marius knew that. In the two July months we had had together, our small drawing room had been filled with them, for Marius bought them for me with a wild abandon during their brief life in the English summer.

I dragged my thoughts away from memories and slid out of the dress. Then I went and drew a bath and lay soaking. I had to get out of the house for the hours that Theodora's guests would be there. Father would be puzzled at my absence, but when he saw Marius he would understand.

I planned to spend the evening with Evelyn Lucas, that grand old friend of my mother's who lived at the Peak top. She suffered badly from osteoarthritis and was housebound, but she had a lively mind and a wonderful sense of humor. People flocked to her small charming apartment, and although friends warned her that the mists which encircled the High Levels for months of the year were bad for her illness, she scoffed at the idea of moving. She would take her guests to her great picture windows and point: "Is there anywhere in the world with such a view as that? The island, the hills, the lights, the sea . . . and strange secret China over there. I can sit here and be happy. I couldn't live without that view."

I dressed quickly, listening to the sounds of activity in the lantern-lit courts. To try to shut out the thought that Marius would be there tonight, I busied my mind speculating on the food. Fish cooked in wine, perhaps; spiced sweet and sour sauces; duck so delicate that the flesh would fall away from the bone; caviar from Russia; strawberries from New Zealand.

So while the hostess and the servants awaited the arrival of the guests, I slipped quietly out of the Pavilion of Apricots, smiling at the puzzled face of Ah Baht, who opened the fortresslike double doors for me.

As I sat in the tram climbing to the Peak, many familiar places drifted into view and disappeared again among the trees. My life in Hong Kong had never been dull for me. I had been an only child but not a bored one. There had been swimming at Shek-O; playing at being a "crew" in someone's small yacht; riding over the great hills; looking for orchids in the hollows.

I spent three hours with Evelyn in her drawing room, surrounded by the Regency furniture she had brought out from England. She had come to the Orient to marry the man called the Sea Devil, because no one could match him in sailing yachts and the wind always seemed to favor him when he entered a race. But the wind had demanded payment for all the trophies he had won, and in the end his green and white yacht had capsized in a freak storm and Evelyn's Sea Devil had been drowned. For her, though, it was then too late to return to England. She had fallen under the spell of Hong Kong.

In spite of painful arthritis, she was still pretty, and now that there was an Art Center and a concert hall on the island, she was utterly content. She had many friends who would half carry her crippled body down the Peak to listen to Yehudi Menuhin or to watch the Javanese dancers.

Evelyn was the recipient of all the gossip of Hong Kong. She would sit and listen to the long stories of the sins and omissions, the intrigues and the scandals, and like the wise and worldly woman she was, she would never criticize. Whenever I returned to Hong Kong it was she who would fill me in with all the things that had happened during my absence, telling me without malice, but chuckling, shaking her snowy white head, tapping her ebony stick with delight on the parquet flooring of her large drawing room.

She had a stimulating mind and a great gaiety, so that being with her was always fun. Yet as we talked, I stole glances at the little brass carriage clock and wondered how long the party at the Pavilion of Apricots would last and whether Marius would give me a single thought.

VII

MARIUS WAS STANDING in the light of the string of lanterns under the acacias. Around the lotus pool, the little potted peach trees had tiny electric light bulbs hidden in their foliage, so that as I stopped abruptly, shocked by the sudden sight of him in Theodora's garden, I too must have been completely illuminated.

The fact that he was always at the back of my mind was something I was trying to accept as a permanent condition. But I had been quite unprepared to come face to face with him just beyond the third moon gate.

I experienced none of the expected reactions—my heart did not begin to thud; there was no pain, no sense of anguish. I had gone beyond all the superficial sensations, and the emptiness I felt was like a desert around me.

He came here to see Theodora. We have met by bitter accident. Oh, Marius . . .

His hair was turned to polished bronze under the lights; his face, with its strong nose and uneven features, was too well remembered, too vivid. "So many months of separation," he said, "and you are still wearing your heart on your cheek." He touched the heart-shaped freckle near my left eye, which had always intrigued him. "It's even more golden than it used to be."

"Lantern light," I said and jerked my face away, resenting the reminder of that old, silly joke that had delighted our first months together. "It's late," I added faintly, needing to fill the moment's silence, to match my coolness with his.

"And you hadn't expected me to be still here."

"No, I hadn't."

"Of course, it could be that I was deliberately waiting to see you."

I moved without speaking toward the little white blob that was the Pekingese, Mister Wu, and bent and stroked the silky back.

"There are still a few people milling around," Marius said. "You should have been there. Theodora gives wonderful parties. She's a gifted hostess, and this must be the loveliest house in all Hong Kong."

I turned my head away from him. Those who said that the alliance of power and glamour had a magic were right. The qualities had obviously charmed Marius. It wasn't just the warmth in his voice that cut through me; I also felt a strange kind of vibration as if, in speaking of her, Marius had brought Theodora to his side, like a triumphant enemy.

I kept my head turned away from him. "You've changed. You used not to like parties very much."

"Oh, I've learned a lot in the past two years—one being that most things are good in moderation."

"I believe Father was also here."

"Yes. And has left. He said he needs his early nights. He was disappointed not to see you."

"I had lunch with him the other day. I'll go and see him again tomorrow. How are you, Marius?"

"Fine."

"Which is really no answer. What are you doing?"

"Studying acupuncture with a Chinese doctor, a master in his profession. He has a small clinic over in the New Territories, near the Sumchun River."

"That's more or less what John Tarquin told me when I saw him in London. He thinks you could have studied there."

"Does he?"

I pursued my questioning against his vague indifference. "Are you living over at the clinic?"

"Some of the time. At others I come here to Hong Kong to enjoy the bright lights for a little."

"John was right," I said. "Why come all this way to study?"

"You knew I was intending to go deeply into the subjects that interested me. I told you that long ago. Or perhaps you didn't listen."

"I did. But I never imagined you would go to the lengths of burying yourself somewhere on the borders of China."

"Why not? Would *you* mind how far you traveled to learn more about jewels and jades?"

"I thought the important acupuncture clinics were in Taiwan now. Why didn't you go there? That's where, so I'm told, some Western doctors go to learn, or you could have studied acupuncture in London."

"Perhaps there are times when a man has to pack up and get

away. They give sabbaticals to people at universities. That could be what I really needed . . . to recoup."

"You were overworked."

"No more than many men in my profession. That's not the point. There are other things to learn here."

"What things?"

"Tai Chi. The art of relaxation—the Chinese way. I told you about that too. It's the principle of constantly shifting weight without strain. Harmony. I've studied it, and I know what it does for some people. You go to a group feeling so damned tired that you decide you want your head examined for bothering to turn up. You come away refreshed."

I listened, thinking: *Marius is doing exactly what I'm doing—talking to cover up tension.* But what was that tension? Meeting me? Or the nearness of Theodora Paradine?

He moved into the shadows. "You're still wearing your wedding ring."

"I'm still married."

He reached out and lifted my left hand. "I wonder how many other women have designed their own?"

I withdrew my hand quickly. "I don't know."

"I'm quite certain you've been asked to copy yours for other weddings."

The lamplight gleamed on the sunrays of thin gold which surrounded the diamonds. "In spite of being asked," I said, "I have never copied it for anyone."

"Does that mean you have a streak of sentiment, Sarah?"

"You can call it that. Or if you like, you can think that it's because I wanted to wear something unique."

"Ah, of course. That's more like it."

There was a burst of distant laughter.

"You should go back to Theodora and her remaining guests," I said formally. "Did you . . . did you bring anyone with you to the party?"

"A woman, you mean?"

"That's what I meant."

"Would you mind if I did?"

I wanted to turn and run. I pretended I was looking for Mister Wu. "I would just like to know how long this is going to last. I mean our . . . indecision . . . neither marriage nor freedom." I waited, but he said nothing. I went on, desperately trying to force some kind of clarity between us, "You once accused me of not believing in marriage."

"*Marriage* is an abstraction," he retorted. "*A* marriage is between people. I have always thought you believed in the first but not the second—or rather, that you persuaded yourself to believe in it and became my wife. But you discovered that other interests were more compelling."

I tried several times to speak. Then my words came out with a rush. "That's not quite fair! Did you wait for me tonight just to attack me?"

"Perhaps."

His tone held such icy indifference that I felt suddenly as if I had touched depths and could not cry out to the only one near enough to save me from drowning.

"It's no use, it never was any use, because you could never understand that I love my work as you love—*loved*—yours."

"Perhaps, for both of us, the goal was right but the route wrong."

"My route was simple. I have always known where I was going. There was no wrong way."

"You used not to be arrogant, Sarah," he said.

I'm not. I'm not. But I'm being hurt and I will not show it. And so I must hold on to my own pride, my own belief in what I am doing; where I am going . . . in myself.

Aloud, I said, "How else can I work with jewels *except* with jewels?"

"The beauty of a stone or of a design—oh, yes. But chasing the world for bigger and better pieces—that is ambition, not creation."

"I work for Theodora. I can only reach the top by doing my best. That's something you must have learned, too, Marius."

"Yes."

His reply was too succinct. I said, hurt and angry, "You haven't told me yet *why* you waited to see me tonight."

"To talk."

"About anything in particular?"

"No. Just talk."

"If you wanted bright party conversation from me, I'm sorry, I don't feel that way." Hurt drove the note of harshness into my voice. "You should have stayed with Theodora and her guests."

"Have dinner with me tomorrow?"

"To talk over old, sweet things? Oh, Marius! Nostalgia is the one thing I would never have accused you of."

"It could be that for a change I want to hear all about your work.

Theodora thinks you're pretty marvelous; she calls you 'the career girl tossing her husband's slippers at marriage.' Her phrase, not mine."

"Heigh-ho!" I said flippantly, wanting to burst into tears. "How clever of her to know me so well." My heels sounded heavy on the marble slabs as I walked away. It mattered, it mattered terribly that Marius had discussed me with Theodora.

"That dinner . . ."

"There's a new floating restaurant out in the New Territories. Try it," I called over my shoulder.

"Oh, we've been there. It has the finest food in the Colony."

"We"—a casual word sliding so easily into his answer. Stung by it, I said, "Then do go again—both of you. And have a good time."

I almost ran through the moon gate into the court of the guest pavilion. I could hear as a background to my footsteps the murmur of conversation from Theodora's late-leaving guests. I stubbed my toe against a stone urn that held a little peach tree, felt a sharp pain rise up my leg and hopped the few more steps into the small pavilion with its string of scarlet-and-gold lanterns.

Lilo was in the hall, leaning against the wall near a bronze jar of arum lilies. She was obviously on duty with Ah Baht, the old gateman, until the last of the guests left.

She gave me her beautiful, secretive smile as I said, "Good night, Lilo."

"I was watching. Did you hurt yourself?"

"Not much," I said lightly. "I should look where I'm going, shouldn't I?" I fled up the stairs to my room.

The lovely gown with the peony pattern was still on the bed. I paused at the dressing table and saw myself as Marius must have seen me. My brown hair was ruffled, my cheekbones glistened a little where the lamplight caught them; my skin was still very pale. Later, when my work here was finished I would burnish my body on the beach at Shek-O.

In the meantime, I was Sarah Brent with a job to be done; Sarah Brent with fingers that could design a ring and win an award; Sarah Brent, trying to get free of a love that was no use to her, and finding herself swimming desperately against a tide too strong for her.

I undressed, put on my robe, and in the blue-tiled bathroom, plunged my face into icy water. It was the finest tonic I knew for a dark mood. Then I went back to the bedroom and peered through the lattice. I could see Marius just beyond the moon gate, still where I had left him. Theodora had joined him. Her other guests must all have left, and as I watched, the lanterns went out and the two people lost their color and became shadows, standing so quietly together. It shouldn't matter. But it did. And it was absurd. I couldn't live with Marius and so I had no right to mind his interest in other women. That I still loved him was my affair and nobody's fault. *But don't, oh, don't let it be Theodora* . . .

I walked around the room, tired yet restless, touching an incense burner, dragging my finger along the blackwood table to a celadon bowl, tracing the little figures of the eight immortals carved round it. I envied those legendary figures their serenity.

The window drew me again. The moon was now hidden behind the acacias, so that small dapples of silver just lit the tips of the trees. Theodora and Marius were no longer there and the emptiness of the Court of the Lotus was like a finger beckoning.

I dragged off my robe, dressed again, went down the stairs and walked into the night. Where the moonlight was unhindered by trees, it flung its brilliance at the bauhinias, turning their flowers to little flurries of snow. It also found the goldfish pool, and like Narcissus of legend, beheld its dazzling self in the water.

Marius must have left, for Ah Baht was locking the heavy outer doors. Then he turned and disappeared in the direction of the servants' pavilion. I was alone in the cool of midnight.

I sat on the marble rim of the pool and closed my eyes, feeling the soft air against my lids.

"Why did you hide from my party, Sarah?"

I sprang up, startled. "I wanted to see Evelyn Lucas, a great friend of my mother's. I had promised her a visit."

"That's a poor excuse." Theodora had taken off her jewels but still wore the brocade gown. Her hair was loosened, and I had an odd sensation as she stood there facing the stark moonlight that she was very like the portrait of Ellen Terry as Lady Macbeth. She had only to wring her hands and the likeness would be perfect. Instead, she flicked the little ivory fan she carried. "I found this just now, lying in the hall. It's charming, isn't it? I believe I saw Janet Vallance with it. She was talking fast, as she always does, to Marius. You did know that Marius was here tonight, didn't you?"

"You told me he was coming. And we met."

She gave me a hard, bright smile, her face so blanched by moonlight that it was like a mask. "I'm glad. I was afraid you would stay away until you were certain all my guests had left—in order to avoid him."

There was barely veiled amusement in her voice, but I made no comment. She elaborated on the point, obviously wanting a discussion. "When everything is over between two people, they should behave in a civilized manner, shouldn't they?"

"Of course."

"I've never been quite certain how you felt, Sarah. But you probably now realize that Marius and I meet often? I find him a delightful companion, in spite—"

"In spite of what?" I asked.

"I was going to say that he really is far too absorbed in all those fancy studies of his. I don't understand the medical world, nor do I want to. I like my lovers charming and amusing, and Marius can be both when he likes."

My lovers? . . . My lovers? I heard the question hammer in my mind, and with it came remembered words. "'Tell me, my heart, if this be love . . .'"

"Marius has only just returned from the New Territories," Theodora continued. "He spends so much time studying in that isolated place, and when I ask him, he doesn't even try to explain why he can't work here on the island. But then, part of Marius's charm is that he never explains himself. Don't you agree?"

I felt that she was talking in order to give herself time to watch my reactions, both to meeting Marius tonight and to her blatant indication of something more than friendship between them.

But when I remained silent, she said, "Now that Marius is back, for a while, from Lok Ma Chau, you won't, of course, mind seeing him around here?"

I minded horribly. "No," I said. "And now I'm going to bed. Good night."

She came toward me and laid her hand on my arm. "Don't go yet. I want to relax, my dear. The party's over. Sit down, just for a few minutes." The softness of her voice was an illusion; I knew that she was using it deliberately to cover her real reason for wanting to talk to me.

She settled herself in one of the cane chairs, the shell pattern of the back and the sides framing her as if she were some shadow queen holding court in a dark garden.

"Did you know, Sarah, that I sold my first husband—and I mean that I literally sold him?"

"Really?" I wasn't in the mood to be interested.

She sat playing with the fan. "He was so good-looking and so charming, but that, and his romantic title of Marquis, was all he had. I was very young at the time and a golden-haired man called the

Marquis de Tasman was something I really couldn't resist. But he had no money to speak of and no intention of earning a living. Nor had I any intention of keeping him. There was a very rich woman who adored him, so I made a bargain with her. 'I'll divorce Hubert and pay his costs and you can have him—if you will give me your Cellini pendant.' It's quite beautiful and was made in the Florentine workshops in the sixteenth century. You may have seen it—a great pearl mounted in enameled gold. I never wear it, but at least it's mine in return for a husband I no longer wanted."

"Well," I said flatly, "that's fine. If everyone was happy . . ."

"Oh, they were. Or at least they were until the silly man went on an expedition up the Amazon and got himself killed."

I knew that this wasn't some tall story for my amusement. The newspapers had recorded the incident in detail.

"My second husband, Viktor, I never see. And my third husband, Oliver, you've met. You know, Sarah, Oliver is the only man—husband or otherwise—who refused to be bought off. Most men have their price. But you've learned that, haven't you?"

"No."

"You will. Perhaps in your case you won't find money the bargaining medium, but there'll be something. So you had better prepare yourself, my dear."

I sat in the darkness, watching the moon dipping almost visibly behind the curved roofs of the pavilion. Nothing that was being said was random, everything, every word, was leading up to the final, paramount point.

"When I was still quite young, my father and I had a very serious talk. 'You are rich. If you like a man enough to marry him, then do so. But pay him off before the whole thing gets stale. I want you to be happy, and life is too short to waste it in boredom.' I never forgot my father's wisdom. *You* were wise, Sarah. You and Marius separated just at the right time—before things turned sour for you. That's why Marius still feels kindly toward you."

"Thank you," I said dryly, meaning quite the opposite.

Theodora lifted her arm, trying to see the time on the tiny exquisite watch which had for a face a fire opal surrounded by diamonds. "It's nearly one o'clock"—she rose from her chair—"and I suppose Célie is wanting her sleep. Good night, Sarah. I'm so glad we've had this talk."

You've had *your* talk, I thought. I said nothing out loud and turned my head away as she left me, walking lightly but firmly.

I swung around on the marble rim and dipped my fingers in the pool, trying to catch the moon's reflection in the water. But it eluded me, and as I lifted my cupped hands, little silver spangles dropped from them back into the pool and danced a moment before tiny waves drowned them.

I touched my burning face with my wet hands, but rage still tore at me, mingling with despair. Theodora's little heart-to-heart had about as much innocence as a serpent's bite.

She had warned me off Marius.

VIII

I CLOSED THE DOOR of my room and leaned against it. I was no prisoner in this palace compound. I could escape tomorrow if I chose, return to London and never see Theodora Paradine again. I had other clients; I had a marvelous world of jewels to study; I was young and strong. I could leave the Pavilion of Apricots, refuse all payment for the short time I had been with her and go to a hotel or to my father's and enjoy myself.

If I walked out on Theodora. The question I had to face, and face quickly, was whether it was more courageous to stay. It was obvious that the point of Theodora's conversation was that Marius, too, had his price, and that she was perfectly prepared to pay it. But he was a man with a good brain and pride. We had lived together long enough for me to know him better than this woman who, with all her vast wealth, had not been able to hold on to her marriages.

But, said a voice deep inside me, *neither have you held on to yours.* Perhaps I hadn't known Marius after all. So conclusion followed conclusion. If Theodora had been able to read Marius's character more accurately in a few weeks than I had in two years, then it was as well I found out. That the discovery would hurt was putting it far too mildly, but at least it could now be a clean and final break.

I slept badly that night, and waking, found that the rare white jade girdle and not Marius was most strongly in my mind whenever I stirred and opened my eyes. It was as though, unknowingly, I had been dreaming of it. I even had a strange feeling that while I slept I found the link between the jade and some memory. But half awake and listening to a distant dog's bark, I lost that link.

In the morning, while I breakfasted by the open lattice window, the jade still troubled me. I sat staring at the stone jars that held dwarf Japanese apricot trees. The nagging half-memory was like seeing someone and thinking, "We've already met somewhere." Or walking into a strange house and feeling, "I have been here before."

Gradually, as I drank coffee and crunched toast, something that had lurked at the back of my mind became clear. There were twelve Signs of the Zodiac, and the Chinese were a meticulous people. They would never have left that symbolism incomplete. So somewhere there must exist a companion belt marked with the other six signs.

While the birds sang in the trees and Mister Wu lay in the sun I gradually grew more and more certain that somewhere, in a museum or even in a private collection, I had seen a ceremonial belt with Signs of the Zodiac on it. As though a fog were clearing, the memory became sharper and more exciting, for I recalled that the one I had seen had been of yellow jade, the stone that was used for the girdle worn for the ceremony at the Altar of the Earth, and together these two—the Earth girdle and the Moon girdle that Theodora now possessed—made a perfect whole.

I needed to look at the jade again. My impatience almost pushed me into rushing to Theodora's bedroom and asking for it, but I knew that she would emerge in her own good time, and that her temper would be violently frayed if I tried to see her before she was prepared to see me.

I heard Ah Lin go to Theodora's room for her orders for the day. The little woman with her creased ivory face ruled the rest of the servants like an army general.

I busied myself in a small room off the drawing room, cataloging the collection of semiprecious stones which had been left to Theodora by an uncle. They had considerable value, but when I had arrived in Hong Kong, I found that she had thrust them haphazardly into the drawers of a red lacquer cabinet. When she showed them to me with an almost bored air, I said they were lovely and persuaded her to let me sort them out.

Almost every conceivable stone was there, and as I handled them, I thought of all the legends and superstitions that surrounded them. Coral, said in the olden days to protect the wearer; amber, the tears of birds; peridots, green as lush wet grass; and topaz and tiger's eyes . . . My fingers touched the cool stones, and I dreamed . . .

"So this is where you are, Sarah."

She was wearing tawny silk lounging pajamas and three long neck-laces, one of garnets, one of yellow topaz and one of green tourmalines. By her standards they were "just things to throw on while I am drifting around the house." To me, each necklace would have been very precious, and the three together extremely heavy to wear.

"Would you please let me have another look at the jade?" I asked. "I'd like to see it in good, natural light."

Her eyes narrowed. "You've had second thoughts? It's a fake, after all?"

"No, it's genuine. But I can't quite place the dynasty, and I like to be accurate. As accurate as I can."

"It's important that you are, Sarah." She turned away, and I followed her into the drawing room, waiting by the Coromandel screen while she went behind it and into her strongroom.

As she handed me the jade, she said, "Be quick. I don't want it left around." She picked up some newspapers from a table and went into the tree-shaded Court of the Lotus.

I took the jade to my room and laid it on the table, trying to remember where I had seen a similar belt to this. Then slowly another recollection formed. I had a feeling that it had not been an actual belt but a photograph.

Memory unfolded and I seemed to see two words on a white explanatory card below a pictured girdle—"Sung," which had denoted the dynasty, and the word "lost." They danced in my mind, as elusive as a will-o'-the-wisp. Something had been lost; something that went back through the centuries to a dynasty that ended in the thirteenth century. I had to trace that belt, or its photograph which I had seen so recently. I had to know why it was vaguely linked in my mind with the one that rested before me on the lacquer table.

The first thing for me to do was to go to the Hong Kong Art Center. I could ask the curator to help me, and I was certain that he would. But before that, I had to tell Theodora what I was planning to do.

I found her sitting in a triangle of mauve shadow under the acacias, reading from a pile of newspapers. I laid the belt on the small marble table before her. "I've got some news for you. Somewhere I know I've seen a belt like this one. And I must find out where. I *must* . . . Perhaps you'll come with me to try and trace it, but if not, I'll go on my own."

"For heaven's sake, Sarah, slow down and start from the beginning."

"I've either seen a similar ceremonial belt, or a photograph of one, very recently. I've got an idea there were Signs of the Zodiac carved on it. And somewhere on the card beneath it, I seem to remember the word 'lost.' So don't you see—?"

"No, I don't."

"There are twelve signs. You have a belt with six of them. Somewhere I'm certain there must be another belt with the other six carved on it. It's possible that the one I remember seeing—or, as I said, the photograph of one—could be the companion piece. It's only a vague memory, but it's nagging at me. I must find it and check."

Her eyes glittered. "Yes, Sarah, find it and get it for me."

I shook my head. "I'm quite certain of one thing. The one I saw was in a museum or some exhibition of Chinese art."

"You didn't mention this to me yesterday."

"I didn't *know* yesterday. Sometimes memory unwraps itself slowly. This did."

"So?"

"The first thing is for me to take this one to the Art Center and see the curator."

Her face hardened. "This belt stays here. I have no intention of having some stranger's hands on my possessions even if he *is* an expert. Not, that is, until I'm dead and the world can see my collections." The thought elated her. She picked up the jade. "And now it goes into the strongroom." She turned and walked away from me.

Behind me, the goldfish darted between the sun specks in the pool and the wind bells danced in the morning breeze that would sweep the last of the mists from the Peak. But Theodora's lovely courts didn't delight me that morning.

I walked through the gates that led from court to court and along the paths between the urns of flowers. Ah Baht opened the main doors and I stepped out into the bustling street. I walked all the way to the newly built Art Center.

The place was fairly empty, and I made for the room where there was an exhibition of photographs of some of the great treasures taken from the Imperial Palace in Peking to the island of Taiwan at the time of the Revolution. These objects were now exhibited in the recently built museum with its green roofs and primrose walls.

There were a few photographs of ceremonial girdles, but they were all from the later Ming dynasty and none of them matched the design on the golden coils which linked the jade pieces of the girdle that Theodora now owned. Nor did any have carved on them the other six Signs of the Zodiac. And that was the most important factor of all.

There was a second, very much smaller room which displayed a few photographs of art treasures found at an archeological site in North China. Moving along the show cases I found a beautiful glossy print of a yellow jade girdle. I stood rooted. Of course. Only a few days earlier I had visited the Center to see for myself the splendid display under the expert lighting. I hadn't remained very long in the rooms that contained only photographs of art treasures, and that was why the cursory glance I must have given the exhibits had meant that I hadn't registered the items photographed sufficiently to remember them clearly. But now I saw, plainly marked, the other six signs, the narcissus designs on the gold links and an identical dragon clasp.

I read the small display card beneath the girdle. "Photograph of a Sung dynasty emperor's girdle discovered at Shensi in 1928. The original is now among the exhibits at the National Palace Museum in Taiwan. A companion belt of white jade used for the ceremonies at the Altar of the Moon is reported to have been discovered recently, at the time of the reopening of an adjoining archeological site. This tomb was looted and certain treasures disappeared before they could be collected and sent to Peking."

And that "lost" girdle had been sold by a cripple on a hillside for a mere fraction of its actual worth.

The fear that had hung over me as we had driven out to Ch'i Pai-shih's hut now took a definite turn. Badly shaken, I left the Art Center. For one thing, although the jade girdle had been bought in good faith, such good faith would not stand up in a court of law. I was now certain that Theodora had stolen property in her possession. And what was even more dangerous, it was property that belonged to the Republic of Red China and to the Chinese people.

I should have taken a taxi straight back to the Pavilion and Theodora, but I was too dazed to summon one. Instead, I walked through the crowded streets, all the way mentally looking over my shoulder. But nothing sinister happened. I was just an English girl in a gray dress and matching sandals, walking in the Hong Kong streets.

When I eventually returned, I found Theodora where I had left her —in the garden. "I have something to tell you," I began, "something important."

The urgency in my voice caught her attention at once. She turned her water-light eyes on me. "What is it?"

"I am certain that the jade Ch'i sold you is stolen property."

Immediately she relaxed, throwing back her head, laughing. "Well, now, that means we'll have to be careful. Wasn't I wise to put it straight into my strongroom, out of sight, so that only you and I and—er—the thief know about it?"

"If I'm right, the belt belongs to the Chinese government."

"*If* you're right? Don't you think you should be certain before you make such statements?"

"Very well, then, I *am* certain. I told you that the ceremonial belt seemed faintly familiar."

"There are probably dozens around."

"Oh no. Only the dynastic emperors wore them. I've just been to the Art Center, and there's a photograph of a belt which was excavated at a tomb in the Province of Shensi nearly fifty years ago. The explanatory note points out that the companion belt was discovered only recently but disappeared from a looted tomb."

"Oh, really, Sarah. Being a designer of jewelry is one thing. But don't let your imagination run riot."

"You know enough about art treasures and about me to be pretty certain that what I'm saying isn't nonsense. The belt you have is unique. The only other girdles I can ever remember having seen usually have designs of musicians or fish or birds."

She stared at me for a moment or two, then flung up her hands in delight. The wide sleeves of her robe fell back to show her smooth arms. "Isn't that wonderful? I really congratulate you. A looted tomb —and I possess a stolen treasure from it which other collectors would give their souls for."

"But you can't keep it. You must know that." I tried to check my growing exasperation. "You could go to the police, or if you want to be quite certain that I'm right, then we'll go together to the curator at the Center and tell him the whole story."

She was silent for a moment, studying her rings. I watched her. Too many rings, too many flashing stones aging her hands. "You know the saying 'Let sleeping dogs lie'?" she asked. "Well, this is a wonderful dog that is going to remain sleeping under my roof forever."

"It will probably wake up and bite you hard."

"Oh, I'll take that risk."

"Shall I tell you what I'm almost certain has happened? I mean, how this one came to be offered to you?"

"I'm not interested."

Her insolence angered me. "I think you should face what is now obvious." I willed her to look at me and listen. "Theodora, *this is important.* I've told you that when I saw that photograph of the yellow jade belt, I *knew* I was looking at the companion piece to yours."

"Then," she demanded, "how did one get to the Museum in Taiwan and the other find its way to me?"

"The card under the photograph at the Center explained. The yellow jade was discovered long before the Cultural Revolution. After that, when all their ancient traditional culture was under attack, Red China closed the sites. No one searched any more for treasures and what had previously been amassed had been shipped by Chiang Kai-shek's government to the island of Taiwan. The photograph I saw in the Art Center was of the belt in the Taiwan Museum."

"And then, when Red China had a change of heart and reopened the archeological sites, the one I possess was found—and then lost."

"Stolen," I said coldly.

"All right. All right. So let it rest. I'm doing nothing about it."

"Theodora, face facts. It's possible this is part of a large theft of art treasures, and if you become involved . . ."

"If China wants her heritage, then let her go and demand it back from Taiwan. Heaven knows there are thousands of jades and bronzes and silks there."

She was implacable, and it was useless to try to reason with her. I made one last effort. "The Chinese are very patient and very thorough people. They could trace the jade to you."

"Ch'i sold it to me, and by now he's probably off the island and away. There's no one who can connect me with anything bought illegally."

"Then you're deluding yourself. Ch'i is probably not the original thief. More than likely, whoever is the brains behind the theft lives somewhere near China, even perhaps just inside the Chinese border."

"It's of no interest to me whether Ch'i or a group of art thieves is involved. The important thing is I have the jade—and I intend to keep it."

I clung to whatever grain of patience I had left. "Theodora, will you please try to understand? The Chinese authorities know that certain archeological finds are missing. Don't you think they'll do all they can to get them back? They won't let them slip through their fingers."

"Oh, but, Sarah, this *has*," Theodora said softly. "This jade that *you* advised me to buy." Her narrowed eyes had a feline glitter; she was baiting me.

I ignored the interruption. "China will have alerted the Hong Kong government, and if they trace that jade to you, you won't be able to plead ignorance. So if you'd just listen to me . . ."

"No. *You* listen." She rose and stood over me. "The matter is at an end," she said. "Put it out of your mind now and come with me to look at some opals I have and tell me how they can be reset to show off their color."

Opals and sapphires, diamonds and rubies . . . "A clandestine collector," I murmured aloud.

She had turned away from me and obviously hadn't heard what I said, for she asked, as I hung back, "Aren't you interested in seeing these stones?"

"Yes."

"Then show it, Sarah. And just remember that the matter of the jade is out of your hands. Now be a good and silent girl." She patted my hand.

The telephone rang and Ah Lin came toward us with her little shuffling walk. "New York, Mistress Lady. They say it's urgent."

"We'll look at the opals later," Theodora called over her shoulder to me. "I have a feeling this is going to be a long conversation."

As she left me I stood with arms folded and tried to work out what I must do. Theodora trusted me and I felt a certain loyalty toward her. On the other hand, both experience and intuition told me that we were caught up in a dangerous situation. The Sung ceremonial girdle was valuable both culturally and financially. I had little doubt that those who watched for any leakage of Chinese treasures would discover in some way or other that Theodora had acquired what rightly belonged to China. I had little doubt, also, that art treasures worth so much would find their way back, by measures that might seem desperate from the standards of the West, to their rightful place in the Forbidden City in Peking.

The slender branches of the acacias laid shadows across the pool. Somewhere beyond the thick outer wall, a child flew a scarlet kite. It soared high in the misty blue sky, silent and free of the huddled houses.

I could see the small, slight figure of Ah Baht in the further courtyard with Ah Tat, the head gardener. His hand brushed lightly across the bauhinias as he talked. I watched two goldfish having a mild altercation; in the trees above me, magpies chattered.

Apart from the birds and the occasional flick of a dragonfly as it skimmed the pool, it was very quiet. Theodora's side of the telephone conversation came clearly. "Then sell. *Sell*. For heaven's sake, what do you think I want to do with my money? Give it away by the truckload? You've told me that Barr Yield shares are falling. It's up to you to know whether it's an inside ruse or not. And if you don't know, then find out. You are my adviser. Damn you, man, *advise* me, then. Don't ask *me*."

I went quietly away from the window from which her loud, drawling voice was hitting the peace of her courts. I walked past the urns of scarlet chrysanthemums and saw, between the branches of the low cherry trees, the golden roof of the little tea pavilion.

Ah Baht was at the outer door and opened it for me. I smiled my thanks to him and went once again into the incessant turmoil of the street.

IX

FATHER LIVED in an apartment block on the Peak. He had his friends and his Yacht Club, and he had his hobby of reading Mandarin, the language of the Northern Chinese. He had even tried his hand at translating Chinese poetry into English and still clung to the hope that one day a book of his translations might be published.

I sat in the cable car and looked out at the thin television aerials, like the skeletons of church spires, rising into the sky. In the distance the sea was lavender-colored and so smooth, so gentle that the violent typhoons that would hit Hong Kong during the summer seemed as remote as old, lost dreams.

I got out of the car at the third intermediate stop and walked along the winding road to Father's block. Between this quiet high place and the nestling city below, there were patches of dark mountain scrub, and above, little silver clouds swam across the sky.

Father's apartment was on the third floor. His housekeeper, Nam Tsao, a small, wizened Cantonese in black silk trousers, opened the door and beamed so widely that she showed her two gold back teeth. She had a sloping forehead and a fly-away chin.

Father was in his large sitting room, the air conditioning under the window burring away softly. He was poring over newspaper cuttings of the many yacht races in which he had taken part at Kellet Island.

He hadn't heard me arrive, and in the moment or two before he saw me, I had a chance to notice how curiously unchanged he was, as if age had stood still for him. His hair shone with the same tawny gilt of old wood as when I had pulled it and played with it as a child; his skin had not yet slackened over his bones; and the only change was the deepening of the spider's webs of lines which hours of sun and reflected light on the sea had given him. Sensing someone there, he looked up and his eyes brightened. When he rose and held his arms out to me, I saw that his body was heavier.

I said, hugging him, "You really have put on weight."

He laughed. "My tactful daughter! You didn't mention that when we met the other day. You delayed the unflattering comment—I suppose to soften the blow." He pushed me back into a deep armchair and went to a mirror and looked at himself. "You can blame Nam Tsao, anyway. She gives me elephantine meals. On the other hand"— he turned and looked at me—"it doesn't look as if *you* feed yourself very well."

"Oh, I do. I do. Especially at Theodora's."

"Ah yes, Theodora's. And why did you hide away from her party last night?"

I walked to the window and looked out over the budding hibiscus and the green hills and the tall masts that guided the planes to Kai Tak Airport.

"All right, I can guess," he answered his question. "It was Marius, wasn't it?"

"Yes."

"But my dear girl, surely you're sophisticated enough to accept the fact that even if you and Marius can't live together, you can meet him in company in a civilized manner."

"We often imagine we're more able to cope than we can when the time comes."

"Nonsense. You can cope. And now the whole of the Island will be talking of how Sarah Brent ran away and hid while her husband attended Theodora's party."

"I don't care what my enemies will say, and my friends I hope will understand."

"Understand that you, a very successful young woman from London, don't even possess the social grace that would allow you to meet your estranged husband at a party? Oh, come!" Father was standing watching me. "Do you want to talk about Marius?"

"No. Nor of my shortcomings as a civilized person. I want to discuss something very important."

"And what could be more important than the fact that you're as in love with the man as you ever were? If you hadn't been, you'd have stayed for the party and met him."

"I did meet him. I had been to see Evelyn Lucas and I got back too early, and he was there."

Father gave a heavy sigh. "I thought you'd find out sooner or later. I just hoped Marius might stay in Lok Ma Chau a bit longer. It would have been more tactful of him to have remained there until you had left. But perhaps it's just as well to know right away."

"Know what?"

"About that budding friendship."

"Between Marius and . . . ?"

"Theodora," he said. "Well, now I've told you. And if I hadn't, someone else would have."

"She has taken pains to tell me already." The words burned my tongue. "But, Father, it can't be really serious? Marius isn't in the least her type."

He stubbed out his cigarette and put his hands on my shoulders. He wasn't smiling. "How do you know, my dear, what type is his or anyone else's? We get very great shocks when we think we know people and find that we don't, after all. You mustn't mind too much."

I moved away as gently as I could from Father's grip. I felt empty, as though plunged into a black void.

"Sarah . . ."

"It's all right, it's all right. I've had to get used to being without Marius. After all, I've got a life to live and I'm damned well going to live it."

"That's fine." The relief in his voice was only too evident. Poor Father. He hated emotional scenes. "That's just the way to take it," he went on jauntily. "Otherwise you'd have been involved in a battle you just couldn't win."

Because Theodora has too many weapons. Because, where I loved, she desired. And desire is ruthless and can overwhelm deeper emotions.

I moved away from Father and stood for a moment with my back to him. Away on the skyline the mountain of Mo Shan was a pale hump. Somewhere beyond, the rice fields ran down to the Shumchun River, which formed the boundary with Red China. And somewhere out there, Marius was living his strange new life.

How enduring was this new existence of his? How strong was Theodora Paradine's power over him? How strong my own love?

"And now," I heard Father's voice behind me, "what is this problem you wanted to see me about?" I was grateful for the question, glad to be forced to put Marius out of my mind. I turned to Father and first made him promise to keep everything I told him to himself. He promised, standing again at the mirror, smoothing his hair. "Go ahead, my dear."

He was a very good listener and didn't interrupt, but his face was grave. When I finished, he went to the door, called Nam Tsao for coffee, and turning back to me, leaned against the wall and shook his head.

"Scruples are all very well for saints, but not for you, Sarah. You live in a world where one has to fight for survival."

"And find myself in jail?"

"Oh, rubbish. Theodora knows how to guard her treasures. Nobody is going to find the jade. There must be many other art treasures that have mysteriously vanished. China is vast."

"Hong Kong isn't."

"Leave it. Ah . . ." He turned as Nam Tsao came in with a lacquer tray on which stood the yellow porcelain cups and saucers I had known all my life. "You see, Sarah, she spoils me. There's always a pot of tea or coffee waiting. Thank you."

"Missy, do you want cream in your coffee?" she asked.

"Yes. And thank you for remembering."

The old servant nodded. "Are you staying a long time?"

"No, but when I've finished my work with Lady Paradine I shall take three weeks' holiday here."

She glided to the door, hesitated and then turned. "The master is not well. I am glad that you have come here," she said and then closed the door behind her.

I looked at Father. "What's this about your not being well?"

He laughed. "Nam Tsao fusses. I'm perfectly fit, just idle. All I do is crew for my friends, enjoy the sun and get mad when typhoons upset the pleasant routine."

"You should be making use of your knowledge of China and the languages," I said.

He gave a faint grin. "You can just about remember, can't you, what they called it at the time? Redundancy. At my age, once you're out, you don't get back. I've got a good government pension, so I can't complain."

"Now that Red China is opening up more to the West, surely you could try your luck at liaison work. After all, they call Hong Kong a bridge to Asia."

He shook his head and his eyes took on the expression of someone looking into the past. "I wish I could have taken you to Peking in the old days, Sarah. You would have loved it all—the Forbidden City, the old jade dealers, the cloisonné workshops . . ."

"A lot of that must still be there. Why don't we try to go?"

He waved a dismissing hand. "It won't be the same, not for me, anyway. The old culture was magnificent. Nothing like it will ever be seen again."

"Perhaps to millions of Chinese, being no longer hungry is important, too. I hear there is no poverty in China now."

"There will always be poverty," Father said. "Give every man five thousand pounds and some will make a fortune, some will end up starving."

The old régime in China was a subject on which Father was relentless, but I made a last effort to shake him out of his pleasant, complacent existence. "The Chinese are now recognizing their past. That's why you could be useful if you made an effort to contact the right people."

He fidgeted in his chair. "It's too late. And I'm too old." He grinned at me again. "It's a pleasant life that I lead, Sarah. Though did I tell you in my letter that we had a pretty awful typhoon in July and it broke up Sam Masterman's boat?"

"That lovely yacht?" I cried, recalling my own happy days on it. "But why didn't he make for one of the typhoon shelters?"

"The auxiliary engine failed and he was too late. The only things he and his crew didn't lose were their lives. And he's got another boat."

Reassured, I returned to the reason for my visit. "Father, please help me. That jade . . ."

He spooned sugar into his cup. "You tell me Theodora has it in her strongroom. Well, then, it's her problem. So stop worrying." He glanced across at me and said with kindly exasperation, "For heaven's sake, you're making a name for yourself. Theodora Paradine is by far your most important client; why antagonize her? It's time you grew up, Sarah, my darling girl."

"I like to think I'm worried for her sake as well as my own," I said. "If the jade is traced to her, she's in for trouble."

"Then just don't dwell on it. And don't get stuck on a point of principle that may prove to be only in your imagination. After all, you have no proof that the jade is stolen."

"I'm three-quarters of the way there."

"It's the other quarter, Sarah, that's important. Get on with your career and enjoy life. And whatever you do, just remember that Theodora is the cream on your strawberries, and the mink instead of rabbit for your winter coat."

The coffee was strong and fragrant. There were some tiny cakes on a dish. I bit into one. "If I lose Theodora, I'll get other important clients."

"Don't be too sure you'll find another millionaire. They don't grow in hundreds, like trees in a forest, so enjoy the one who favors you. She said at dinner, just before you came out here, that she liked you because, besides being so knowledgeable, you are amenable—*her* word." He chuckled. "Go on being that way, my dear."

My fingers stiffened around the handle of the little cup. I set it down very carefully. "Father, did you say you and Theodora were dining?"

"That's right. We quite often do, didn't I tell you? Now, aren't you going to eat some more of those cakes? Nam Tsao made them specially because she knew you liked them, and she's psychic in some ways. She knew, for instance, that you were coming to see me today. Oh, and I've got something to show you. As you know, I've always been interested in photography, but I've now taken it up in quite a big way and I'm proud of my latest results. Some are of Theodora taken at Shek-O."

He got up to get the pictures and I ate a second little iced cake in silence, disturbed that Theodora obviously had also enlisted my father in her flattering entourage.

"Now . . ." He came back, sat down and took some photographs from a pink folder. "Look at these." He spread them fanlike before me. "There she is. Doesn't she look magnificent in that green beach robe? And there she is with me and—oh . . ." He tried too clumsily to slide one of the photographs under the ones I had already seen.

I whipped it out. In the picture Marius stood against a white Mediterranean-style villa with Theodora by his side. Her arm was through his and her face was turned to him, laughing.

My husband and my father . . . The thought lashed me to anger, but I hid it because I didn't want more argument.

I glanced very obviously at my wristwatch. "I really must go. Keep the snapshots for another time, will you? Theodora wants me to advise her about some opals."

Father said, "Of course, my dear. Of course." And then he gave me an odd, oblique look. "You know, I'm not really taking Theodora's side. I just want you to get ahead, succeed—which is more than I ever did. Your mother was the one with drive, and now it's up to you to make a big thing of your life. Do you know what someone said to me the other day? 'Robert, how is your jeweled daughter?' I liked that."

I said lightly, "You make me sound like Tiffany's. I doubt if any jewel of size is in my possession for more than two weeks."

"If you stick to your ambition, you'll remedy that. And whatever you do, don't let your broken marriage get you down. You and Marius couldn't live together. All right. Accept the fact and go right ahead with your own life. And that will mean not following in *my* footsteps."

I said anxiously, "But your life has been happy."

"Of course. And still is." He nodded. "But when I think when I came out here as a young man, when I remember Peking . . ." His eyes grew dreamy. "The old houses and even the sand which some-times blew across from the Gobi Desert. As I've said before, it was part of a charm, a graciousness and culture we'll never see again." For a silent moment his face was remote, and it was as if I were being allowed a glimpse of a man who not only provided a home for my mother and myself, who enjoyed his friends and his pleasant life, but someone with his own dreams, secret and beautiful and gone for-ever.

I remained very still, not daring to break the old lost magic. Then Father shook himself and gave a brief laugh. "But the secret of en-joying life is to adjust, and that is something I've done. I've got the sea and boats around me and friends—" He stopped short and gave me a slanting look. "There's one thing, Sarah."

"What?"

"Talking of friends, Marius comes here occasionally, for a drink and a chat. I think when he can get away from that clinic near the China border, he likes to relax."

"Have you seen it?"

"The clinic? No. I gather it's a very small place, though I can't re-ally say. No one around here seems to have seen it. Marius doesn't talk about it, either. He likes to hear me tell yachting stories. Maybe one of these days he'll take it up as a hobby. It would be good for him."

I gave Father an overbright smile and said firmly, "About that jade . . ."

"I thought we'd finished. I gave you my opinion."

"But I can't take it. I've got to report to someone that I believe it's stolen. I know we don't agree on what I should do, but please, would you come with me to the Art Center? I'd like to talk to the curator there first."

"Since when have you wanted your hand held?"

"*Please.*"

"If you do what that troublesome conscience of yours is nagging you to do, then you'll end up regretting it."

"Very well." I kept my voice light. "If you won't help, I can't drag you with me."

"It looks," said my father, "as if that's just what you're going to do, doesn't it? Come on, let's get going. The first thing I suggest we do, though, is to find this man Ch'i. He may be perfectly honest, and if so, you'll be saved a lot of unnecessary trouble, my dear. Shall we go? You can direct me."

Father's small, compact car was far more practical than Theodora's huge Rolls. As I got in, I said, "You take an awful lot of persuading. But thank you. I really do need someone's help."

The sun shone from a gauzy blue sky, and on the deeper blue of the sea a bat-wing junk was being swept by a soft wind. The rest were huddled, bobbing and swaying, on the waterfront.

Although Father's presence by my side gave me a sense of sharing my misgivings with someone wiser to the world than I, I had little faith that our visit would achieve anything. I said, "I hope we're doing the right thing in going to this man Ch'i."

"A cripple, you tell me, in a wheelchair? What do you think he can do to us?" He took a hand off the wheel and patted my knee. "When there's any question, it's always wise to go first of all straight to the source of it. I'm afraid if I don't try to help you, you'll only take matters into your own hands and go rushing to the authorities. If you do that, as I've already told you, you'll regret it. Theodora will break you, somehow."

"Well, so I'll begin by dealing with Ch'i."

"No, you won't. You'll just keep quiet and let me do the talking."

"He might not be there."

"Then you'll just let me think out the next move."

"And if he is there, what can you say to him? You can't ask him if he has been getting rid of stolen property. I wish we'd gone to the curator at the Center and asked his advice."

Father shot me a swift look. "I am a pretty good judge of the Chinese character, and besides, since I know both Mandarin and Cantonese, I can gauge him in his own language. It makes a difference, you know, a vast difference. Inflections in a voice, hesitations, choice of words—they can all reveal whether a man is speaking the truth or not."

We passed the great apartment blocks and came to the little group of fruit and fish stalls, but the man with the blue umbrella wasn't there. Instead, a young boy was in charge of the ginger stall. Some way past the town, I found the place where the track ran steeply through bamboo and wild banana to Ch'i's hut.

"This is it," I said.

We pulled the car to the side of the road. Once more, this time with Father by my side, I climbed the steep hill.

The door of the shack was wide open, but there was no sign of anyone and no shadow moved across the dark interior. When I had first entered with Theodora, I had looked around for another door, half anticipating that Ch'i would have a companion with him, but there had been no other room.

As we stood in the doorway, I said helplessly, "So Ch'i *has* gone."

"Well, I'm damned!" Father strode into the room. "I suppose he was so sure he could sell the jade to Theodora that he had already made his arrangements to leave this dump. But if, as you say, he's a cripple, how the devil did he get down that hill?"

"He walked."

"What . . . *what* was that?"

"I said he walked." I had my back to Father, and was staring at a bundle of sacks. Two wooden arms protruded. "The chair is here," I said.

Father strode across the room and lifted the sacking. "Good God, it is! That bundle of wood and rattan would never have made it to the road."

"It's obvious that he wasn't a cripple. That game was in order to get *us* to visit *him,* because he was in hiding and in fear of his life—at least that's what I think. Father, that jade was stolen property. It's all as I thought."

I stood in the doorway and watched as he prowled around the small room, opening the broken drawers of the cabinet, poking into every corner, exclaiming, "This place isn't fit for a pig, and there's nothing to be found here that will give us a clue to this man."

"Do you realize," I asked, "that there's no bed in the room? I think Ch'i came up here only to meet Theodora."

"Ch'i Pai-shih." Father bent down, tugged at a piece of long, dry grass and flicked the air with it. "Somewhere I've heard that name." He stood grinding his teeth in a way he had when he was thinking. Then his face cleared. "Of course! It's the name of an artist who was famous before your time—I'd say about fifty years ago. I remember seeing some of his work at an exhibition at the Mandarin Hotel."

I said, "I suppose the man I saw here assumed that name . . . So he turns out to be anonymous."

"I'm afraid so. And with four million Chinese on a small island, how do we go about trying to locate one man?"

I started to turn away when something flashed in my eyes. The sun on glasses, binoculars, a car's windshield—I couldn't tell, for there was nothing and no one in sight. Scrub hid the folds and slopes of the hills, and anyone who might be watching us. I shrugged it off as my imagination and went down the path after Father, who was striding ahead of me.

I caught up with him. "You see now, don't you, that I've no alternative but to go to the authorities? Of course, I'll explain to Theodora first. She'll rage, but I can't help that."

"It's Theodora's responsibility, not yours, Sarah."

Argument was futile. I gave up and climbed with him down the long rough track. And although I watched the distant hills for any sign of movement, I saw none. Only a few butterflies danced across our path, and clusters of gordonias swayed in the wind, their polished leaves gleaming.

X

WHEN THEODORA WAS ANNOYED, her eyes seemed to darken and her lips tighten into an even thinner line. "Where have you been, Sarah?"

"To see my father."

"But I wanted you to wait here while I took the telephone call. I needed your advice about the opals."

"I'm sorry, but this was urgent."

"Why? Is your father ill?"

"No. But I had to talk to him."

She broke in swiftly. "Don't tell me that you told him about the jade? I warned you to say nothing and if you have . . ."

I interrupted her. "Please understand. I had to ask somebody's advice and Father is the one person I can trust not to spread anything I might say all around Hong Kong. I'm so involved that I had to do something about it. *I* advised you to buy, and the more I think about it, the more convinced I am that the jade is stolen property."

"Yes." She looked at me with a long, thoughtful expression, her lips faintly curved into a secret smile. "You *did* advise me to buy it, didn't you, Sarah? And *I* couldn't have known that it was stolen, could I?"

"But now that you do, you must see that it's impossible to keep it."

"*You* are saying that I know it's stolen. *I'm* not. After all, there is no real proof. And anyway, however the jade got into Ch'i's hands, it's mine now. That's the only important point to me. And it should be for you, too. Don't you understand loyalty?"

"Yes. But I understand danger also."

She stubbed out her unsmoked cigarette on a little plaque of lavender jade—long ago it had been a Chinese scholar's handrest. "From now on, you will please talk to nobody about yesterday morning."

"But you *can't* keep the jade."

"Oh, I can—and I will."

In spite of the arrogance of her tone, I knew by the way she immediately lit her second cigarette that she was either nervous or angry.

"I've been out to Ch'i's shack," I said. "Father went with me. Ch'i Pai-shih is no cripple. His wheelchair was there, but the place was empty. I remember that he was impatient for me to be gone when I went there to collect the jade and pay him. He must have fled immediately after I left."

"I'm not interested."

"That isn't his name, either. Father remembered that there was a famous artist called Ch'i Pai-shih who lived about fifty years ago."

"I don't care if his name is Uncle Sam or John Bull," Theodora said and choked lightly on her cigarette. "He had what I wanted. The chapter is ended."

"We can't keep it."

"*We!*" As she walked across the room she looked down at me, her eyes cold. "My dear girl, I don't give up what I've paid big money for."

"But I've told you—and you must know—that the belt might easily be traced to you."

"So?" She paused, stood staring out of the latticed window. Then she swung around. "Let's get one thing straight, shall we? You talk glibly about going to the police, but you dare not. Do you hear? *You dare not go to the police.*"

"I'm sorry, but I can."

"Don't try to fight me, Sarah," she warned. "I reminded you just now that *you* advised me to buy the jade. *You* took the initiative. I was only the collector who bought it on your recommendation."

I shook with anger at the cool way she was making me the scapegoat. "You suspected from the beginning, didn't you, Theodora, that the jade was stolen—even when Ch'i telephoned to tell you about it? You involved me deliberately because you so desperately wanted it."

"Oh, do stop being righteous about it all."

"I'm not being righteous. I'm being realistic—and scared. That's why I have no intention of staying on here and advising you any more. I'm not so hungry for clients that I'll do anything for your patronage. Thank you for all the excitement I have had in the past. Now you must get someone else to advise you on your opals, and fly to Thailand. Wasn't that what you asked me to do before I took my holiday? But one thing I have to do immediately, and that is to call on the curator at the Art Center."

"Do that, Sarah." She reached out and slapped my hand lightly. "But if you do, I shall go and see him, too. I'll tell him that you bought the jade on a commission basis for me, but that it was I who decided it might have been stolen and forced you to report it. I shall be very upset that you tried to make money out of stolen property and then resorted to this foolish act of trying to place the blame on me. I'm a rich collector, my dear, universally known in the art world. I'll be believed because I have never been known to handle stolen works of art."

I turned my back on her. "You can say and do what you like. But I intend to report the jade."

"Sarah . . ."

I was in the doorway. I stood quite still, my back to her. There was a long silence. The scents of the house enveloped me softly, of Oriental woods, of flowers, of sandalwood and jasmine.

"Come here." She leaned against the wall, her head on a level with an embroidered scroll of orioles and mocking birds. "There are two kinds of people," she said. "Those who let their heads rule, and those whose emotions control them. You are one of the latter, aren't you, Sarah?"

"Am I?" I edged away, wary of the narrow, amused eyes.

There was a long silence. Then, very quietly, Theodora said, "I wonder how far you would go to protect someone you love?"

I received the words like a physical blow. Outwardly, I probably gave no sign of shock. Inwardly, I recoiled and froze.

"Well," she went on as I remained silent, "now is the testing time."

"You are testing my faith in someone I love?"

"You understand perfectly."

But that, I thought desperately, was something I could not do. I kept saying silently to myself, *"But I don't understand . . . I don't . . ."*

"You realize what you've done by being so high-minded, don't you, Sarah?"

"What have I done?"

She tilted her head back, laughing. "Kicked a stone and started an avalanche. Oh, not that I shall be caught in it. But *you* will. You see, it wasn't Ch'i who telephoned me. You've guessed now that I wouldn't be so foolish as to go 'blind,' as it were, to see an unknown man on a lonely hillside. I was assured beforehand by someone we both know well—or rather, *I* know well and you thought you did— that it would be perfectly safe."

I tried to steady my reeling thoughts. Theodora wouldn't dare lie about an involvement because she knew I could call her bluff. And so I believed her.

Someone I loved . . . Marius . . .

"I'm sorry to shock you, but it's no use pretending any longer. The cards are on the table, my dear, and I have all the aces."

I wasn't aware of moving, but I left her somehow, and went out into the court under the spread of acacia and orange trees. Bright birds skimmed past me in the warm sunlight, and beyond the Pavilion wall, the scarlet kite again limped and swayed drunkenly, seeking a wind to lift it above the housetops.

Theodora's compound faced south and east, and the symbols for those points of the compass—the phoenix for the south and the dragon for the east—were carved in stone against the walls. Only money could have created such beauty and kept it intact against the pressure for more space to house the fantastic population explosion on the Island. Only money could create such a place of silence when the streets outside teemed with people.

What other power did Theodora's money exercise? Marius was not a man who felt anything lightly. He would take their relationship seriously and Theodora would destroy him; perhaps had already destroyed him.

"Sarah." She stood at the lattice window. "We will leave discussing the opals until later, after I have rested. And by the way, the call I had just before you went out was from Marius."

"I'm not interested." Dear God, I had learned to lie with emphasis! And Theodora must know it. She was too sophisticated not to be perfectly aware that, in spite of our separation, I still loved Marius. Women like Theodora Paradine did not miss a give-away look, a hesitation, a tone of voice. But she couldn't know yet that I would cling to belief in Marius's integrity until I had proof that I was wrong.

"He mentioned you," Theodora's voice carried across the bright air. "He said it had been interesting to meet you again last night. 'My pretty, ambitious once-wife,' he called you."

I turned on my heel and left her and went up to my room. The air came in softly through the open window and I crossed to it and sat down with my head resting on my folded arms. Looking back on my days here with Theodora, I realized that the sanest thing for me to have done would have been to free myself from Marius because Theodora had caught him in her golden trap. As soon as I had known of their friendship I should have left the Pavilion and put both of them out of my mind.

But I knew I couldn't. A frantic urge took hold of me. Now I had to stay in order to discover the reason behind what Marius had done. I was too bewildered at the wanton recklessness of a usually cautious man, at landing himself in such a situation. I couldn't go away and shut the whole affair out of my mind. It was easy to ask myself, "Why should I bother with a man who has walked out on me?" My only reason was that my love for him was deeper than all the superficial arguments about pride and hurt. At this time, which was so dangerous for him, neither of those things mattered. I had to try to understand his situation. I had also to face that I was perhaps partly responsible for Marius being on his own in Hong Kong. I . . . and Theodora Paradine. If it hadn't been for her demands on my time, Marius would not have left me. And now, if it hadn't been for her, Marius would not be in this situation. The two truths linked me with whatever had helped to involve Marius in what could be danger and dishonor. And so *I* was involved, also.

Marius's dissatisfaction with the limits of orthodox medicine and his dream of working somewhere where he could have absolute control must have led him to this, to carrying out his nonconformist ideas, to experiment. For that dream, it would be necessary to have his own clinic, and such a place would mean a great deal of money. If Theodora had spoken the truth—and I believed she had—then it was this dream of Marius's that had involved him in the stolen jade.

And that brought me to the shattering realization that if I walked out on Theodora, she would immediately suspect that I would be going to the police to denounce her. In that case, she would go, too. And she was right. She had the authority of riches and a name. She would be believed, not me. And as well as destroying my career, she would probably, somehow, destroy Marius.

I had very little to say, after all, in my own justification. I had advised Theodora to buy the ceremonial girdle; I had been the one to hand the money to Ch'i. And if he were caught by the authorities, he would corroborate that.

Yet she had asked me a question. "I wonder how far you would go to protect someone you love?"

I answered her to myself. "A long way. Oh, a long way . . ."

XI

THEODORA HAD GONE OUT for the evening, and at half past eleven, on edge and restless, I went to bed.

I lay listening to the sounds beyond the wall—the click-clack of mah-jongg pieces from the teahouse, the laughter of passers-by. I heard the thin reed music, plaintive and tuneless, conjuring in my imagination centuries of an Orient that was rich in culture when my forebears in England had not yet been invaded by the Romans.

Occasionally I drifted into a light sleep, and three times I woke for no apparent reason except that my mind must be turning over with anxious, unremembered dreams of Marius. The fourth time I woke, I knew that something had disturbed me.

An old cottage in the English countryside and an ancient Manchu palace were the same when it came to the stress of hardwood that seemed, like humans, to relax and stretch in the cool of the night. But the sound on that waking was slightly different. I leaned on an elbow, listening, wondering if perhaps Theodora had returned and had brought someone with her to spend the night in one of her guest rooms.

The sounds became more clear. Someone was crossing the parquet flooring below. I tensed, holding my breath so that the sound of my breathing wouldn't intrude upon the furtive steps.

Had it been Theodora, I would have heard talking and most certainly Ah Lin would have been roused from her bed to see that the guest had every comfort.

I swung myself to the edge of the bed and put out a foot to test for creaks. Then, assured that I would make no sound, I got up and stood again, listening. The stirrings from below became more clear. I crept to the window.

No light shone out from the room below, but suddenly there was a small, muffled thud. Something had been dropped. I tensed, visualizing the room. Porcelain plates of Imperial Ming green; ancient Sung carvings of dragons and phoenix; lacquer and lapis lazuli—all valuable enough for a thief's delight.

I still clung to a faint hope that one of the servants, perhaps seeing a light, had come to turn it off. But I was sure I had not left a light on when I came upstairs.

The footsteps sounded again. From where I stood, I could see down into the court and, well hidden, watch whoever left the guest pavilion. I would wait where I was, and when the intruder was making his way through the various courts to the doors to the street, I could dash to the hall and sound the alarm, which would ring in the servants' quarters. Whoever was down there had little chance of getting away from the complicated pattern of courts unless he had wings. Ah Baht was old, but on one occasion I had seen him move swiftly as a leopard. And the French chef, Maurice, was a Kung Fu expert.

But no one came out from the hall beneath me; nothing stirred. In the beating silence I began to lose my fear. I crept out of the room and switched on the stair lights. The narrow hall with its silk scrolls and crimson and gold lacquer furniture was quite empty. Only a bronze Buddha looked my way, eyes unseeing.

I went down into the small guest sitting room. The windows were closed and the moon filtered only a pale glimmer through the latticed windows. But as I felt along the wall for the light switch, something moved in the shadows between two tall cabinets.

No one had been sleepwalking through that room; no one had entered innocently. Whoever it was had heard me come down the stairs and was waiting for me. I should have run, but I didn't. My mind had frozen. And the shadow slid to the door and remained there, barring my escape. It had taken on too much substance, rising black and featureless and silent.

For a moment that seemed an eternity, neither of us moved. Then a shadow arm lifted. I saw, with a kind of rooted horror, the gray shape of a hand on the wall. A huge, magnified hand holding a thin blade.

There was a swift, sudden movement, and in the faint moonlight I saw the arrow-swift glitter of metal. By one of those miracles that sometimes happen in times of great danger, I ducked in a flash before the knife reached the spot where I had crouched. The blade dug into the parquet flooring where I had cowered a moment earlier.

Immediately, as if certain that the knife had found its target, the attacker disappeared into the hall. I heard the swift padding of feet and then the click of the front door opening.

I raced to the window, my mind blank, my movements mechanical. I unlatched the window, fumbling with shaking fingers. Then, keeping myself well hidden against the wall, I looked into the court. It appeared deserted. The dying moonlight made milky patches on the flowers and the urns and the marble paving; the trees cast black shadows. It was possible that whoever had attacked me was hiding behind one of the great banks of bauhinias or coxcombs. I had sufficient control of my senses not to race out into the court and shout for help.

I tore up the stairs to where the bell connecting with the servants' pavilion was concealed between two painted panels of Mongolian hunting scenes. As I pressed the bell I could hear, through the night's stillness, its jangling in the distance. Although the sound reassured me, my legs shook as I returned to the sitting room and checked the art treasures. I was fairly certain that nothing had been disturbed. The silver wine goblets with lions' head handles, the porcelain and the *famille rose* pieces were all there.

But someone had entered the pavilion for something. And I had disturbed him. Or else he hadn't found the specific thing he was looking for.

Clattering feet sounded along the paths from the servants' court. The front door burst open and both Ah Lin and Maurice entered.

"What happened?"

"Someone broke in here," I said. "I heard footsteps and came down. Look."

The knife still lay on the floor just at the spot where I had stood in the glimmering moonlight.

My wits were not at their sharpest at two o'clock in the morning. The instinct which had sent me reeling sideways when the knife had cut through the air deserted me at that moment. "Look," I repeated and broke all intelligent rules and picked the knife up. "*This* was thrown at me."

Maurice dived for the front door, muttering, "*Mon Dieu,* I'll get him . . ." Lights began to flash on everywhere, both in the house and the grounds.

Ah Lin ran to me. "Are you hurt?"

"No. I dodged the knife. But someone wanted to stop me from turning on the light and seeing him."

"He tried to kill you. He tried to kill *you*," Ah Lin moaned, and arms across her thin chest, rocked herself backward and forward.

"He was disturbed. But he has probably left some identification. Fingerprints or footprints. We must telephone . . ." I stopped, hearing a sound. A car had drawn up outside the walls. Theodora had returned from her party.

It was only as I was crossing the Court of the Lotus, hugging my robe tightly against the cool night, that I realized I still had the knife in my hands. I stood in the shadow of the main pavilion, and now that I had probably destroyed all previous fingerprints, held it carefully between finger and thumb.

It was a steel-bladed knife with a carved amber handle, and I had seen it, or its twin, on a table in the hall of the guest pavilion.

"Sarah, what *is* all this? What is Maurice doing storming across the courts? I called to him but he was making too much noise to hear me."

Theodora swept past Ah Lin and then past me and into the drawing room, calling back. "Has Maurice gone mad?"

"There has been a break-in."

She turned slowly and looked at me. Her blue gauze cape slid from her shoulders to the floor. Ah Lin rushed to pick it up and carried it flowing over her thin arms out of the room.

"*What do you mean?* A break-in?" She looked around the room, her eyes swiftly taking in every treasure lying under the glowing lamps.

"I heard a sound in the guest pavilion and went downstairs. Someone was there but it was dark and before I could find the light switch he threw this at me." I laid the knife on the table by her side.

As she reached for it, I said quickly, "Don't touch it. It will have fingerprints on it. Mine because I handled it to bring it to you. But someone else's too."

"But my dear Sarah, nobody could get through the main doors. You surely know that by now. Had you been asleep and something woke you?"

"Yes."

"Then you had a nightmare."

Maurice came to the door. "I've searched the courts, Madame. There's no one there."

"You can go, Maurice."

"But, Madame—"

"I said, you may go now."

Célie appeared in the doorway as he left. Her thin face was twisted and frightened. "Oh, Madame, it is terrible. There has been—a—" She broke off as Theodora shot behind the great screen.

We stood silently listening and waiting. After a time, the strongroom door closed and Theodora reappeared.

"I was quite certain everything would be safe there—and of course it is. And for heaven's sake, Célie, stop shivering like that. Tell me, did you hear anything?"

"No–no, Madame. No. I was sitting up waiting f–for you. I'd have known if anyone entered the pavilion here."

"So what are you shaking for?"

"Ah Lin brought your cloak to me and she told me. All I heard was someone running and when I went to the window I saw that it was Maurice. He had turned all the lights on outside. Ah Lin told me that someone broke into the guest pavilion. It is terrible . . . it frightens me. If thieves can get in, perhaps they will kill us next time."

"You're talking nonsense. If you're going to have hysterics over an imagined break-in, then you had better have them in your own room. Now go." She seated herself, then turned to me. "What happened, Sarah?"

I was watching her hands. For all her harsh words to Célie, Theodora was tense. The long, heavily ringed fingers clutched each other as she sat there.

"I intercepted someone," I said, "and he threw that knife at me."

She glanced down at it. "It's the one I keep on the hall table in the guest pavilion."

"The man must have heard me come downstairs, felt around in the dark and picked it up either in order to attack me or, in case I were a man, to defend himself."

Theodora looked over my shoulder. "Fetch Ah Baht."

"I'm here, Mistress Lady." The old man entered the room.

"Show me your keys."

He fumbled at his waist, unhooked them from his belt and held them out to her.

She nodded, pushing his hand away. "All right. They're all there. And do you keep them right by your side at night?"

He nodded. "As you have always told me to, Mistress Lady."

"You may go, then." She let out a soft breath. "Well, Sarah, now you see, don't you, that you must have had some kind of nightmare. The doors were locked and there is no other way anyone could enter this place. The walls are unscalable and electrified. There are just two sets of door keys. I have one set; Ah Baht has the other."

"It was no nightmare. The paper knife is always kept on the table in the hall of the guest pavilion. But it fell clattering at my side in the sitting room. Isn't that proof enough? Someone *was* there and whoever it was wanted to stop me from turning on the light and see-ing him . . . or her. Even if it meant killing me."

Theodora's face seemed to have an unusual pallor. It was possibly because she was tired or, since her skin was almost dead white, because her pinkish make-up hadn't lasted too well.

"I was just about to telephone the police when you arrived," I said. "You *must* call them quickly. Shall I do it for you?"

She seemed not to hear me. She sat very upright in her chair. "Lilo, I must see her." She was suddenly very alert. "Ah Lin, are you there?"

I glanced over my shoulder and saw her in the doorway.

"Fetch Lilo," Theodora said.

"But, Mistress Lady," Ah Lin glanced at the small malachite clock. "It's late and—"

"I don't care if it's Judgment Day. Get Lilo."

Theodora and I were alone again. I said, "You surely don't think that she had anything to do with a break-in?"

"At the moment, Sarah, I am convinced that you dreamed the whole thing. I think that our conversation tonight upset you more than I imagined it would."

"That doesn't come into this."

She gave me a long covert look. Her lips smiled. "My dear, I'm a woman of the world. I can see expressions that are hidden; I can read behind spoken words what is really meant. Of course I upset you."

Exhausted and furious, I remained silent. There are times when acts of violence can be involuntary. I could have hit her.

Lilo, in scarlet pajamas and flowing hair, entered the room.

"Once," Theodora said to her, "you let some relations of yours into my home. Do you remember?"

"Yes, Mistress Lady."

"And I told you never to dare to do such a thing again."

"I did not. I did not."

"You didn't let them in tonight?"

Lilo shook her head vigorously. "No. I would not dare. You were so angry with me before. And I said I was so sorry. But I did not *really* open the door for them that time, either. Ah Lin crossed the street to get grapes and my Second Uncle and Third Cousin came by. I only asked them to look at the beautiful flowers where I lived. That was all, Mistress Lady. And I have never let anyone in again." She spread her slender hands. "I have no key. You understand?"

Theodora had sat quite still as Lilo's words had rushed from her in a kind of scared torrent. "Very well, Lilo. You may go. All of you go."

The small crimson clad figure fled with Ah Lin and Célie.

Theodora turned to me. "I questioned her for your benefit, Sarah.

As you heard, she let her relatives in once, when Ah Lin left the doors open for a few moments. But I knew she would never dare let her family over my threshold again. So we're back with you and a nightmare, aren't we?"

"No."

She sat frowning at me. Then suddenly her face lightened. "All right, no. Which brings me perhaps to the real reason for what was supposed to have happened tonight. You said you were about to telephone the police when I arrived."

"Yes, I was. And we must."

"Because, all along," she said softly, "that is what you've wanted, isn't it?"

I watched the small shadows of the Cantonese servants pass by the fretted windows. "I want nothing but to find out who broke in tonight and who threw the knife at me. I happen to like my life and I want to keep it."

"Perhaps I can tell you the whole story."

I backed to the wall, tired and cold, but still putting a mask of bravado over my fear.

She said in a tight voice, "This charade was your ingenious idea, wasn't it, for getting the police into the house? You wanted to tell them about the jade, so you devised this method. Once they arrived, it would be easy enough for you to explain that you suspect the attack was because of a rare jade I possess; that the intruder was searching for it. You would be so frank about it all—and the police would ask to see it." She gave me a long speculative look. "I never dreamed you could be so subtle, or so imaginative."

My first reaction was that Theodora must have got a little drunk at the party. And then I heard myself shout with violent laughter that was merely a wild alternative to hitting her.

"Sarah, stop that." A shade of alarm crossed her face.

I stepped back, colliding with a table, stumbled and righted myself. The laughter ceased as suddenly as it came.

"A supposed attack," she continued before I could speak, "in order to bring the police here. Because you dare not go to them with your story of a stolen jade. So you decided that they could come here and that from their questions and your answers, they would learn about the jade girdle. But surely, Sarah, you must realize that if you had carried this idea through and called the police, it would have been foolish in the extreme. Whatever wild idea you had for contacting them, you would be involving not only yourself and me, but someone else."

She had drained my anger from me, and I leaned against the wall for support. Some curious ragged pride would not let me sit down and so, as it were, face her on her level. I remained standing. But her devious mind had seen deviousness in mine. She had defeated me. I could not call the police.

"And now, my dear," Theodora said, "go to bed. In the morning you'll feel more calm about things." She rose in a cloud of sapphire gauze.

Words were of no more use between us. She had the answer for anything I might say: *If you bring the police here, under the pretext of an attack on you, then you will involve and destroy not only your largest source of income, but this man.* This man, Marius.

I left her without another word, went through the hall and out of the pavilion. The courts were in darkness and nothing stirred. The birds, the flowers, the leaves of the trees were as if suspended in an enchanted sleep.

It was incredible to me now that I could have done that mad and thoughtless thing; that against all my training I had advised Theodora to buy something that should have roused my immediate suspicions by the obvious secrecy of the meeting and the sale. But such mistakes happened. In a single moment a career—a life, even—could be destroyed. Apparently experience had not yet taught me the vital lesson of caution.

I went into the guest pavilion, flicking on all the lights, alert to any movement. But of course there was no one there. By now, the attacker would be well away, in the twisting streets of Wanchai or in a building that housed one of the many secret societies that abounded on the island.

I lay in my bed, restless and tossing. Then for the second time that night a sound roused me to complete wakefulness. I started up. It came, distant and yet disturbing. A woman was in one of the courts and, in the absolute silence, her weeping came clearly through my open window.

The hands of the bedside clock pointed to three. Once again I slid into my robe and went to the bedroom door and listened. My first thought was that this could be some trap to get me out of the house. But no one could force such sobs that seemed to touch rock-bottom despair.

Lilo—weeping for some broken love affair? Célie—sent to bed at last by Theodora and anguished by her biting tongue over some slight and unimportant error? Ah Lin, even?

I opened the front door of the pavilion and walked between the marble urns of peonies in the direction of the sound. There was no one in the guest court; no one on the white carved seat under the acacias. But the sound grew louder as I approached the Court of the Lotus, and I saw a tall shadow move quickly into the house, her hands over her face as if to stifle the sounds she was incapable of controlling.

It was impossible to tell from that distance and in the now moonless dark, who it was. Only Theodora lived in the main pavilion, but Theodora never wept. I crept to the latticed window and peered through the elaborate arabesques of cedarwood carving into the drawing room. What I saw was scarcely believable. Theodora Paradine was weeping her heart out among her jades and her bronzes and her gold.

I turned silently away from the window. I could do nothing for her. She was far too proud to want me as a witness to some secret grief and I was much too bitter about her blatant threats to Marius and me to want to comfort her. Our isolation was mutual.

XII

THE LOCAL NEWSPAPERS carried stories about Pandion Dioscuri, the Greek millionaire who had arrived on the Island. He had brought with him on his yacht a party of friends, all glamorous and colorful. Their expeditions to the various islands made fascinating reading for the foreign residents in Hong Kong, though very few of them were ever invited aboard the lovely, sky-blue ship, the *Endymion*.

Theodora had known Dioscuri for some years and had been invited to join the yacht party on a visit to the outer island of Lantau, to the Buddhist monastery, and to the ruined Sung dynasty fort on the far side of the island.

The morning following the intruder's attack, I was in the court when Theodora came out of the pavilion, ready for the cruise. Nothing either in her looks or her manner could possibly remind me of that wild, convulsive weeping.

She was cool and sleek in gray and white and black—which on her, with her bright make-up and the great flashing blue diamond in her ring, were the essence of sophistication.

Whatever she might suspect happened in her palace while she was out the previous night, Theodora had no intention of carrying her questioning any further. It was quite possible that she had persuaded herself that I really had planned the whole thing in order to get the police into the house and subsequently report the jade as a stolen treasure of Red China. And if by any chance I mentioned the fact of surprising an intruder, I could guess what she would say.

"Sarah is so imaginative and so caught up in her work that of course she dreams about it. She's so absorbed in collecting for me that she's nervous about being left alone with all my valuable collection."

Oliver Farache arrived while Theodora was indulging in one of her eternal telephone conversations. I guessed it was a social chat, since the Pavilion was the one place where her managers and her secretaries only called her when there was a matter of supreme urgency.

Her rich laughter mingled with Oliver's footsteps on the marble slabs of the court. I uncurled my legs from one of the fan-backed chairs.

"All right, say it," I called defiantly. "I look as if I'm posing for a portrait of an idle woman. But I'm not. I'm thinking."

"Then thinking becomes you," he said. "Anyway, you don't have to justify yourself to me. Are you coming to Lantau with us?"

"I fit into this chair much more comfortably than I'd fit into the cocktail hour on a luxurious private yacht. I'm not 'jet set.'"

"Neither am I. But I never say no to invitations that allow me to see how other people live."

"The monks at the Golden Lotus Temple?"

"Yes, though saffron robes and shaven heads are not my idea of good living."

"Oh, no, I couldn't see you as a monk. As Theodora's husband . . ."

"But not even that," he said, and picked up Mister Wu. "You smell of French perfume, you sissy," he said to the little dog.

"I accidentally spilled some on to his coat," Theodora said, coming out of the Pavilion. "You're late."

"Am I?" Oliver didn't apologize. "You look rather splendid. But Theodora, my darling girl, do you have to wear that egg-sized diamond? It's a cruise, not a royal ball."

I waited for a show of anger. Instead she said lightly, "Pandion has an Oriental love of jewelry. He probably likes his mistresses to wear sapphires with their bikinis." She darted a laughing glance at him.

I watched her, amazed at her tremendous range of moods. The arrogance, the obsessions, the storm of despair last night, and now the gaiety as if, although she had divorced Oliver, he still had the power to make life a laughing place.

He was saying to me, "I remember when Theodora bought that ring. There was a court case over it."

"I know," I said. "It's the Marengo diamond. I was apprenticed to Felix at the time of the quarrel over who possessed it."

Theodora said lightly, "That Spanish princess with the name a yard long and quite unpronounceable claimed it belonged to her, but her nephew wanted to sell it. And in the end, *I* got it."

"The triumph, Theo, wasn't yours. Fate took a hand, didn't it?" Oliver asked. "It merely struck the princess dead with a heart attack at the very moment when the case was being heard in court. So since the nephew was her heir and she hadn't done what she threatened and changed her will, even if it *was* her property, it passed to him. Do you realize that if the Spanish judge had taken a few less minutes over his breakfast, that jewel might never have been yours? The princess could have been alive until the case was finished. So you could say that eggs and bacon probably won you the Marengo diamond."

"You talk too much, my dear. Come on." She took Oliver's arm and said over her shoulder to me, "Sarah, you could spend your time thinking about those opals. Célie will show you where they are. I'd like a few ideas for a ring and earrings." And then she was gone.

Mister Wu waddled a few steps after them, changed his mind and came back to me. We sat together and the sun poured a gentle morning blaze on to our faces.

I spent about an hour with my pencil, pad and the case containing the opals which had been in the Creech family for more than a century and a half. They had never been reset from their original heavy, haphazardly arranged plume brooch. Each opal was beautifully marked and fiery.

But I couldn't concentrate. The pavilions with their gay painted roofs, the flowery courts enclosed in the great high wall gave me a sense of being trapped. I had to get away, out of the city and into the hills; I needed to breathe, to feel free of tension.

I handed the case with the opals back to Célie and fetched my purse. Lilo was sitting in the servants' court grooming Mister Wu and Ah Tat's little conical straw hat was bobbing about as he cut off the heads of the last of the lilies. They were deepening to ivory, the first sign of their dying; Theodora hated anything that was not in full and healthy bloom.

A loud hiss made me jerk round. Ah Lin was hurrying toward me. "I'll tell you, missy, but you must not tell anyone."

"Tell me what?" I looked down into the little puckered face with the web of lines.

"Lilo," she said. "That Lilo. She lied to Mistress Lady last night. She opened the door last night after Ah Baht locked it. She had to tell me because early this morning I found her picking up some food that had been dropped. She said that her Sister and Third Uncle came last night and she gave them some food. It is not easy, missy, to get Lilo to tell the truth. But she was scared. She said while she went to fetch food for them, they came into the court to look at the flowers. She said she saw me come along and she pushed them out.

That is when they must have dropped the food. I must tell Mistress Lady."

"*No,*" I said, looking into the troubled old face. "I think we'll forget it now."

"But someone came and tried to kill you, Missy. That's terrible. Célie tells me that he took nothing."

"I disturbed him. Probably that's why."

"Mistress Lady must know about Lilo," she insisted.

"*No.*"

"But she lies!"

"Ah Lin, please let it rest. Lilo was very frightened last night and I'm quite certain she won't let her relatives in a third time. We must forget it." I saw doubt on her face. "But thank you for telling me. Someone could have slipped in while the door was left unguarded— probably some casual thief who hid until night when he thought everyone would be asleep and he wouldn't be disturbed. These courts are very easy places for hiding. But the man saw me and panicked."

I drew a deep breath as I gave her a reassuring smile and walked past her to the outer door. It had been a weak explanation, but Ah Lin appeared to accept it. I was relieved, for I felt that to tell Theodora would help no one and would probably cost Lilo her job.

I took the cable car to the Peak top, got out and walked without aim past the villas and the radiant gardens and on to the hills.

Up there the view was breathtaking, opening out on to the China Seas and the islands, some shadowed by cloud, some green and bright. I passed the last of the villas. Bulbuls flew among the casuarinas and the orchid trees, and magpies broke the stillness with ceaseless chattering.

I picked my way over boulders and through golden bracken, weaving among groups of trees, bamboo and wild banana. A few of the Island's famous hoard of butterflies danced around me, and with each step I seemed to shake off the dark mood of fear.

I was free. I was young. I was in Hong Kong. I took deep breaths of the sweet hill air, which on the Peak was free of the sea and wet wool and cooking smells which permeated the city below.

I passed few people. European tourists looked at me with cool curiosity since I walked alone. It was different with the Chinese families I met.

Perhaps it was my love of a country in which, although I was not a native, I had lived for most of my life, that gave me the feeling that the spirit of the people was so much warmer here than in London—

the smiles more swift, the narrow eyes kinder, the gaiety more spontaneous. So I smiled back at a little Chinese girl holding an emerald kite shaped like a bird, and an old man with mere slits for eyes and a shoulder pole heavy with melons he was delivering to the villas.

Yet for all the charm that the Chinese had for me, I knew that on the Island there was as much menace as anywhere else in the world. Corruption tainted Hong Kong as it tainted all the world's cities. A new bribery racket was being run among the Chinese authorities—the demand for what they called "tea money," bribes of more than two hundred pounds for exit permits to Hong Kong. Was that how Ch'i Pai-shih had come to the Island, perhaps by selling some less valuable jade piece he had "acquired" to pay for his migrant visa? There were other ways too, devious and adventurous. Many of them were labyrinthine, involving slipping from island to island, bribing boatmen, weaving through the China Seas and landing eventually on some dark night in an isolated bay. It was all too possible, too probable. And I wanted to forget it.

I lay down in a hollow that faced the sea far below. The grass was harsh, but it was also warm and enfolding. As a child I had spent so many happy times with Father and my friends on these hills. We would go on photographic expeditions, tilting our cameras at everything from birds in flight to lady slipper orchids hiding in some green hollow.

Then the lovely, youthful days of running free were exchanged for study in London, for a small apartment with a kitchenette the size of a cupboard, a shared bathroom and a chestnut tree outside the window. There were good times and bad, excitement and disappointment. But my work developed, my life was enriched, and when I married, the world seemed to hold nothing more that I wanted.

And here I was, back in the hills of my youth, because I needed to think quietly. But lying there with the sun golden on my face, my arms stretched out on either side of me, my fingers plucking and teasing the dry grass, I found that it was thoughts of Marius and not the jade which came most easily to my mind.

Whenever I had asked myself, *How did we lose one another?* there had always been the same answer. *We pursued different dreams.* But so did hundreds of other married couples, and it worked with them, so why not us?

The answer could be in the one word "pursue." Happiness was not a race but a state of mind. Perhaps we had killed it by ceaseless activity, talking of "doing," always "doing." Instead, perhaps happiness lay in being still and letting the world in.

I took a long, deep breath and remembered something Marius had once said to me. "There is so much you miss by constant activity, Sarah. Life isn't just a battle, my darling." And then he had quoted his favorite phrase, written centuries ago by Sir Thomas Browne. " 'Ready to be anything in the ecstasy of being, ever.' " I had retorted that love was ecstasy and so was work. Marius had not replied and when I looked round for him, he had vanished.

"You've got an ant crawling over your foot."

I leaped up, spun round and saw Marius. "Oh, no . . . no . . ." I cried, overwhelmed by a feeling that I had conjured him up from out of the translucent air. "Don't tell me you just chanced by."

"I followed you. I saw you catch the Peak tram, so I drove up. You know that dress of yours is a bright green patch on the landscape. I couldn't miss you."

"Why didn't you try?"

He bent over me and pushed me back onto the grass. Then he flung himself down by my side. But he didn't look at me. He sat, his eyes narrowed in the sunlight, staring ahead of him toward the golden, dancing sea. "How long are you staying here?" It was a harsh, peremptory question.

"About three more weeks. Do you mind?" I asked.

"Would it matter if I did?"

The old pattern was beginning, the sparring, the cautious holding up of masks so that our emotions were not naked on our faces.

"Why did you follow me, Marius? Was there something you had to say? I mean, something that couldn't be put into a letter?"

"Letters can be even more fatal than speech. You can write down the truth as you see it, address the envelope and post the letter on impulse. In speech, the words die on the air; in a letter they are there for all time."

I stared ahead of me, not wanting to look at him, not wanting to hurt myself by seeing the long mouth, the blue eyes, the short but magnificent hair like fire seen through dark-brown gauze. For I would be seeing in my mind's eye, Theodora by his side.

He began to speak. "I wanted to see what the past two years had done to you, and it wasn't possible at Theodora's party. But now that we're alone, perhaps we can talk."

A cold ghost's finger ran down my spine. I thought, He is going to ask for his freedom. I waited, my eyes on the green and purple islands and the sampans, like ladybirds, crawling over the dark blue water.

A dragonfly skimmed across Marius's face and he ducked. Suddenly I laughed, too loudly, too gaily.

He said matter-of-factly, "It was flying so fast it could have knocked itself out if it had hit my head. So, you see, I have probably saved a life." Then he added, "Your laughter has changed."

"It depends on what I'm laughing at. Whether it's funny or odd or . . ." Or, I finished to myself, *whether it's to cover up the terrible awareness of being so near you. I've got to stop loving you. But something must help me. I can't help myself.*

"Tell me what's been happening to you, Sarah. I hear you're doing great things."

"It takes a long time to get to the top—maybe I never will. But at least now I can afford to work on designs that aren't actually commissioned. And I have a larger studio."

"Where you work alone?"

"Yes." Unthinkingly I turned and our eyes met. I looked away. "Why did you want to talk to me, Marius?"

"Are you happy?"

"I have my work which I love; my life which I enjoy. I have my demons too, but who hasn't? And I suppose you'll tell me that one of my demons is independence."

"I would say it's a lack of ability to have a deep relationship."

"Oh, no." The two words seemed to fly out, echoing among the crags of the granite hills. "Marius, you never before accused me of that."

"Because it took me quite a time to work it out. But it's true. You want a relationship, yes. But you also want the freedom that cannot accept compromise."

I was frightened. The threat was there in the words we spoke. "Did *you* ever accept compromise?" I asked, trying to keep my voice quiet. "You hated it if I had to go off to an auction abroad. It was part of my job, but you wouldn't see that. You wanted me at home all the time."

"I never asked for a doormat. That would have bored me. But I didn't want a wife who was constantly rushing off to Paris or Vienna or God knows where to buy an icon or a jade or to win some dead queen's gee-gaw over the heads of all the other buyers who bid for it. You want to fly high, Sarah. That's all very well for eagles, but you need strong wings and a hide like a rhinoceros to play equal with the experts."

"Don't we all want to win? And isn't it only by keeping that in sight that you get even halfway?"

"Oh, Sarah, if you only knew. Your face is made for laughter, not philosophizing." He touched my cheek and I shot away as if he held a lighted cigarette too close to me.

I struck back. "You accuse me of something which—since you make it sound a kind of sin—you were also guilty of. You're ambitious too, or at least you were once."

He didn't answer me. We sat in silence and I had no way of knowing whether the tension was just mine or if something also emanated from Marius. We had loved and had been parted for some time, and yet I still longed for him to touch me and to feel the warmth of his body. But only the outward, visible Marius was with me. The other—the closest, the one from which his love had once radiated—was hidden. Or destroyed.

I said, without looking at him, "I was attacked last night. Did you know?"

He looked at me sharply, eyes narrowed against the sun. "Tell me about it." It seemed to me that his voice was sharp with curiosity rather than anxiety.

I gave him an exact account. He listened keenly and quietly and when I had finished he said, "You disturbed the man and he tried to frighten you, not to harm you. Had he intended to injure you, he would have manhandled you."

"I saved myself," I said indignantly. "I moved quickly and that saved me from injury or worse."

"When he found the knife had missed you, he could have attacked you himself. That would have been the obvious thing. So that's why I think he only meant to frighten you."

"Theodora went one better than you," I said bitterly. "*She* believed I had a nightmare."

"Stranger things have happened. Nightmares can sometimes seem very real."

"Not as real as this was. There are treasures in every room in the Pavilion, yet he took nothing. I think he was after one specific thing."

"Do you?" Marius spoke with an aloofness as if, since he no longer cared for me, he was not interested. Or as if he wanted no discussion that involved Theodora and, incidentally, himself.

I hugged my knees and stared unhappily at a distant butterfly with carmine wings. "I can't talk to you any more, Marius."

"I'm sorry. What do you want me to say?"

I didn't know; that was the awful thing. Perhaps I had wanted what he could no longer give me—reassurance. *I will guard you, Sarah. I will always guard you.*

I changed the subject. "You asked me, now I ask you. How long are you staying in Hong Kong?"

"I don't know."

"You threw away a career, and it was a good one. Marius, you had a dream."

"I still have."

"The clinic. 'Anywhere,' you said. 'Anywhere in the world where it is most needed.'"

"I've told you. The plan is still there, a hundredfold more intense. When I decide to do a job, I do it thoroughly. But now that job is not limited to Western methods of medicine."

"And you know the way you want to go?" I kept my face turned away from him.

"Yes."

Stung by the finality of that single word, I said, "I wonder, were we ever really close?"

"Don't you think it's too late now for questions like that, Sarah?" He paused and then asked, "Are you as interested as ever in jade?"

"Yes."

"Your father tells me that I should go to Taiwan and see the art treasures there. You've probably already been, even if only to see the jade. I'd like to see them."

My heart gave a lurch. "Since when have you been interested?" I spoke with deliberate lightness. "You once said, 'Put a piece of soapstone next to a jade and I wouldn't know the difference.'"

He was silent for a moment. "Perhaps one of the things all this new study has taught me is that one-track minds belong to cramped characters and I don't want mine to be that."

"It never was."

"In my own field, no. In others, yes. And now, because my interests have broadened, so have the questions I ask myself. And there is one that to me is tremendously important."

"What is it?"

"Just that, in any action, if the aim behind it is morally right, then is the method of attaining it justified—whatever that method is? Well," he asked after a moment's silence, "what do you think, Sarah?"

"I don't know. Murder and cruelty must be ruled out. No aim could justify those. And cheating and . . ."

He made a quick gesture with his hands. "All right, let's drop the subject. It's far too loaded a question for a bright day. I shouldn't have asked it."

I knew that tone only too well. It was as if he had half opened his mind to me and then closed it again. The weight of fear for him and for myself pressed down on me. He was too near, too loved, too difficult. I wanted more than anything else to escape. "I must go," I said. "I want to look in on Father."

Marius rose and pulled me to my feet. For a moment he held me, head bent, face shadowed. Then abruptly he let me go.

I was walking away without saying goodbye, when he called me back. I paused, and for that moment, everything around me seemed to stand still. The lovely hills, the trees, the grasses. The world was not mine, my own body scarcely seemed to belong to me. Just one thing was dominant and imperative. As we stood facing one another across the grass spangled with sunlight, my will-power to free myself of him rose like a storm inside me. "In the future, Sarah, whatever may happen, temper your criticism if you can. Whatever I do, God help me, I must do. All men have their faith and have to fight for it." He turned and walked away, disappearing over the crest of the hill.

Nam Tsao opened the door of Father's apartment. "The master is not here. He's gone with that Greek gentleman to Lantau. But come in, Missy. I've made some rice cakes."

She fussed round me, pushing a chair forward on to the terrace. "It's a warm day. I'll bring the tray out here."

I thanked her. I loved her cakes and the green tea which would inevitably be brought with them. It would be welcome before I made the journey back to the jostling, crowded town center.

The view from the terrace was marvelous and familiar, reaching out over the city toward the harbor, where masts and sails were spread like a rich abstract painting with the hills of Kowloon like the humped backs of green whales across the skyline. I wandered into the sitting room and glanced at the pile of magazines on the table. There was also Father's miniature camera, no bigger than a cigarette packet, and some enlargements of photographs. I picked them up.

Nam Tsao brought the tray and then went off, leaving me with the fragrant tea, the little round cakes and the photographs.

I flicked through them, dropping them one by one onto the table. They were mostly color views of the hills and one that I recognized as the Sumchun River at Lok Ma Chau, on the border of the New Territories with Red China.

Father's skill at his hobby had improved enormously since the early days of fuzzy prints and out-of-focus poses. The colored prints I was looking at were clear and beautifully balanced.

I laid one down and picked up the next. On the right-hand side of the photograph there was a car standing on the roadside and I could see part of the registration number. There was a six and a seven, but the rest was out of the picture.

Two men stood by the car, one turned three-quarters toward the camera. I recognized the Chinese who had been at the wheel of the dark Avenger car cruising past the place where I had visited Ch'i's shack, the face of the man who had seemed just a little too interested in me. His companion in the photograph had his back to the camera, but I knew only too well the set of the shoulders, the copper-colored hair, the strong square hand resting on the car's hood. I would know Marius even if he were masked and cloaked.

Shaken, I turned back to the six enlargements I had glanced through so casually and looked at them again. But the one taken at Lok Ma Chau was the only one with people in it. The others were just views taken with Father's new telescopic lens and I recognized almost all of them as of the hills in the south of the island.

Shock shared with others is painful enough. Shock received alone carries with it a terrible sense of isolation. There were two things that were linked in my mind—Marius's last words to me about not condemning him were I to discover something about him that might shatter me. And now this discovery that Marius and the Chinese were known to one another and, judging by the companionable stance in the photograph, were friends.

I felt as if I had found another important piece in some jigsaw. And I was sure that it was no coincidence that Marius and the Chinese had been photographed together.

I needed a name for this man for my own identification, so I called him by the make of his car: the Avenger.

My thoughts went back to the night of the attack on me. Whoever had broken into Theodora's Manchu palace had taken none of the treasures lying around for the picking. The deduction was uncomfortably obvious. The Avenger had seen me leave Ch'i's hut, had taken a very good look at me and had followed me back to Theodora's home.

There was, then, a probable connection between the man in the car and the attack on me in the guest pavilion. I wondered whether I was perhaps imagining too much. But the fact remained, steady and only too obvious. There were links—and strong links at that—between Marius, the Avenger and Ch'i Pai-shih.

XIII

I HAD SCARCELY SEEN THEODORA since her return from Lantau two days previously. In between appointments with the hairdresser and masseuse, there had been luncheon engagements and a dinner party out at a villa at Deepwater Bay.

It was now early evening and I was sitting in my favorite place on the edge of the lotus pool, watching a kingfisher. Theodora drifted out from the main pavilion and sank with affected exhaustion into one of the yellow fan chairs.

"I haven't had a chance yet to ask you how you enjoyed Lantau," I said.

"The one thing I have never wanted is a yacht," she said.

"I hear that Father was in Dioscuri's party."

"That's right. I asked if I could bring him." She laughed. "My charming elderly chaperone. I have no liking for amorous battles in dark corners."

"I suppose Father enjoyed himself. I haven't called him today."

"Your father"—she laughed again—"should have been a merman with a fish's tail. The sea is his idea of paradise."

I let her talk about Lantau and Dioscuri, who had invited her again that night to dinner. She said, "I can't resist. His chef produces the most wonderful Greek food." Then she told me about the Buddha in the temple on the Island of Lantau which she would have loved to possess. "It always seems so strange to me to see people kneeling before these images and shaking out the sticks that tell their fortune. So primitive."

"There's a primitive element in all religions," I said. "Anyway, Buddhism isn't a religion, it's a philosophy. I like it."

She said in a clipped voice, "Then you'd better go and shake the sticks and tell me something about *my* future, Sarah. I have plans, and I need to know . . ." She stopped, gave me an oblique glance and waved a dismissing hand. "Oh, never mind. Let's get down to something more practical. I have to be in London at the end of November for the Duchess of Hellenbar's ball. I think I'd like to wear my diadem. Would you get it out of the bank for me and have it cleaned by the time I get to London? I'll give you a note of authorization before you leave here."

"A signed note won't be enough," I said. "Your bank doesn't know me that well. I'll probably have to show them my passport, and you might have to call them, too."

She gave a little gesture of exasperation. "Oh, the complications of ownership!"

"You can't possess fabulous jewelry without them, you know."

She said plaintively, "Well, I can't travel with everything I possess. You have caught the sun, Sarah."

"I've been walking a lot in the hills since you've been away. The other day I ran into Marius."

She made no visible movement and yet I knew she had tensed. "Well, coincidences are not unusual on a small island. I suppose he told you about his plans?"

"For what?"

"The clinic, of course."

"No."

She spread out her hands, separating her fingers, watching the glitter of her rings. "Perhaps you aren't so patient at listening to a man's ambition as I am, Sarah. I admire it. But, of course, the gossips here do say—"

"What do 'they' say?"

"That the study of acupuncture isn't the only reason Marius goes so often to Lok Ma Chau. It's only a stone's throw, more or less, from China. Why travel all that way to learn what you could learn in Hong Kong, or even in Europe? That's what people ask."

"Do *you* ask that?"

"No. But then I think I understand Marius rather well. Ambition is a great link between two people."

"This man who is his teacher, Dr. Hai," I asked, "what is he like?"

"I've never met him."

"Marius has never described him to you?"

"Except to tell me that he is a small man and I believe bald but with a beard. *If* that's an accurate description. It sounds to me as if Marius made up that picture after seeing some of those old scroll paintings of ancient mandarins."

The man in the black Avenger had most certainly not been old and bald and small for, in Father's photograph, he had stood shoulder to shoulder with Marius.

"I'm going to Dioscuri's dinner party on the yacht tonight," Theodora said. "He has anchored off Shek-O. Oliver will be there—and Marius."

"Oh."

"You sound surprised."

"Yes," I agreed. "Perhaps I am. The Marius I knew wouldn't be interested in the jet set. He seems to have changed very much."

"Or is himself," she said. "Maybe you never understood him, Sarah. You probably wanted to see Marius the way you wanted him and the way he never was."

"I don't think I was given to illusions."

"Oh, but you're young, and the young are full of them in some form or other. No, dear, you never understood Marius. *I* do. Shall I tell you the absolute truth?"

I took a few more steps away from her. Her voice reached me, cool and clear. "That one-time dedicated surgeon husband of yours will do anything—*anything*—for what he really wants."

"What did he tell you he wanted?"

"The clinic, one that will eclipse all clinics. Do you know what he once said to me, Sarah? I was wearing the Gioconda emerald at the time and he looked at it and said, 'That would buy my clinic.' And then he added, 'Don't worry, I'm not coveting it. Come hell and high water, I'll get the money.'" Her mouth twisted into the long, secret smile I had grown to know so well when there was a thrust or a barb coming. "And he will, Sarah. Oh, he will."

I changed the subject quickly. "There are some stones I want to buy while I'm here," I said, "and I have a list in my room. I want to check it."

"Stones for me to see?"

"No. I planned to look for some good amethysts, royal purple ones, and perhaps some alexandrites. They would fetch good prices in America."

"What are alexandrites?"

"They're chameleon stones, green by day, crimson by night. And rare."

I had uttered the magic word. "Rare?" Her eyes sharpened.

"Yes. They're found in the Ural Mountains and they're called alexandrites because the first one was discovered on Tsar Alexander's birthday."

"You must find me some, Sarah, and make me a necklace."

"They don't come by the sackful. It takes a long time to collect fairly rare stones."

She smiled. "I'm prepared to wait." Then, as I moved away, she asked. "Where are you going?"

"To look for the list of stones I told you about." I left her and went through the courts to my room. When I had closed the door, I leaned against it. What I felt was beyond tears, beyond anything physical—a kind of emptiness and a betrayal. Marius had asked me to understand that whatever he did, he had to do. It seemed only too clear that it concerned a clinic, a very great deal of money, and the wherewithal to find it. Three pointers to Theodora Paradine.

The room was, as usual, immaculate. Fresh flamingo-pink chrysanthemums stood in a celadon vase; a few sprays of bauhinias made a white cloud on a table top. By their side was a Hong Kong newspaper. I hadn't seen one that day. I picked it up and found that it was folded to an inside page.

In the second column there was an item about a man, a Chinese, aged about thirty, whose body was found floating in the sea off Repulse Bay.

There was no identification on him, but in the pocket of his coat had been found a great wad of sodden Hong Kong notes wrapped in a piece of cloth dyed with red and blue colors that had run into each other. The man had a long, livid white scar at the side of his face.

No one knew who he was; no one had reported him missing nor come to claim him. Even I didn't know his real name, only the name he had given us: Ch'i Pai-shih.

It could, of course, be a case of suicide, but I didn't believe that—not for a man with a sum of money in his pocket that would be a large fortune to him and would give him the freedom of the world. The answer must be accident—or murder. The first I ruled out. The memory of the obvious attempt on my life the other night was too real for Ch'i's fate to be a coincidence.

And someone had placed the newspaper in my room. It could be any one of the servants, but their positions in Theodora's household were far too valuable for any of them to risk the least thing that would give her displeasure. Whoever had entered the Manchu palace and attacked me could have done so again, this time in order to leave that brief report as a significant message for me.

I know you are involved. And now you know that I know. Invisible words for me to read between the lines of a newspaper paragraph.

I flung myself on the bed and closed my eyes. Sanity pointed only one way for me to go, and that was out of Hong Kong as quickly as I could. But in this jet age mileage mattered little. If I were suspected of being involved, no sea or land mass, nor desert nor thousands of miles of forest could prevent me from being in danger.

I turned over, stared at the ceiling and faced the fact that I was trapped. And caught in that trap, the result of a few minutes of thoughtlessness when I had held a rare jade in my hands, was also—I was sure—Marius.

A country's ancient marvels are a matter of national importance. A country was its past, its history and its art and crafts. To lose these was to lose identity—as the Chinese would say, to lose face. And God help any country which let that happen. China had pride. Oh, damn, damn that emperor's girdle which had adorned the ceremony of that moon that would soon shine like a child's silver ball outside my window . . .

I got up and went to turn on a bath. I flung jasmine scent into the water and lay counting the fishes fashioned in gold leaf on the heavily decorated walls. Made drowsy by the warm water and smoothed by the calm, flowing lines of the unidentifiable fish, I thought of my work. Because I was staring at gold leaf, I remembered how I had watched a goldsmith hammer gold between two pieces of pigskin until the gold was transparent. Then, suddenly, I jerked out of my reverie. I had no time for dreaming.

I needed to find out who put the newspaper in my room. The hands of the bedside clock pointed to seven. Theodora wouldn't be leaving for Dioscuri's party for a while. I dressed quickly, seized the newspaper and ran down and waited for her in the Court of the Lotus.

She came minutes later, dressed in rust and gold silk, a Persian necklace of rubies and turquoise round her long white throat. Glancing at the newspaper I held out, Theodora nodded. "Oh, yes, I forgot to tell you. I read that and told Célie to put the paper in your room. Interesting, isn't it? But at least my jade is safe now."

"Is it?"

"Of course. The man is dead. It's extraordinary, isn't it, Sarah?"

"No, I don't think so. It seems to me to be all part of a pattern."

"Oh, my dear, do stop letting your imagination run wild. No one else knows that I have the jade—no one, that is, but you and I."

"And the man—or woman—who killed Ch'i."

"He was probably trying to get away on some boat that works illegal passages, slipped and fell into the sea. The boatman would leave him. He probably sank before they could get to him. They might not even realize he had money on him. You know yourself how illegal immigrants go back and forth to these islands."

"I also know there's such a thing as murder," I said. "I think Ch'i must have been a member of a gang raiding a tomb in China. Perhaps he kept the money for himself instead of going to some meeting place where it should have been shared out. And the others caught up with him."

"That's guesswork, my dear." She gave the impatient shrug that was characteristic of her when she couldn't find words to win an argument.

I pressed my point. "I'm frightened that the people involved in this business might resort to anything, even violence, to get that jade girdle. The other night, for instance, whoever broke in made no attempt to take anything that lay around."

She laughed. "Oh, Sarah, do stop! How do you think I could manage my affairs if my nerves played with me every time the stock market dropped?"

I answered in a rush of anger. "Ch'i is dead. Someone saw to that. And someone attacked me. Can't you *see* that the Pavilion isn't as burglar-proof as you thought? Someone got in. I'm quite certain none of your servants threw the knife at me."

She rose and stood over me. "And *I'm* certain, also, my dear Sarah, that no one did." Her eyes were brilliant and mocking in the lights from a dozen lanterns. *"I know, without any doubt, that the whole thing was a good story invented by you.* And there is no argument you can use to persuade me to think otherwise."

A wave of something electric quivered between us. I felt my blood boil and my face flame. Theodora saw and checked her arrogance, making a small gesture toward me. "Keep calm, Sarah. I'm sure you mean well, and I suppose I should tell you that your high principles do you credit. But I'm not going to. So let things be, please." Her smile was as winning as her strong features could make it. "Let's drop all this talk. I've a feeling that in spite of our disagreement over the jade, I'm going to be instrumental in making you very, very happy. I feel certain that in the end, you will be grateful to me. And I'm not talking about your career. You'll see . . ."

She walked away from me and into the house.

A few minutes later, as I came out of the guest pavilion, I saw her disappear through the great double doors to where the Rolls awaited her.

The car could barely have turned out of the narrow street before the bell began to clang. I knew that Ah Baht and Ah Lin would go at once, the one to open the outer doors, the other to receive and question the visitor.

I paused by the main pavilion, listening. The man's voice came from beyond the second moon gate and was too far away for me to recognize. But my heart turned over as I thought. Marius . . .

A moment later I breathed more freely as I heard Oliver Farache's laughing protest. "Oh, but I haven't come to see 'Mistress Lady.' I've just seen her leave. I'm calling on Mrs. Brent. Is she in? Ah"—he caught sight of me at the door and approached with an easy grace—"do you know that standing between those two temple candlesticks—they're as tall as you are—you look quite dramatic. Oh, don't mind me. I'm full of compliments. I can't help it. I suppose in an earlier century I'd have been engaged by some inarticulate princeling to write flattering love letters to his princess. Will you come out with me?"

"Shouldn't you be dining with the other guests at Shek-O?"

"I pleaded a hangover after a party last night. I don't suffer from them, but I gave a good dizzy interpretation of one. Anyway, there will be so many people there that nobody will miss the one that got away. And Theodora won't mind; she has other interests. And now, where would you like to take me tonight?"

"You're the visitor to the Island. Choose."

"Oh, I don't know this place well enough. Just show me the night life."

"The Mandarin and dance?" I asked. "Or a restaurant boat and food and talk?"

"That was the whole idea of asking you out. I want to talk and I want to eat Chinese food."

"Let me change. I'll be quick."

"Oh no, don't do that. So few women can wear that chartreuse green. It's lovely on you."

I thought, as I sat in front of the mirror combing my hair, that tables at society dinners were always carefully planned and a missing man would upset the placements. But to Oliver, that was Dioscuri's problem. Oliver had wanted to see me. I smiled at my reflection, flattered and a little excited.

I had hoped that we would drive over to Kowloon to dine, but Oliver gave instructions to the hired chauffeur to take us to the gay and gaudy Aberdeen Harbor. It didn't matter. I was no longer nervous of that village and the hills beyond. I would be with a man who looked well able to protect someone twice my size. In any case, Ch'i was dead and the attack at Theodora's home could, after all, have been made by a casual thief. It was all easily explained—except to my nagging semi-subconscious, which said: *There is danger in complacency*.

As we drove along the road, salt-tanged with the sea air, soft with the balm of the Orient's gentle autumn, Oliver's gaiety infected me. He had the manner of one who had always found life easy, and he accepted, without apparent vanity, that women enjoyed his company. It intrigued him that I was working for Theodora.

He admired my topaz ring. "The setting is superb." He took my hand and traced the curves of the ring's golden shoulders which held the sunny stone. "You know, the only real quarrel I ever had with Theodora was over her jewels. I told her that, to me, diamonds were rather like decorations on a Christmas tree, sparkling but without personality. I told her to get stones that had richness of color, but no glitter. She didn't know what I was talking about." He laughed. "She flashed her great pink diamond at me and said, 'What about *that*?' And I said I'd rather she wore an aquamarine. My great-grandmother had one she claimed had been presented to her by Queen Victoria, who once gave her a lift in her landau when her carriage broke down outside Cadence Manor." He stopped a moment, then said, "Don't you agree with me about Theodora's jewels?"

"Theodora is my client."

"You're very tactful. I'm told you're also very ambitious. Are you?" There was a faint touch of amusement in his voice.

"No one could exist in a competitive world who wasn't. Of course I am."

"What would you like to do more than anything else?"

I nearly said, "Live with Marius again," but I stopped in time and kept to the topic of my work.

"More than anything, I would love to find a new stone. I even dream of the color—brighter than a flawless emerald, deeper than a peridot. I think jewel jade comes nearest to it."

"You should have been around when Henry Platt discovered the tanzanite. Have you ever seen one?"

"Yes, in New York at Tiffany's. A lovely blue."

"But not for you with your color eyes."

"Not for me with any colored eyes." I laughed.

The junk village of Aberdeen came in sight, the sampans busily ferrying the visitors across to the brilliant restaurant boats.

Oliver asked, "Why don't you join some big company instead of working on your own?"

"Because I like it this way. I get commissions for jewelry from wholesalers. My favorite kind of work is when I am given a stone by a dealer or a client and I have to create a design around it. I offer some sketches and work from the one chosen."

A boisterous, beaming Cantonese woman took us in a sampan across the water. Oliver and I sat side by side under the little matting domed roof while the boatwoman *yulah-ed* us toward the huge boat with its hanging banners and strings of lights suspended from the curved roofs. This was Mr. Yun T'ao's fine floating restaurant.

Mr. Yun himself greeted us and took us to the fish pens slung at water level, where we chose our lobster and watched it being borne off to be cooked for us in sweet sauce. Or so we thought. Cynics said that fish were already in the pot awaiting us, and the live one was thrown back. It didn't matter. The display was convincing.

We sat at one of the tables in that animated place with the lanterns trailing ripples of light on the water. We ate our lobster, drank wine, talked and laughed. Then, when it was very late, we drove back to Theodora's palace.

At the door, Oliver kissed me. "Will you come with me tomorrow to buy some presents for me to take back to England?"

"I think I could if Theodora doesn't need me. But I *am* here to work for her, so I must make certain that I can take time off."

"Of course you can," he said easily. "I'll see to that."

We arranged our meeting provisionally for eleven o'clock.

"And afterwards," Oliver said, "lunch with me. We'll go over to the New Territories and stare into Red China."

I said, leaning for a moment against the ancient russet-brown wall, "I have a dream."

"What's that?"

"That I'm walking in the Forbidden City in Peking."

"Then we'll go together one day." And so he left me with a gay promise I would have given the world to have heard from Marius.

Ah Baht opened the doors and I crossed the first court. The trees and the moon-blanched flowers seemed to close round me in that enchanted prison of wealth. But I felt better, lighter, freer because I had laughed a lot and felt a man's interest in me.

XIV

I WENT TOWARD THE LIGHTS of the main pavilion.

Theodora had returned. She was sitting by the lotus pool with Marius. He was teasing Mister Wu with a chrysanthemum leaf and the little dog was loving it.

Theodora glanced up and saw me and continued what she was saying to Marius. ". . . and he's nearly six now. They do say that if I bothered to show him at Crufts he'd be a champion. His real name is Hsiao-chuam, which means 'small seal.' But it's such a mouthful that I christened him Mister Wu."

Marius saw me and rose, tossing the leaf into the pool.

"Don't do that," Theodora said sharply. "I hate untidiness."

"It will eventually sink without trace," Marius said easily. "Here's Sarah back from her evening on the town."

Theodora glanced up at me. "You look like a girl who has walked on air."

"I've dined well," I said, "and listened to Chinese music and drunk wine." I added, "We went to a restaurant boat at Aberdeen."

"I knew you and Oliver would get on well together." She lay back in the lounging chair. "He's charming, but"—she turned with amused exasperation to Marius—"he's extremely stupid where money is concerned. There's cash in his name in the Chase Manhattan Bank in New York, and because I put it there for him, he won't touch it. He says he likes the challenge of earning his own money."

Marius gave up the chair next to Theodora for me and sat down on the rim of the pool opposite us.

"After all," Theodora added, "his family can't make much money running that manor of theirs as a weekend guest house."

"It probably just about pays its way," Marius said.

Theodora flashed back at him, "Then it wouldn't do for you, would it?"

"Wouldn't it?"

She reached out and touched his hand. It was the first affectionate gesture I had ever seen her make. "Question for question? But if I'm wrong, and you ask little of life, then all the things we were talking about before Sarah joined us are just fantasies."

"We all fantasize and dream," he said. "That's right isn't it, Sarah? *We* did. Oh, and hell, how we did . . ." He got up abruptly and walked away. Mister Wu fullowed, giving tiny sneezes, his coat like long strands of snowy silk gleaming in the light of the temple candlesticks in the Pavilion doorway.

Theodora seemed scarcely to notice Marius wasn't there. She said a little dreamily, "So you enjoyed your evening with Oliver? I thought I understood him, but I never did. What sort of charming idiot is he, Sarah, to refuse money from me? Did you manage to decipher that one tonight?"

"No. We didn't discuss money."

She lifted her hand to brush her hair back from her forehead. "You think it's a vulgar subject, don't you, my dear? But the public loves to hear just how many millions I have. When you have a reasonably nice bank balance—but not too much—it's bad manners to talk about it. But when you've got millions, that's different. Envy and curiosity go hand in hand." She gave a small fretful laugh. "And when you've got a title as well . . ." She stretched her arms and the light fell on the Fabergé ruby; I had never really liked it because its glow was dulled by the heavy setting. Theodora loved it because by owning it, she again was linked with history. The stone was said to have been given by King Louis II of Bavaria to his cousin the Empress Elizabeth of Austria. Rumor, warming to its subject, had it that she had worn it at the time of her assassination at Geneva. Rumor, perhaps, but Theodora believed it. To wear a piece of history and to possess a title—she had so much that she wanted.

The light played dully on the stone as she sat back, spreading her hands as if she were counting her fingers. I knew the sign. It was a mannerism of hers used when she was bored with the company. And she wasn't bored with Marius. I took the hint.

"I'm tired," I said. "Good night."

"Good night, Sarah. Sleep well." Then, as I turned to go, she called after me. "I've heard of some wonderful old silk scrolls, faded but very rare. I'd like you to go with me to see them."

"Silk scrolls? Not jade this time?" Marius was some distance from us and yet he heard.

I called to him, "I never before realized that you have primitive hearing. Can you put your ear to the ground and hear footsteps miles away like some jungle tribes?" I was talking to cover up a feeling that Marius had not asked his question lightly—in fact, that it was no question at all, but a message. And the only one to whom it could be given was Theodora. The implication was: *Why talk of scrolls when there are jades to be had?*

Theodora said firmly, "I'm told these scrolls are seventeenth century and have been carefully preserved. They're embroidered with the Eight Buddhist Symbols."

I doubted, as I walked between the mimosa trees by the moon gate that led to the guest pavilion, if Theodora even knew what the Eight Symbols were. To stop thinking about Marius, I named them to myself: the Wheel of the Law; a conch shell; a state umbrella; a canopy; the lotus; the vase; a pair of fishes and the endless knot. The last had a chastening significance for me. The knot that tied us together—Theodora, Marius, a jade, a dead man and myself.

I hated that moment when I had deliberately walked away and left Theodora and Marius together, but the memory of the photograph in Father's sitting room of Marius and the Chinese, the Avenger as I had named him, had become overwhelmingly disturbing.

I had no idea how long my husband stayed with Theodora that night, and I tried not to listen for the sound of the outer doors closing. Sleep was difficult, and when morning came, I felt as listless as if I had stayed too long at a boring party.

Theodora's plans had changed. Pandion Dioscuri had invited her to join a group that was flying to Japan. The scrolls, she said, could wait. She wasn't particularly interested in them because she felt they were like many she already had. If they were there when she returned to Hong Kong, she would make an offer for them.

Célie was behaving like a fussy little hen. "My Lady has such quick whims," she complained to me as she scuttled toward the sewing room in the servants' pavilion. "And now she has asked me to take *this* to that Lilo," she added jealously.

"This" was an evening cloak that had been made from a beautiful piece of old Chinese brocade. Lilo had mended the frayed embroidery so that it looked almost as beautiful as when it was new. But a few strands of scarlet silk had become snagged and needed to be resewn into the pattern.

As I passed the gate that led to the servants' quarters, I glanced in. Lilo sat like a young Oriental queen under a mimosa tree, her little sewing cabinet on a chair by her side. She looked so serene, waiting for Célie.

I had told Theodora that I was going out with Oliver to help him buy some presents to take home, and she had waved at me airily. "Do go, Sarah. I shall be too busy this next few days to need you."

It was a relief not to have to see those scrolls because I knew relatively little about Chinese paintings. I had repeatedly resisted Theodora's attempts to persuade me to study different branches of Chinese art. I knew that if I once dissipated my interests, I would end by knowing something about a lot of things, and not enough about the one or two that really absorbed me. Jewels were my joy; jades my love.

Oliver came for me about eleven o'clock. To see Hong Kong with a stranger's eyes was always fascinating. Oliver refused to go directly to the shop I suggested. "There's something so exciting about the city," he said. "I feel I shall never stop wanting to walk the streets and see all that bright laundry hanging over crooked balconies; men carrying black fans, laborers wearing huge floppy hats with flowers painted on them . . ." He lifted his head and sniffed the air.

"Incense," I said. "We are near a joss stick factory."

"And is it still all fascinating to you?"

"Yes." I skipped round a basket of dried fish swinging from a pole. "Someone I knew once said that Hong Kong slides into the spirit like some exciting, teasing drug." There was laughter in my voice because, unaccountably, I was suddenly happy—as if being with Oliver had helped me shed my fear.

We spent the first hour wandering the streets aimlessly. Oliver stopped many times. First, he found a herbalist's window full of strange, unlikely goods. Then a snake shop drew him to the glass tanks. I stopped only once and that was to look at an enchanting jade model of Ho Hsien Ku—the Immortal Maiden of Chinese legend—surrounded by peach trees.

In the end, by a roundabout route, we reached my favorite shop in Queen's Road. The owner, Mr. Jack Kee, had known me since I was a little girl. Father used to take me with him when he bought some gift for my mother. So much of the really good modern jade was lovely, but I doubted if any of today's craftsmen would do what the old ones did and study a piece of perfect jade for months before deciding how to carve it.

Mr. Kee dealt in good-quality modern jade, intricately cut and copying old designs, expensive, but not as prohibitive in price as the glorious jewel jade.

Oliver was fascinated by a lovely twentieth-century copy of an ancient *k'uei*—the archaic dragon. He stood turning it over and over in his hands, saying, "It really is rather splendid, isn't it, Sarah? And, you know, I thought dragons were fierce. This one looks extremely benevolent."

"Of course," said Mr. Kee, his beautiful ivory hands spread out on the display table. "It is recorded that when Confucius was born, in five hundred and fifty-one, two dragons kept watch. They are good, dragons are good. They guard and they bless."

I picked up the second jade piece lying on the black velvet pad. "And here's the phoenix. They go together, the dragon is the emperor's sign; the phoenix is the empress's."

Oliver shook his head in protest. "Which do I choose, Sarah? They're both rather expensive. But after what you've told me, how can I possibly buy the one without the other? They must go together. Oh well, I'll buy them. But for myself."

I pointed to some smaller pieces. "These are what you could buy for your friends."

A little jade cat took his fancy.

"The word for cat is *mao* in Chinese," I said.

"Mao . . . meeow . . ." He exaggerated the syllable. "How apt!" We both laughed, as children would.

Even Mr. Kee, who had been educated in England and was in so many ways Westernized, expected us to bargain. It was part of the fun of selling. Oliver listened to me, fascinated. But I knew that the jade pieces he was buying were genuine nephrite and not some synthetic material, like cleverly dyed soapstone or the soft serpentine so often sold as jade and so different from it. Jade broke at the slightest knock, but never scratched; soapstone could be marked by a fingernail.

When the price was agreed and Oliver was feeling for his wallet, I asked Mr. Kee about the recent excavations in China.

"So little information comes out," he said. "But the sites have been reopened and I believe wonderful things have been found. And so, of course, the light-fingered move in for possible pickings."

"There have been thefts?" He didn't answer me and I urged him. "What has been stolen?"

Mr. Kee shot a quick look at Oliver and shook his head in a noncommittal way. Apparently he was being deliberately cautious in front of a stranger, though if he knew, it was I whom he shouldn't trust, not Oliver.

"Mr. Farache," I introduced him. "His family owns a lovely home in England which is open to visitors. I've been there."

Mr. Kee's tilted eyes smiled. "I, too, have visited stately homes in England, Mrs. Brent. Hardwick Hall and Chatsworth—very beautiful. You are fortunate, Mr. Farache."

"Oh, ours is a miniature place compared with those"—Oliver slid an arm lightly around me—"and we don't possess a Turner or a Picasso. We just have a charming old house, with the accent on the 'old.' "

I said, "These thefts you mention, Mr. Kee. I don't suppose it will be long before they catch the thieves."

He shook his head. "Where you have a vast country like Red China and so many tiny islands around, it is far more difficult to trace things. And, as you know, on the art market, works of age and beauty fetch astronomical prices." He turned away to find wrapping paper for the gifts Oliver had bought.

I felt it was vital to know as much as he could tell me. "There really have been vast finds in China recently, haven't there?"

He nodded. "Archaeology is a fairly young science in China, Mrs. Brent. The old General Chiang Kai-shek took shiploads of treasures with him on his flight to Taiwan and only recently have the remaining sites been reopened. Chairman Mao has said, 'Let the past serve the present.' The buried palaces and tombs have been brought to light and all the finds have been carefully recorded. But sometime—oh, a few months ago, perhaps—some valuable jades vanished."

"They have been stolen?"

"Probably."

And "probably" meant "certainly" . . .

I asked him, "You have a list of what is missing from the recorded artworks?"

"No. Details are not given outside China, except, of course, to investigators they have sent over to search."

"You know that I'm collecting for the Viscountess Paradine?"

"Oh, yes. All Hong Kong knows." He smiled at me.

"I wondered if I, too, should be given details of what art objects to look for. It's possible that, as Lady Paradine is a very rich collector, something that . . . that is stolen, may be offered to her. If I could know . . ."

He shook his head. "You are an excellent judge of jade but you must be careful. That's all I can say to you. Apart from probable stolen pieces, there are some magnificent fakes now on the market."

The ceremonial girdle was no fake.

I stood in the cluttered little shop and felt as if a thousand eyes were on me. Guilt? Oh, I felt guilty. But I clung to my self-justifying argument. Whatever I might discover (and I had to do all I could to find out the truth), I could not betray someone I felt deeply about— not even for the sake of a few pieces of jade that had lain buried for centuries.

With a start, I realized that Mr. Kee was asking me a question and I hadn't heard it. Oliver, too, was looking at me and waiting for me to speak.

"If you have not been to Taiwan, Mrs. Brent, then you should go. The Museum is magnificent." He spread his eloquent hands, "And the walls inside are of marble. Very fine, very fine."

"Then let's go," Oliver said.

I shook my head. "I can't just take off like that. I have work to do here in Hong Kong."

"A fine excuse! What work? Theodora is on her way to Japan, so you're free for a few days."

"I want to look for turquoise. A London jeweler has commissioned me to buy some for a client. With Theodora occupied with her trip to Japan, it's a good opportunity. I might even be asked to design the settings when I get back to London."

"Turquoise," Oliver said. "A dull stone. Mother has a bracelet of them."

"Come with me and I'll show you how beautiful they can be."

"It's a challenge," he said. "When?"

"Today."

"All right, then. But later. I don't want any more shops yet. After all, I've come thousands of miles, and I want to see China."

"You shall—if only from a distance, across a river."

For the next few hours we did what tourists did. We visited the walled city of Kam Tin, drove past rice paddies and farmlands, and at Lok Ma Chau, looked through the telescope into Red China. Somewhere nearby was Dr. Hai's clinic where Marius spent most of his time. Only a river separated him from the green fields of China . . .

Our morning was packed with interest, but I was determined to visit the turquoise dealer. The wholesaler I knew in London had already been in touch with the owner of the shop in Hankow Road. We found the place—a kind of jeweler's workshop.

About half a dozen Chinese worked at benches, sorting amethysts, and in a huge bronze tray lay a little pile of aquamarines and some stones which I guessed, from a distance, could be rather poor quality yellow sapphires.

The owner of the workshop was a Northern Chinese, Mr. Hsu K'o-liang. He greeted us with great courtesy and led us into an inner room. It was untidy, but I knew that more than likely such a place held far more valuable stones than a smart, chic shop in one of the fashionable areas.

Mr. Hsu crossed to a large, badly worn lacquer cabinet and unlocked a drawer. From it, he drew out a cedarwood box. This he set on a table before us, opened it, and unfolded a piece of dark velvet. The turquoise that lay there, about fifteen in all, were magnificent. Turquoise is not my favorite stone, but only once before, when I was visiting America, had I seen any so fine, and they were in the Smithsonian Museum.

These before me were large cabochon stones, rich and deep in tone. I knew, as I examined them, that this color wasn't fabricated by the common means of dipping the stones in blue wax. These were rare, and pure.

Oliver was looking over my shoulder. "They really are the most marvelous blue. Where do they come from?"

"I'd say these were found in Persia. That's where the finest turquoise come from." I looked at Mr. Hsu, who nodded.

"From Nishapur."

I held a stone between my finger and thumb. "Do you know," I said to Oliver, "that it's said that a turquoise should be a gift and never be bought for oneself?"

"Then I'll buy you one."

"No, thank you," I told him lightly. "There are so many stories about them, though. Long ago, in the East, it was supposed to betray the infidelity of a wife if a turquoise changed color. Dyed stones do change color, so perhaps when a husband was tired of his wife, he gave her a poor-quality turquoise and then, when it became pale or greenish, he accused her of being unfaithful and got rid of her."

"That's a thought!"

The little room rang with our laughter.

I turned to Mr. Hsu, asking what his price was for the stones. He named a sum which I knew was far larger than the London jeweler had anticipated; the jeweler would probably refuse. But I also knew that such lovely stones would find a swift market.

I asked Mr. Hsu if he would wait a few days while I called London. "In the next three days," I said, "I will have found a buyer for them. Oh, Oliver, if only *I* could buy them myself. I'd love to set them in a necklace of diamonds—small ones so that the marvelous sky-blue color wouldn't be overpowered."

"Well, then, why don't you?"

"Because I haven't the money, of course."

"Then get it, and buy all the stones you want."

We had left the workshop and I paused in the street and burst out laughing. "I'm Sarah Brent, not Theodora Paradine."

"But I've a great deal of her money lying idle in a New York bank. I won't touch it for myself, but it would be different if it could help *you*. Now, wait a minute"—he stopped my swift protest—"I'll make a guess. Theodora uses you pretty thoroughly and keeps all her so-called friends away from you in case they'd take you over. Theodora only gives where she knows she'll get a good return for the money she spends. She won't risk losing you. So, in a way, it would be rough justice if I let you use some of her money. And you don't need to think I'll keep it dark, I'd tell her."

"Oliver, stop!"

"When you're rich you can pay me back."

"It won't come to that, because I've no intention of borrowing money to buy turquoise or diamonds or any other stone."

"You're a pretty little idiot," he said, "and pride is an illusion that ambitious people can't afford."

I began to walk on.

"It will serve you right," he said, catching up with me, "if none of your London contacts will buy the stones. And why should they, sight unseen?"

Quite suddenly he bent and kissed my cheek.

I knew what would happen next. It always did in that crowded, confined community. Coming toward us down the street was one of the Island's greatest gossips. She moved in a circle of acquaintances who knew Theodora and who also knew that Oliver was around. The next step was all too obvious. I faced the thought that all Hong Kong would now know that Viscountess Paradine's third husband was attracted to Sarah Brent.

Taiwan was the next place I must visit. But before I went, I needed a detailed photograph of the belt in Theodora's strongroom. I had to compare the workmanship, the state of the jade and the type of carving of the Taiwan exhibit with that on the belt in Theodora's possession. I hoped wildly, and without much optimism, that I had made a gigantic mistake and that the two jades were not companion pieces . . . the one in the National Palace Museum at Taiwan, the other hidden from sight in Theodora's strongroom.

To ask her if I might take the jade while she was away in Japan would be to court a curt "No." There was only one thing to do. I must ask her to let me see it while she was still at home. Then I would photograph it.

I remembered the shop in Connaught Road where Father had bought his photographic equipment. And the morning after my shopping expedition with Oliver, I dropped in there and bought a good-quality camera.

That evening I asked my favor of Theodora, wording it carefully. "While Oliver was choosing presents to take home," I said, "I talked to Mr. Kee. He owns a modern jade shop in Central District. He told me that some brilliant fakes had been made—not many, of course, because the men who made them wouldn't want to flood the market. But he says only the experts can tell them from the genuine. I want to have another look at the girdle you bought from Ch'i."

"In case, after all, it's a fake? Sarah, really! After persuading me to part with a great deal of money, you . . ."

"I don't doubt that it's genuine," I said quickly. "But please, just let me see it once more."

"And if it proves to be one of those clever fakes, am I to be the loser?"

"I've told you. I'm certain it is genuine. But it can do no harm to let me see it again. I promise you it can go back into the strongroom before you leave for Japan."

Theodora had kept me waiting, but I didn't mind. In the end, the white jade belt was in my hands and I took a dozen colored photographs of it. Then I chose the most detailed, tore the others up and threw them away.

I knew that there were many thousands of treasures from the palaces of Peking and Jehol that were on display at the National Museum in Taiwan, but I also knew that because of lack of space, countless more were stored in great underground caves. The exhibits in the Museum were changed every few months in order that visitors could see as many as possible. All I could do was to hope that the ceremonial girdle for which I searched, the photograph of which was in a room at the Art Center in Hong Kong, would be on exhibit when Oliver and I went to the National Museum.

Theodora left for Japan with as much luggage as I would take for a three-month cruise. I fretted for my visa for Taiwan, but because of the demand at the Commissions' offices, it was three days before I could fly out. Oliver had insisted on coming with me, and I was glad. I needed his gay companionship.

It took us only forty-five minutes to reach the island by jet. The plane was always slowed down from its maximum speed for the journey. Otherwise, it had been laughingly explained to me, it would have landed in Siberia.

Oliver clutched a book he had found which gave a short history of some of the treasures of the Palace Museum. I had only my purse, and inside it, the photograph I had taken of Theodora's jade girdle.

The taxi was climbing into the foothills of the mountains and I sat watching the plantations of banana and sugar cane. Then, not so long after we had left Taipei, there it was—a classical palace with primrose-colored walls and glazed green roofs dipping and curving in the grand and ancient manner of Chinese architecture.

Inside the building we both bought copies of the Museum bulletin and studied the guide to the various galleries. Oliver, who knew little or nothing about Chinese art, was drawn to the bronzes on the first floor and I stood mutely by while he exclaimed at the Shang and the Han treasures; a buckle shaped like a leaping tiger; a deer about to spring; an owl. All the time I fretted for the Archaic Jade Gallery on the second floor.

I could scarcely believe I would find what I was looking for, and as I walked between the priceless pieces in the Gallery, I did not see the particular emperor's girdle. Then, at the far end, just as I had given up hope, there was the original of the faded yellow jade whose photograph was in the Hong Kong Art Center. As cautiously as I could, I opened my purse, took out the close-up I had made of Theodora's belt and compared it with the one on display.

The workmanship was uncannily similar—the same sweep of a circle, the same deep indentation of carving, the same heavy type of buckle. I peered down into the glass case and identified the other six Signs of the Zodiac—the dog, the cock, the monkey, the goat, the horse and the snake. This, then, as I had feared, was the companion to the emperor's girdle which Theodora had locked in her strongroom. I slid the photograph back into my purse and closed it.

Oliver had been poring over an exquisite carved table screen, and finding me by his side, said, "Have you had enough?"

"Yes."

"Good. So have I. There comes a moment of mental indigestion when one sees so much."

We left the gallery, pausing together to glance down into a small garden. Oliver lifted his head, looking about him. "The setting is really fine, isn't it? Those hills . . ."

I cared nothing at that moment for the hills or the treasures around me. A Burmese cat, fur gleaming like bronze, crossed in front of us.

"That's luck," Oliver said.

"Is it?" I asked, and laughed and shivered. "Come on, let's go and look around the town."

XV

THE MORNING AFTER my visit to Taiwan, it seemed as if the courts of the Pavilion were even more radiant. The pavilions and the gardens had changed their aura, and as I wandered in sandaled feet between the massed flowers, I realized how powerful Theodora's personality was, overshadowing even the beauty of her surroundings.

I kept catching sight of the servants, so invisible when she was there, scuttling in and out of the four pavilions, freed from the restrictions of having to be seen and heard as little as possible. Their uniforms of black silk trousers and short coats were immaculate; their hair glistened in the sunlight; their wrists, delicate but strong, moved the lovely Coromandel screens, heaved the lacquer cabinets. But they were laughing and chattering in Cantonese as they worked.

I was of little importance to them. I was somewhere between classes—neither employer nor servant—and so the silence that the Chinese found so difficult to hold could be broken because I was not Mistress Lady.

With Mister Wu's tiny claws pattering on the marble by my side, I wandered back through the moon gate, past the guardian cloisonné stork.

The ornate yellow-cushioned chairs stood in the shade of the acacias, and I sat down, lying back and feeling a strange and lovely peace. There were many things I could be doing that morning. I needed to check the cataloging of Theodora's collection, I should be asking Célie to let me look again at the opals Theodora wanted me to reset. I had planned that, instead of a letter, I would telephone the London jeweler about the turquoise I had found in the shop in Hankow Road, though that could wait since Hong Kong morning was night in England.

I lay listening to the birds in the red-frescoed eaves. I felt washed of all hurt and all fear, although I knew that I couldn't remain so.

The bell at the side of the great outer door gave its deep gonglike sound. Perhaps it was the flower boy bringing in new pots of poinsettias, to grow and flower in the winter.

I listened disinterestedly to the roll of the great outer doors and then, eyes closed, heard nothing more. No one called me, no sound disturbed me. I turned my face and laid my cheek against the yellow silk cushion on the chair back.

" 'Tread softly, because you tread on my dreams,' " said Marius.

I hid my startled dismay, opened my eyes and tried to look as if his arrival didn't disturb me.

"You walk like a cat," I said.

"I dislike loud noises. You should know that, since you've lived with me."

"Theodora isn't here."

"I know, but I've brought something she asked me for." He laid a small glossy book in my lap. "You'll probably be interested, too."

I picked it up, riffling through the pages. It was a catalog of a jewelry sale to be held that week. A Mr. Peter Tsin, one of Hong Kong's millionaires, had died and in his will had left instructions that his already dead wife's valuable collection of jewelry be auctioned for the benefit of St. Cecilia's Hospital, "where I received the most wonderful nursing and extreme kindness."

While I glanced through the finely produced catalog, Marius sat down next to me. Mister Wu came up to be greeted, and I was aware of the broad, sun-tanned hand caressing the little dog.

"But this is a superb collection," I cried. "Look." I showed him a page and began to read. " 'A very fine necklace of jonquil-colored diamonds interspersed with pigeon's-blood rubies.' I'll make a guess that a Chinese wrote those descriptions—they have a touch of poetry." I turned a page. "Oh, Marius, and *this*." I was looking at a bracelet of vivid green peridots and rubies, the kind of color combination that brought out the richness of each stone.

"Now you'll be in your element." Marius spoke without malice, but with a kind of gentle indifference. He had tossed the promise of an Aladdin's cave into my lap as casually as crumbs to a sparrow.

I laid the book on the wrought-iron table by my side. "I'll let Theodora see this when she returns. She'll be back in time for the party she is giving on the night of the Moon Festival."

"And this time you won't run away?"

"I'll probably go and see Father. We might take the car and drive somewhere just to watch the fun. And you?"

"I don't know. Here or there." He lifted his shoulders. "You and I never liked to be tied to promises, did we?"

I stared out across the golden light to the high fronds of the palm trees by the outer wall. "No. But that was only the outward and visible sign. The real, deep trouble was that we never really belonged. We should have been lovers and never have set up housekeeping together."

"You could have said that earlier." Marius flicked at a flying insect. "And then, perhaps, we would have held onto our half-relationship—for what that would have been worth. A herring instead of caviar."

"We might have been very happy with the herring," I said. "But how could we have known . . . *I* have known? That's the awful thing about being young. You have to make mistakes in order to find out that they *are* mistakes."

Marius said nothing. We sat side by side quietly, like old friends or people married for so long that passion had given way to passive friendship.

Mister Wu lay on the cool marble close to my feet, watching a butterfly; his tongue tip was like a pink flower petal caught on the end of his nose. I bent down to him and he accepted my fondling graciously but without fawning. He had the independent character of a cat.

"Now," Marius said, "what happens next?"

I turned in surprise. "As far as I'm concerned, nothing. I mean, I'm here and I've got a few commissions for buying good stones. I've found some turquoise but I also want to buy some red tourmalines—old ones that centuries ago were cut and used as buttons for mandarins' hats. I don't think they're particularly beautiful, but there's a rather chichi wholesaler in London who wants them if I can find any."

"And jade?" Marius asked.

I could not answer. I turned involuntarily to look at him, but only his profile was etched against the mass of bauhinias—a quiescent yet alert line of forehead, nose and jaw.

"Well, tell me what you've been buying for Theodora," he said.

"Oh, jewels and . . . other things."

"She runs risks having her treasures collected in an old house without guards or guard dogs."

"The place is marvelously protected." And thought: *But it wasn't the other night*.

The telephone bell began to ring. I heard Ah Lin's footsteps coming toward us. "It's Mistress Lady, for you."

"But she's in Japan . . ." I began. Then I ran into the hall and picked up the receiver.

"Sarah? Is everything all right?"

"Perfectly. Where are you?"

"In Kyoto and we leave for Gora tomorrow morning. I was just checking to see that you're looking after my house."

"With so many servants, I don't think I'm very essential. And, Theodora, Marius is here."

Her voice became suddenly explosive. "But he knows I'm away. Why has he come?"

"He has brought over the catalog of a jewel sale that's being held in aid of the hospital. You apparently know about it."

"And *he* knows I'm away." She said it again, her voice so loud that it racked my ear. "Why didn't he wait until I returned?"

"You'd better ask him."

"I will. Call him, Sarah."

I laid the receiver down on the lacquer table and as I turned I saw Marius's shadow thrown on to the ground outside the open lattice window. "Theodora is on the line. She wants to speak to you."

He came round to the door and, passing me, picked up the receiver. As I went out into the court I heard him say, "That peculiar crackling accompanying your voice isn't exactly a symphony orchestra. How are you enjoying Japan?"

After that I was too far away to hear more than just the murmur of Marius's voice. I had an uneasy feeling as I sat waiting for him to finish his telephone conversation, that this was no casual visit. I also knew perfectly well that Theodora was angry that Marius and I were together in her house. Her friendships—or love affairs—were always violently possessive, and no wife, particularly not a discarded one, should share in it.

For now Theodora wanted Marius. And it was not even that which troubled me most. It was his sudden interest in jade and in Theodora's acquisitions. The terrible thing that tore at me was that I had begun, in spite of desperate efforts to trust him, to question Marius's integrity.

I was so closed in with my own mistrust that I was quite unaware of the golden garden.

"I think"—Marius came out of the house toward me—"that Theodora only telephoned because she is a little bored with the company."

"I doubt if Theodora is bored. She finds Pandion Dioscuri rather—as she puts it—'ugly but fascinating.'"

"Maybe. But he has his own particular interest with him in that party, and by heaven, is she beautiful!" He leaned his elbows on his knees and looked at me. "Is there anything worrying Theodora?"

"What could?"

"Oh, plenty. The weight of responsibility of possessing so much, for one thing."

"I think she enjoys everything she owns."

"But fears she might lose it?"

"Not unless the whole world went bankrupt," I said. "Her wealth is spread over so many international banks. And, anyway, everything is insured."

"Everything?"

"Well, almost." I hadn't thought. Of course, she dared not insure the jade.

Our faces were carefully turned away from one another. Marius said, as if he were changing the subject, "It's strange, isn't it, how the fate of one small object can upset the lives and hopes of many people."

"What . . . small . . . object?"

He said calmly, "Sometimes I think aloud. Random thoughts. But take no notice."

They weren't random. They were linked with what we had discussed before. The idea struck me like a blaze in my mind. Theodora could have promised Marius his clinic as payment for his help in passing on to her the stolen jade. It was the only way I could make sense out of the sequence of events and hints and threats.

But I didn't know the right questions to ask; I had no knowledge of the subtlety of inching my way into someone else's mind. And that, in itself, showed how little I knew Marius; that I didn't dare be honest with him because I had no idea how he would react—and I was afraid.

The silence between us was overlong. I was too aware that I loved him. I said desperately, "What will you do when you've finished your researches here?"

"Start thinking about my clinic back in the West."

"England?"

"Maybe. I don't know yet. It depends on many things."

"Such as?"

"The situation there. Politically, I don't want to be hamstrung by officialism or medical prejudice. I must be free and I must succeed."

I said sharply, "Your ambitions have changed. Theodora has taught you to enjoy the thought of success."

"Oh, no, Sarah, *you* taught me what ambition was. And mine has grown from a flame to a fire. Now when I make up my mind to do something I go all out for it."

"Aim for the stars—and crash."

He said, as if thinking aloud, "Health is the most important factor in the life of every human being. I need my clinic to put my ideas into practice. Maybe I'll find that it's all misguided, but nothing is ever achieved without experiment and I'll have a damned good try." He looked at me half over his shoulder. "I shan't fail, you know. I *can't* fail because what I want will be worth while for so many people. Whatever it costs me, I'll succeed."

"And the money?"

"Ah, yes. The money." He trailed a finger in the pool, grave, lost in a thought I knew he would not share.

I asked, "Is Theodora interested in the clinic?"

"People with perfect health are seldom interested in sickness."

"But you've talked to her about it?"

"Yes."

I knew the tone only too well. The clipped, succinct word was like a warning to me that the discussion was over. But I was in no mood to be pressured into silence. "Theodora must have shown *some* interest in your plans."

He got up and walked a few steps from me. Then he turned abruptly. "And you, Sarah? Are *you* interested?"

"Of . . . of course."

"Ah, but that moment's hesitation gave you away, my dear. Your world is utterly remote from mine."

In spite of the life we had had together, he had no idea that my hesitation was a nervous reaction—a fear for *him,* for his profession and his wild ambition.

Was it that we had both loved not a person but a myth, some dream we had formed in our minds and fastened on to the human being we found most nearly filled the illusion? Was that all it had been? And was it that from which I was now fighting to free myself?

I closed my eyes. We had had such moments of joy, but we had never questioned what lay behind it. We called it love and for a short while believed in our luck at finding one another. But luck proves fickle, rises and falls, fluctuates and dies.

I opened my eyes. Marius, walking silently, had disappeared. Moments later, I heard Ah Baht locking the outer doors.

I went to see Father, and halfway through the evening Marius arrived. I heard him talking to Nam Tsao in the hall.

Marius, twice in one day. Coincidence? Stranger things had happened, but I didn't believe he had just chanced to call. As Father went into the hall to greet him, I got up and walked to the window, standing with my back to the room.

I had begun to fear Marius. I feared that he had come to the apartment because he had been watching my movements and knew I was there. Just as he had joined me that day on the hillside. I felt that he was waiting for me to drop some remark, let out one tiny sentence that would reveal his suspicions that I knew too much for my own safety. That he was the tool of the Avenger, watching and reporting back.

"Oh, by the way," Father said, coming into the room, "Sarah is here."

"Hello," I said to Marius. "Twice within a few hours is quite something, isn't it?"

"Yes, isn't it?"

Father was an easy conversationalist, but as he poured out drinks, I sat quietly and cautiously, only listening. I wondered if Father, with his previous diplomatic associations with the old China and the Chinese border, knew the clinic where Marius spent so much of his time.

The conversation was desultory and seemed to me studiedly commonplace, as if each man was being careful in what he said to the other. They talked of a new block of apartments being built at Mid-Levels; of the retirement of an old doctor who was returning to a cottage in England with his collection of volumes of Chinese poetry . . . I stopped listening.

On Father's desk was a carved ivory rose paperweight with a base of ebony. I picked it up and began playing with it. My thoughts wandered. Ivory . . . From the Chinese themselves had come the words "Ivory is the elephant's beautiful, generous excuse for his clumsiness."

". . . what's your opinion of it, Sarah?"

"Opinion?" I hadn't an idea what they had been talking about.

"The new Art Center," Father said. "Do you like it?"

"I think it's beautifully designed. Yes." I put the ivory rose back on his desk and felt awkward and alien in that big room with the two people who should have been closest to me. The hall clock struck ten and I sprang to my feet.

"I must go now. But I'll be in touch."

Father said, chuckling, "The striking clock was almost like a signal for you—Cinderella at the ball at midnight. Good gracious, girl, you aren't in some little English village where they go to bed at nine—that is, if there are any such places left. But off you go if you must."

"I'm leaving, too," Marius said. "I've promised to meet someone. I'll run you back to town, Sarah."

"Thanks, but I can take a cable car."

"Don't be such a little idiot," Father said. "Why wait around for that and then trudge back to Theodora's place when you can get a lift to the door?"

I had no convincing reason for refusing. I climbed into Marius's small car, keeping myself carefully pressed against the door, fearful even of the casual touch of his arm as he reached for the gear shift.

As we drove down from the Peak toward the glittering waterfront, we talked indifferently. I watched the city grow closer as the car took each curve.

A car roared past us, driving too close, and Marius swerved to avoid it, jolting me against him.

"The moon is so lovely," I said. "And I suppose next week, when they hold the Moon Festival, the sky will be full of cloud and the Chinese will beat their drums to their invisible goddess and, being Chinese, will cheerfully make the best of it."

"You've got your facts a bit mixed, haven't you?" For the first time that evening Marius laughed. "They beat their drums to frighten the devils of the air so that their beloved moon can be seen again, not to pay homage to their goddess."

"I know that," I said crossly. "I was just making conversation. If you prefer, I'll just sit quietly."

"You won't." Marius slowed down. "And so we'll touch earth. As you so rightly say, the moon may be behind clouds on the night of the festival. Let's make the most of it now." He stopped the car and leaned across me to open the passenger door.

I seemed to move like a sleepwalker, obeying Marius, ill-at-ease, lost for words. Walking through the bracken, the camphor trees stark against the illumined sky, we should have played the romantic lovers' game. Instead, we were an estranged husband and wife and a world of misunderstanding and suspicion separated us.

I bent and picked a spear of tall wild grass. Marius paused, watching me. " 'In such a night Medea gathered the enchanted herbs.' "

"This," I said, "is a very ordinary blade of grass and you needn't call me Medea, because I'm no sorceress."

"Once you were."

"Fantasies don't last." The hardness of my voice spoiled all that beauty, denigrating it. But it was my only armor against him and the dangerous luminous night. *I don't trust you, Marius* . . . I cried aloud, "My God, why did we have to meet and imagine we were in love?"

"Because we're human and the moods and passions of life are what seize and control us all."

I saw a cruise ship way out on the black horizon, lights blazing from bow to stern, and remembered how Marius and I had sailed by sea to Hong Kong on our second visit. We had dreamed through the long days and danced through the nights and made love. Marius's favorite dress had been my green chiffon, and when the ship put in at Bombay he bought me a necklace of garnets.

I turned abruptly, saying, "Let's get back to the car." I stumbled over a small granite rock as I spoke, and fell against Marius.

He steadied me and lifted one of my hands. "How incongruous. Millions of dollars must have passed through those lovely fingers."

"I don't work in a bank."

"Gems," he said.

I snatched my hand away. "Rubies and emeralds, aquamarines and turquoise—the lot. And all in order to buy butter with my bread."

"At the rate you're going, my darling girl, you'll soon be breakfasting off caviar."

We had paused by the car and for a moment we looked at one another. My face must have been in the shadow, but the moon's blaze poured onto Marius so that every bone from hairline to chin stood out as if they, too, were luminous.

He bent and kissed me.

Driving the rest of the way home, we scarcely spoke. Marius stopped the car outside the thick wall and turned off the ignition.

"Perhaps," he said, "one day you will ask for your freedom."

"And you'll give it?"

"Of course."

I sat, my head half averted. In the houses opposite, all the family washing had been taken in, and the bamboo poles stood out like giant pins. There was a smell of fish cooking. "I'll give you your freedom if you want it," I said to Marius.

He nodded. "Yes, I suppose that's the way it will be. You see, I like the idea of being married—I mean to someone who happens to stay around."

I said, too quickly, "If there is anyone now . . ."

"I'll give you fair warning." He spoke lightly and with complete indifference, not even glancing my way to watch the effect of his words.

I got out of the car. "Goodbye. Let me know when you've decided. I suppose we'll be civilized and remain friends. I may even like your second wife."

I pulled the great bell at the side of the door three times, the signal that whoever waited there was resident at the compound. Ah Baht let me in.

"It's a lovely night, isn't it?" I said, and heard the car behind me drive away.

"Next week is the Moon Festival. I hope that it will be a very fine night," said Ah Baht, who with the rest of the servants would probably not be allowed by Theodora to leave the Pavilion but would celebrate with mooncakes and their own private ways of greeting the gods.

As I walked through the first moon gate, Mister Wu came toward me, his curled tail flicking against the cloisonné stork. I spoke to him and he pattered ahead of me. Then, as we passed the pool, I swooped him up in my arms, and bending my face into his thick white hair, burst into tears.

XVI

A SMALL ROOM was set aside in the Art Center for the preview of the jewels to be auctioned for the new hospital. Most of the pieces of jewelry were of magnificent precious stones in such ornate settings that the stones lost their brilliance. The display tables were guarded by detectives and police. Mixing with the wealthy of Asia I recognized a few well-known dealers from as far away as Europe, although I doubted whether the extreme elaborateness of the jeweled settings would appeal to European taste.

Beneath one velvet-lined case containing a single magnificent blue diamond set in a ring, the card read: "In the seventeenth century in India, the Rajah of Kufah gave this to his wife upon the birth of her thirteenth child. It is said that this particular stone was known as 'Fragment of Eternity.'"

Oh, no, it wasn't, I said silently to the unknown writer, for the name had applied in India to diamonds right down the centuries. But someone would buy and believe that he owned a single diamond bearing a name that might become as strongly historical in the jewelry world as the Cullinan diamond in the British Crown Jewels or the great pear-shaped Tiffany diamond.

I moved to a necklace of emeralds, the most fragile of all precious stones. "The trouble with emeralds," I said, "is that they are almost always flawed."

Oliver, who was with me, was looking about him. Theodora had wandered off to join a crowd at one of the corner tables. By the time I reached her she had managed to edge her way to the front of the group.

A collar of jewels at least five inches wide lay on a blue satin bed. It was made up of moonstones and peridots with a scattering of fair-sized pigeon's-blood rubies.

A woman near us said, "For my money, that's the most beautiful thing in the room. Are those green stones emeralds?"

"No, peridots." The voice was so very English that I guessed he was a dealer from London. "They come from the Red Sea, and they're sometimes known as 'evening emeralds.'"

I said softly to Oliver, "I didn't know that. You learn something at every turn of life, don't you?"

Oliver said, "The light seems to move on those stones like water."

"It's known as the *Schiller*," I told him, "and it's a mysterious vanishing light you only see on moonstones."

Theodora was at my other side. "Bid for it, Sarah. Bid high. I want it." She left me and pushed through the crowds.

Oliver said, "She'll get it, you know. Or rather you, my poor sweet Sarah, will get it for her. And you know what will happen? It will never be worn."

I wandered to the next object, which was an Indian hand ornament of delicately chased gold chains studded with rubies, a legacy from the days when high-born Indian women used their hands only to express an emotion, never to dust a shelf or even to dress themselves.

There was a festive air about the small room, as if the riches that one man had poured on to his wife were like a drug that lifted everyone out of the matter-of-fact world into an amazing paradise of luxury.

I looked across the room. Theodora was in a far corner, talking to a man. At first, seeing only his back, I supposed him to be a Hong Kong dealer, but something about him was vaguely familiar.

Then Theodora laughed, and at the same moment the man turned slightly my way as if sensing that he was being watched. He was about forty; his face had an Oriental calm and his hair was very black. He wore a well-cut suit and I knew that his eyes, seemingly so indifferent, missed nothing. It was the Avenger.

"There's Pandion," Oliver said, "and with another beautiful girl! Hey!" The hand that reached for mine slid off my fingers as I darted away from him. My action was purely instinctive. I had no thought of why I should join Theodora and the man I least wanted to meet. But I edged my way toward them.

". . . and I occasionally lend some of my most interesting pieces for exhibitions," Theodora was saying. "Not often, of course, because when one loves one's possessions as I do . . ." She caught sight of me and stopped; there was annoyance on her face.

I didn't let it worry me; I was far more anxious about the Avenger's presence. But he barely seemed to notice me. I might even have been attached to the group standing next to us.

"You are a very famous collector, Lady Paradine," he said. "We all know that. One day perhaps you will grant me the pleasure of see-ing some of your treasures."

"One day," she said, "I might have an exhibition here in Hong Kong. I haven't made up my mind yet. But tell me, are you a collec-tor or a dealer?"

He smiled. "Neither. You might say I'm just a lover of beautiful things. I believe, by the way, that your main interest is in jade."

"Oh, no." Theodora flung the crimson gauze scarf she wore more for effect than necessity round her throat. "Jade is only one of my in-terests, and not by any means my chief one. But Mrs. Brent,"—she pressed my arm tightly—"is really an expert. In fact, sometimes I have to curb her craze for it."

"I'd like to put it," I said quickly, "that I love jade. I hope I'm reasonably expert. But I'm not possessive."

"Sarah dear," Theodora remonstrated, "I've seen those fingers of yours touch jade as if you couldn't bear to part with it." She might be merely talking for effect, to show the Avenger that she chose her ad-visers well. But she was on dangerous ground, both for herself and for me.

I moved away from them, saying, "I had better look around and see if there is anything else that might interest you."

"So far, all I want is the moonstone collar."

The Avenger was looking at me. "You have been to Taiwan, Mrs. Brent?"

"Yes," I said brightly. "How could I resist?"

"We have rare jade treasures in China, too," he said, "a great many. Sites have been reopened and wonderful things found."

And lost . . .

Theodora was saying formally, "I'm so glad that your country has now decided that its ancient decorative arts are to be preserved."

"We have had to learn to be proud of our past as well as our pres-ent, Madame. And we guard our treasures." Beneath his polite com-ments, I was certain that there lay a meaning which he hoped would get through to me. I really feared this man. I wondered what he and Theodora had been saying before I joined them and how they had got into conversation.

"Come, Sarah. We really must finish going round this collection. Good morning, Mr.—"

"Good morning, Lady Paradine," said the Avenger, and gave her no name.

I felt the bruised flesh where Theodora had gripped my arm. Her powerful fingers had borne a command. *Take care what you say, Sarah . . .*

I had no need to be careful. I was certain, although I still had no real proof, that Ch'i had been given the task by the robbers of contacting Theodora in order to sell jades—probably cautiously, one by one—but had tried to sell this girdle for himself. I remembered how anxious he had been for Ah Lee-ming and me to leave the hut; it must have been because he was terrified of his fellow robbers catching up with him. But at least one of them had. And Ch'i was drowned.

There had been no one on that lonely hillside and only one car passing at that time, the one that had followed me to Theodora's palace. The Avenger must have been involved with Ch'i. He must think that I was the one who acted as messenger between Ch'i and the innocent Theodora. Ch'i was dead. And there had already been one attempt on my life.

"Sarah, where *are* your thoughts? I've asked you three times what you think of that ring."

"I'm sorry. Who was the man you were speaking to?"

Theodora shook her head. "I don't know. Someone interested in the sale, I suppose. That's why he didn't give his name. A dealer, wanting to find out the things that *I* was interested in—probably someone commissioned to buy for a jewel agent in New York or London. Now, this ring . . ."

It lay in its black velvet case, heavy and old-fashioned, probably made in seventeenth-century Italy, a complicated mass of sapphires, emeralds and pearls.

"What do you think?"

I shook my head. "It's overdecorated and the cutting of the stones is bad."

"The catalog says that it once belonged to Charles the First. That makes it really historic."

"I would advise against it because I don't believe it is English, so I doubt if Charles the First ever owned it. The design and the cut is entirely antique Italian. Of course, I could be wrong."

She shrugged. "Never mind, you're right about the cutting of the stones. So far there is only one thing here that I must have, and that is the moonstone collar. I'd like you to bid for it at the sale tomorrow." She looked about her. "Where is Oliver? Ah, there he is. And Pandion is here. I wonder what he is aiming to buy, and for whom? He's got a Chinese girl with him."

She was very beautiful and she was also being noticed by everyone.

Photographers had not been allowed into the room, but men were jockeying for a chance to speak to Pandion and so get close to her.

The girl had smooth ivory skin and lovely hair unusually braided in a coronet round her head. She had a mouth that was neither too small nor too sensuous and her eyes were large and light in color.

Oliver saw Theodora's imperious wave and returned to us. "That's Fay Mi," he said. "She's an actress."

"Another one?" Theodora asked acidly. "Pandion really does go in for them."

"But this one is different. She's no starlet. She's one of the most important actresses of the Shaw Studios in the New Territories. Pandion must have talked about her when you were with his party in Japan."

"I did hear her name mentioned."

Oliver laughed. "When Pandion has a crush, he really falls for a girl. Temporarily, of course."

On the morning of the sale, I sat alone in the third row of the heavily guarded room. The atmosphere had the same hushed reverence that I had experienced so often in Sotheby's or Christie's in London. The auctioneer was a handsome and elegantly dressed Chinese who looked down on us from the platform. His manner was at once benevolent and alert, and I was sure he was a master of his profession and intended to get full benefit for the hospital out of the sale.

Theodora had refused to come with me. "If I were there the dealers would know what I wanted and would push up the price."

As if seeing me, who so often bought for her, wouldn't have the same result . . .

I glanced about me. There were a few familiar faces, dealers from some of the finer jewelry houses of Hong Kong and Kowloon and from Europe. The Avenger was nowhere to be seen, but then he had no need to be there. He had known our names and appearance. Now he knew our voices also. I wondered whether, because of her inability to stop boasting about her possessions, Theodora had made some small slip that could have put my life in even greater danger.

The bidding for the more important pieces was swift and rose high. I remained interested throughout the sales of the ornate, exclusively Oriental jewelry, because although I wasn't buying, it was always fascinating to watch the way the dealers would feint and fence, playing their expensive, nonchalant parts in the game of acquisition like players at a poker table.

I was waiting for the moonstone collar. When it was brought to the auctioneer's table, offers were brisk, but one by one the bidding fell away until there were two of us. The price rose: tensions sharpened.

One hundred and thirty thousand . . . this was crazy. But Theodora had said, "Get that collar." I made my bid with a nod.

"Two hundred thousand Hong Kong dollars . . . Two hundred and fifty thousand . . ." The auctioneer looked my way.

I held my breath and my heart began to turn over with nerves. Auctioneers didn't wait while minds hovered between the "Yes" and the "No." I shook my head. The bidding had risen beyond all reason.

A stranger, a European whom I guessed to be a dealer, had acquired the jeweled collar.

XVII

"YOU LET IT GO? *Just like that?*" When Theodora was angry she went very white beneath her make-up and the skin around her lips and at her temples gleamed like milk against the faint suntan of the rest of her face. Her lashes swept up like dark shadows as she looked at me standing before her. "You let that collar go?"

"For a quarter of a million? Yes, I did."

"And since when have you been in a position to tell me how much of my money you'll spend. *My* money?"

"The price was ridiculous. The piece of jewelry was beautiful, but it wasn't worth half that. And, although the rubies were lovely, the chief stones were semiprecious. You have never liked wearing those."

"I wanted that collar. I told you to get it for me at any price."

"I'm sorry. But there comes a time in sale rooms when something on offer reaches a price that is more than just outrageous. This was. You want a necklace of moonstones and peridots and a few rubies? Give me time and I'll see that you have one."

"Ah, so that's it." She sat up straight, like a blanched goddess, her long neck stretched, her eyes on fire. The whole scene was out of proportion, and I felt outside anger, a spectator at a fury. I knew perfectly well that even if she possessed the moonstone collar, Theodora would probably never wear it.

As I turned away from her, a thought struck me. She could have wanted it just to impress Marius; to say, in effect, "Look what I have done towards the hospital you are interested in; look what I have given for something not worth half the price."

If that were so, how much more would she give him for his dream, his final aim, his clinic? For that would be the way she would impress him. "This was the show piece, Marius. This, that is now mine."

Only it wasn't. Because of my final silence at the sale, Theodora had lost it.

"Sarah, are you listening to me?"

I was wearing dark glasses because the evening sun was very bright. I pushed them up on top of my head so that they held my hair back. The light dazzled me for a moment, but I could see Theodora better and marvel at her unbreakable assurance, her savagery.

"You were saying?"

"I want you to find out who bought that collar."

"What good will it do? Within twenty-four hours it could be anywhere—in Florida, in New York, in London, in Buenos Aires."

But Theodora was right. I had let my own feelings interfere with the job I had been sent to do. I added, in an effort at self-justification, "I'm sorry if you think that I've let you down. But you see, to me it was a principle."

"With *my* money, you accept *my* principles, Sarah. Always remember that."

I crossed to a chair and picked up my purse.

"Where are you going?"

"To find out what you want to know, who has bought the moonstone collar. If I can, that is. It may be some private buyer, in which case we shall probably never know."

The bell at the door began to peal as Theodora was about to speak again. She slid forward quickly, glancing at her reflection in the unruffled water of the lotus pool and smoothing back her hair.

"I'm not expecting anyone. Oh . . ." Her voice changed as she saw who came through the first moon gate. "I might have known. Oliver never makes appointments." But I saw her faint smile of pleasure. "Come and cheer me up."

"I'd be delighted, providing you'll offer me a drink. I need one. And I also need an hour of relaxation in your quiet courts. I've had a long day on the yacht with Pandion and his beauties. Unfortunately, that's all they are, just beauties. So I thought I'd like a little intellect to round off the day."

"Then you've come to the wrong place," Theodora said easily. "I'm no intellectual, and I'm perfectly content with being myself."

Oliver sat down near her, laughing. "Only at the moment you're out of temper with someone or something."

"Yes, I am. I sent Sarah to bid for that moonstone collar. Do you remember seeing it at the jewelry preview?"

"I remember seeing one hell of a lot of baubles. Theo, dear, what about that drink you promised me? The afternoon is hot and I'm parched."

"I promised you nothing of the kind."

"Very well." He gave her a good-natured grin. "Then I'll go to the Mandarin and take Sarah with me. We'll have splendid iced drinks in frosted glasses."

"Sarah has a job to do for me."

"At this time of evening? It's half past six."

"Time is different in the East—or perhaps you haven't noticed. I want her to find out who has the moonstone collar that she should have bought for me at the auction."

"Well, I can save her the trouble. I know."

Theodora leaned forward, eyes on his face. "Who?"

"Pandion Dioscuri's new love, Fay Mi. He gave it to her. Surely you remember seeing her at the jewelry preview with him?"

Theodora gave a small, sharp hiss. "Damn that man!"

Oliver rose. "And now, my dear Theo, since you have forgotten your art of hospitality, I'm taking Sarah with me for that drink."

Theodora reached out a foot and pressed a bell that was fixed into the side of the marble basin. Almost immediately, Ah Lin wheeled the drink trolley into the court. Oliver mixed martinis with a neat, practiced hand.

"Theodora is angry," I said, "because I failed to get the moonstone collar for her. I lost my courage."

Oliver lifted his drink lightly in a toast to us and said, "I saw the necklace, and quite frankly, if it had been my money involved, I'd have said that Sarah needed a spell in a mental home if she had offered even half what it fetched."

"But," said Theodora softly, "it wasn't your money that was involved, darling Oliver. Yours is tucked away in a New York bank where you're too proud, or too stupid, to use it."

He said happily, "Pride and stupidity are both my prerogatives. They always were."

"Yes, you're right." I watched her smile and wondered, as he seemed to soften her temperament, whether their divorce had been a mistake and Theodora knew it.

"Pandion has invited me to the yacht tonight," she said. "There is to be a Chinese opera performance. Are you coming?"

"No," Oliver told her cheerfully. "And he won't miss me. He only ever misses the young and the beautiful."

Theodora's heavy lids closed over her eyes in slow motion. "I'm neither young nor beautiful, but he has asked me."

"My dear Theo, you are ageless—that makes you the exception to every rule."

"You see?" she turned to me. "Oliver knows all the answers. And he was just the same when we were married. He never slumped into a dull 'now we are married attitude' which so many wives have to put up with. Very well, Oliver. Stay here with Sarah. I told you once before that you two should get on excellently together."

"You know, Theo," he said lightly, "I had every intention of doing just that, whether you had asked me or not."

I waited, expecting her to make the acid comment that it was she who did the inviting to her house. Instead, she sipped her drink and watched Mister Wu twitching an ear at a fly.

An hour later, Theodora left for the Chinese show on Pandion's yacht in a flurry of embroidered ruby silk, sapphires and perfume that killed all the scents of the garden.

When she had gone, Oliver sat down again, stretched his legs and commented, "Strange, isn't it, that someone owns all this and far more, and yet is so restless that she always has to be chasing around to the next place? I hear it's to be New York soon."

"She has a vast business to control."

"Oh, rubbish! All she has to do is to rake in the money. Her directors and her managers do the rest."

"I'd still say a great fortune is a weight to cope with, especially in today's economy. You should know that better than most, since you were her husband."

"It's old history," he said, "and I'd like you to forget it, too. I've got a house of my own, or rather a share in it, and I happen to like Cadence Manor. All I want is to hold on to it."

"But you will."

He shrugged. "Maybe. My parents and I find our home a place where we want roots for life. My brother isn't so interested. I think one day he might clear off and leave it to the three of us."

I said softly, "I remember it so well. That lovely curved drive of elms . . ."

"Limes."

"I never was very good with trees." I laughed. "And your square hall with that glorious eighteenth-century furniture. I remember your father telling me that possessions meant nothing to him except the ones that had been handed down in his family. He said, 'You can go out and buy a Regency table or an old oak chest or even a bit of Italian Renaissance—but it's only yours because you've paid money for it. The things in Cadence Manor have been ours since Charles I's reign.'"

"One day, Sarah, I hope you'll grow to love it all as we do."

"I'd have to save up for one of your weekends. They're not exactly cheap."

"Oh, you'd be our invited guest. And after the first visit . . ." He broke off, leaned forward and kissed my cheek. "It's warm where the sun has touched it. Did you know you've got a freckle shaped like a heart?"

"I prefer to forget it," I said quickly.

Theodora returned early. Oliver and I were still seated under the acacias, enjoying a laughing argument about sports.

"Riding," he said, "with a fine, spirited horse that only you can tame."

"Tennis and swimming . . ." I stopped and turned to see Theodora sweeping up the path toward us.

"That's the quickest visit I've ever known," Oliver said. "Don't tell me that you and Pandion have fallen out."

She sat down in the chair he had vacated. "I don't understand a word of Chinese nor, I suspect, did many of the other guests. They sat on, but I escaped. The scenery was rather makeshift; they couldn't fit the full sets into the confined space of Pandion's little yacht theater. But the costumes were magnificent. When I got bored with looking at them, I left. I told Pandion that I had unexpected visitors." The long red dress swirled around her feet as she moved restlessly. "I'm hungry. Pandion's guests are having a buffet supper halfway through the evening. I've eaten nothing yet. Sarah, ring for Ah Lin, will you?" Then, to Oliver, "Are you staying?"

"Have you asked me?"

"More or less." Her voice was casual.

"Then thank you. I never say no to your table."

When she had given her orders to the housekeeper, Theodora turned to me. "I knew perfectly well that Chinese theater wouldn't be my idea of entertainment. But I hoped Fay Mi would be there. She was, and I had a chance to speak to her. She was alone for a few moments and I asked her how she liked her expensive moonstone gift. She just said, 'It is pretty.' I might have been talking about a bauble from a cheap store. I'm convinced that if the opportunity came to her, she would prefer money." She smiled to herself and rose. "Come, let's eat."

We had avocados, delicious seafood and peaches in brandy. It would be a very long time before I ate as I did at the Pavilion of Apricots.

I left Theodora and Oliver at about ten o'clock and went to my room. I was sitting by the window writing letters to friends in England when Ah Lin knocked on my door. "Mistress Lady wants to speak to you."

Theodora was alone in her drawing room, and her usually neat hair fell about her face, softening her features. A luxurious Mandarin coat served as a robe.

"Were you there when Oliver said that Pandion Dioscuri is returning to Europe in three days?" She didn't wait for me to answer, but went on. "And he isn't taking Fay Mi with him. I never imagined he would." Her eyes had a sudden excited look. "Don't you see? He has 'thanked her for the memory' with a moonstone and peridot collar."

"For which," I added, "he has paid many times its worth."

"Oh," Theodora replied, "that was a gesture to a charity. The important thing is that I have made arrangements for you to meet this actress, Fay Mi," Theodora said. "I had a word with Pandion and also made efforts to be charming to one or two guests who are part of the Shaw film establishment. I have managed an invitation for you to go to the studios, ostensibly just to look around because you are interested. I have sung your praises as a very fine gemologist who has won prizes for her designs. And where there is money, there is usually an interest in jewels. When you go to the Studios, Fay Mi herself will show you around and then you'll have the opportunity, quite naturally, to drop the piece of information that if she ever wishes to sell the moonstone necklace, she has a buyer ready and waiting. And one who will pay her far more than a dealer."

"It's possible that she might like to keep it. After all, she's a star and stars don't earn a pittance."

Theodora smiled dreamily, pursuing her own plan for me. "And, Sarah, drop every hint you can think of that she can make herself two hundred and fifty thousand Hong Kong dollars for the jeweled collar she probably never wanted, anyway."

"You'd pay all that for it?"

"Of course."

This was avarice gone mad . . . I stood by the window and saw the colors of the garden and glimpsed the crimson and gold of the tea pavilion between the trees. Then, turning away from Theodora, I put a direct question to her. "*Why* do you want that necklace so much? It's not worth all this effort to get it. It really isn't."

"A purchase for a good cause."

"Then you could have let me bid for *anything* that was being auctioned. Or just have given money to the hospital without even buying."

She turned a secret smile on to me. "Yes, I could, couldn't I? But there's something else, Sarah. If I had got that necklace I would have defeated Pandion Dioscuri, and he doesn't like women to do that. To him, they are the receivers, the little girls who hold out their hands for treasure trove. Oh, Pandion must have amused himself enormously when you let yourself be outbidden." She leaned back in her chair, half closing her eyes as though she were looking into the future. Her next words proved that that was exactly what she was doing. "One day," she continued, "it will give me great pleasure to let Pandion know that in the end I got what I wanted; that I beat him over the jeweled collar." Then she laughed and reminded me, "The appointment at the film studio is for half past ten tomorrow morning."

"I'll go," I told her, "but I won't plead your cause."

"Oh, yes, my dear, you will." She got up and stretched her arms above her head, looking down at me. "Because, as I mentioned to you when we talked about the jade girdle, I can make life very difficult for you if you don't do as I ask. And not only difficult for *you*, Sarah. Now, let's stop arguing and get down to practicalities. Ah Lee-ming will pick you up here at ten-fifteen."

For the time being I was caught in the prison of Theodora's threats, but when I returned to London, I would free myself, even if it meant a considerable loss of income. I was ambitious, but I would never again place myself in a position where a rich woman could blackmail me because of the thoughtless valuation of an ancient jade.

I sat beside Ah Lee-ming in the great car taking me to the Studios in the New Territories and hoped that a little of Theodora's elegant air would rub off on me so that I wouldn't be turned back at the gates as an unwelcome stranger.

As we approached the huge studios I wondered about Run Run Shaw—the first name "Run" meaning "sincerity," the second "Run" (written differently in Chinese) meaning "honesty"—who had built an empire of studios and cinemas, amusement parks and hotels. I wanted to see this place he had created where lovely hand-picked girls lived in their own special block and were fed and clothed and trained, where stars were groomed and luxurious sets were built.

Theodora had done her preliminary work well. As soon as I mentioned her name I was allowed in without any further question. All around us were buildings and sets: pagodas and painted dragons the size of elephants, as well as a few half-dismantled Western sets. There were girls everywhere, each one outstandingly pretty and animated.

"Much is done by paint," said Ah Lee-ming lugubriously. "Doctors open Chinese girls' narrow eyes."

Fay Mi, I felt certain, had needed no cosmetic surgery. Before, I had only seen her at a distance in the artificial light of the room at the Art Center. Now at the studio with the sunlight directly on her, she was even lovelier. Her eyes were beautifully large and well-spaced, her nose small and straight. She wore her hair short and slightly waved, like fluffed-out raven's feathers. The braid she had worn at the Art Center must have been a hairpiece pinned on that enchanting head. Her dress was very feminine and Western, with ruffles at her throat.

She greeted me charmingly, speaking good English, and led me to her apartment which looked over a garden where coxcombs made brilliant splashes of color under the orchid trees. I explained that I had spent my childhood in Hong Kong and had always wanted to see the Studios.

She nodded. "Lady Paradine told me about you, how you buy beautiful jewels and jade for her. She says you are clever and that maybe one day I will be so rich I will want special jewels and that perhaps you will get them for me."

"Of course, if I can."

When I asked her about her work, Fay Mi told me she loved acting. She had won a Shaw brothers' talent competition some years before. Mr. Shaw was making long feature films now for the Oriental market, and dramatic stories and comedies. It was all very hard work and the hours were long, but she didn't mind. She was happy.

With the thought of Pandion Dioscuri in mind, I asked her if she ever considered coming to Europe. She nodded and turned to accept the tray of jasmine tea the amah had brought in. "Oh, yes. One day I will go all over the world; I will see everything."

I was silent, leaving her momentarily to her dream as she poured out tea. "Lady Paradine said when I met her at Pandion's that one day she will show me all her jewelry. It is very rare, isn't it? Pandion tells me it is beautiful."

I said it was so.

She shook her head. "It is strange. I would not know what to do with so much."

It was an opening. I said, "But now you've got a most lovely moonstone collar, Miss Mi. I saw it at the auction."

She sipped her tea, her hands small and delicate, her nails long and bright pink. "Pandion won lots of money at some horse race in Europe, I don't know where. He says he does not want the money his horse made by winning, that he is old and cannot use what he already has. It must be so wonderful to have too much money." She gave a little dreamy laugh at the thought. "Pandion tells me he bought the collar because it was his way of helping the hospital. It is such a good cause."

"You really like it?"

"I think it is beautiful," she said softly. "Those stones are bright like the moon and the green ones . . ."

"Peridots."

". . . shine nicer than emeralds," she said.

"I thought the same when I saw it," I told her and tasted the delicately flavored tea. "Lady Paradine admired it so much that she wants me to try and find one like it for her."

Fay Mi shook her head. "But that is not possible. Do you understand? Pandion told me it was made for a very rich man, specially for his wife."

"Oh, well, I suppose if Lady Paradine is so keen to have one, I shall have to try and find the stones to make one for her. Though that won't be easy. Peridots are very scarce."

"Why does Lady Paradine want a necklace like that," she asked with disarming charm, "when she has so much?"

"Rich people are sometimes great collectors. And if they want something, they are prepared to pay highly. You know, do you, that I tried to bid for the collar at the auction?"

"Oh, yes, Pandion told me. But the man who bid for him won."

"And now," I said, setting down my empty cup, "I may have to find the stones for such another collar. Lady Paradine is prepared to spend a quarter of a million dollars—Hong Kong dollars."

Not a muscle of Fay Mi's lovely little face moved. "That is silly . . . surely silly? They are not like diamonds and although the red stones are rubies—are they not?—the necklace is not worth so much money."

"No, it isn't."

"I wonder. Do people who are very rich want something because they love it? Or because they don't want to lose?"

I said, "I think it's a little of both."

We laughed together like conspirators.

"I am sorry she lost the collar," she said, "but she will forget it. Soon she will forget."

Our eyes met and in that moment I realized that Fay Mi knew perfectly well why I was there. But I had said all I intended to say. I had stated a price, explained Theodora's interest. And Fay Mi had smiled at me, finished her tea and shrugged off the mass of dollars as though they were chicken feed. She intended to keep the jewel for her own lovely neck.

She rose and asked if I would like to see her apartment. It was furnished with rather more European taste than I would have expected, but it was charming and not in the least opulent.

Just off the hall was an alcove in which three joss sticks burned before the gilded Buddha. I wondered if this was Fay Mi's household altar or her amah's. The scents of herbs and sandalwood seeped through the whole apartment. As I followed her from room to room in the apartment that looked on to the garden, I also wondered how Fay Mi had felt about the fickle Greek she had known for such a short while. Whatever the depth, she had no intention of showing her feelings to me. She was bright and animated and chatty. But then, a star in the Oriental world would be as sophisticated as any in the West.

I left her, promising to ask Theodora if she would invite her to the Pavilion.

XVIII

"YOU BUNGLED IT, SARAH. Of course you did." Theodora stormed up and down the parquet floor of her drawing room. "That girl Fay Mi didn't strike me as a fool. She must know that when her looks leave her, she'll need all the money she can get hold of to live as she has become used to living."

"She likes the collar, and that's a good enough reason for keeping it. I've told you the Studio looks after their girls, especially their great stars, so I doubt she'll ever need to sell anything to buy bread."

"You were far too tentative."

I nearly lost my temper. "What did you expect me to say to her? 'Lady Paradine wants that moonstone collar. She'll pay you a quarter of a million Hong Kong dollars for it. Now, will you please get it for me?' And then hold out my hand and wait?"

Theodora saw nothing outrageous in what I said. "I'm not certain that that wouldn't have been a good approach. Shock her into giving it up before she has time to think."

"Then you don't understand the Chinese temperament."

"I understand women, my dear Sarah."

"Fay Mi wants to see the Pavilion. Perhaps you'll invite her here and then you can make the offer for the collar yourself."

There was a long silence. With nothing more to say, I walked to the door and through it. I had an odd feeling that I had won a battle. I had tossed the onus on to Theodora.

I was in my bedroom when there was a tap on my door. Lilo entered. "Missy, I could not help hearing. I was in Mistress Lady's dressing room and I heard that you went to the Shaw Studios."

"That's right."

"Then, Missy, you can help me. Please. I often see Fay Mi in movies. She is beautiful and perhaps if you would help me meet her, she would talk to Mr. Run Run Shaw." She watched me. "Don't you *see*? He would listen to her if she said I am pretty. I *am* pretty . . . ?"

"Yes, very."

"If she spoke to him, he would take me into his Studios. I could live there and be a big star."

"Lilo, I'm sorry, but I'm not going to the Studios again."

"But she is coming here. I heard you say she wants to see Mistress Lady's house. When she comes, tell her I am beautiful and a good actress. You could bring her to see me somewhere Mistress Lady won't know."

I shook my head. "I'm not even certain that Fay Mi will ever come here."

"But she wants to and Mistress Lady wants those jewels."

"That's over, Lilo," I said firmly.

She didn't understand. "Missy, I know something. If I tell you, will you help me?"

I sensed a sudden tightening of the atmosphere. "What do you know?"

She gave me a sideways smile and shook her head.

"Lilo." I made my voice stern. "You heard me talking to Lady Paradine. What else have you heard by listening at doors?"

"A lot." She gave a little giggle. "I need to practice my English. I want to speak well."

"And you heard something that is important, something you think I should know? Please, Lilo, tell me."

She sauntered to the door. On the dressing table lay an amber bracelet I seldom wore and was intending to give to the growing-up daughter of a friend of my mother's. I picked it up. "It's real amber," I said. "Would you like it?"

The word 'amber' meant nothing to her, but the word 'real' did. It was synonymous with 'valuable.'

She reached out for it. I held on firmly. "On one condition. Tell me what it is you heard and thought might interest me." I was, without the slightest sense of guilt, encouraging her in eavesdropping.

"The telephone rang," she said. "When I picked it up I heard Mistress Lady talking and laughing. She was saying, 'There is nothing you can do. Oliver has his use. Marius and me . . . we are together.' The man at the other end was angry. He said bad things to her as if he hated her. He said, 'I will not let you hurt my daughter. I'll go to the police.' Mistress Lady laughed, 'Oh, no, you won't.' Then she kept saying, 'This second jade . . . jade . . . jade.' I think whoever it was talking to her, hates her. But she went on laughing and said your name, missy. She said, 'Sarah.'"

"Yes. Go on."

"There was a noise somewhere outside and I didn't hear the next bit. Then Mistress Lady said something about the Night of the Moon Festival. But Ah Lin came and saw me and I ran away."

Lilo reached out and plucked the bracelet from my hands and put it over her wrist, holding out her arm to admire the glow. "Will you speak to Fay Mi?"

"If she comes here, yes," I promised. It was the least I could do in payment for the shattering words that confirmed my suspicions.

Lilo left me, walking softly, but every word of what she had said remained clear in my mind. It was exactly as I had dreaded it might be. Marius was involved in some way with Theodora's purchase of stolen jades. My father had dared her to . . . to what? But I knew. To involve me in blackmail over the buying of the jade girdle. And it seemed that there was another jade I was to value—and Father was not to interfere. It was to happen on the night of the Moon Festival.

So there it was. What use Oliver could be was something I could leave for the moment. Marius was my concern. Marius, and my own danger.

I thought of the photograph taken of Marius and the Avenger. It was now imperative that Father tell me what he knew. Somehow or other—probably in his wanderings over the hills to find fresh subjects for his photography—he must have seen something or overheard something that had made him suspicious. Theodora could have been there, or her name mentioned. But whatever it was, she was now trying to silence him with threats.

I had to talk to Father. The time had now come for each of us to realize that we had to pool our knowledge. He could not help me by hiding what he knew. I looked across at the telephone by my bed, but I didn't go to it. It was an extension line, and anyone in the house could pick up another receiver and listen. Lilo had been adept at that.

Seated in the Peak tram, I wondered if Lilo could have misheard or even made up some of the conversation. But I rejected both ideas. Lilo was too watchful, too alert to her own main chances, and at the same time too unsophisticated to invent a conversation.

I watched the scenery which I knew so well, the golden haze still lying over trees and the great hills and the far-down shining sea. But when I got off at the stop near the Peak top, I almost ran to Father's apartment.

Nam Tsao, opening the door to me, pulled me in with quick, anxious words. "Are you ill?"

"No. Just in a hurry. I must see Father."

"He's gone sailing. I think he said they were going to Cheung Chau and that they might stay around the island for two days."

"Whose boat is he on?"

She shook her head. "I do not know. Master has many friends with boats."

And even if I caught the ferry to Cheung Chau, I wouldn't be able to contact Father because he would be on the yacht and have no link with the island.

Nam Tsao pressed me to stay. "I'll make you some tea or coffee. Sit on the terrace. It's a fine morning."

"Thank you, Nam Tsao, but I have to get back. As soon as Father returns, will you please ask him to call me? It's urgent."

I stayed another five minutes chatting as brightly as I could to re-assure her, because Nam Tsao worried about me almost as much as she worried about Father.

It was nearly lunchtime when I returned to the Pavilion. Theodora had gone out with friends and I ate alone. In my absence the post had arrived and there was a huge pile of letters. I guessed that they must be replies to Theodora's invitations to a party on the night of the Moon Festival.

She had issued a strange order to her guests. "The men are to wear dinner jackets. The women must come in Chinese costume—either copied from some early dynasty or from one of the Chinese operas."

Célie came down the stairs as I left the dining room.

"My Lady has put out two costumes for you to try on for the party." Her gaunt face looked at me, assessing my size. "They'll both be too big for you, but if you would please try them on now, there will be time to alter them before the night."

"I've a feeling I'm going to be very uncomfortable in Chinese cos-tume. European figures aren't made for them."

"But you are *petite*," she said.

I went up the stairs and along the passage hung with silk scrolls. I could well imagine the fuss among the prospective guests. Where would they get such costumes? Where to hire them? How to make them? I had little doubt, however, that they would manage to find something to wear, even if it were only a cheongsam, with a piece of elaborate embroidery swathed round them like the pictures of the Chinese dynastic court ladies. I could imagine the silk boutiques being besieged. Theodora would have no such problem. In her ward-robe room she had clothes made in rare tribute satin, in brocade and even a lovely lama priest's robe which Lilo had made into an evening coat for her.

There were two costumes lying on the wide divan in the wardrobe room. One, which I had not seen before, looked like a costume made for a Chinese operatic character, shimmering with blue and gold thread; the other was a copy of an Imperial Dragon robe in silk tapestry. I picked it up wondering why Theodora possessed it, for as a copy, it had little value, and although the embroidery was delicate with its weavings of the five-clawed dragon of fourteenth-century China, it was ill-cut.

I put it round me and Célie put her hand to her mouth to hide her laughter. I laughed, too. "You could get two of me in that." I picked up the other. "And this is a bit bright. But since I have to dress up, I'd better try it on."

I did. It wasn't as heavy to wear as I had thought. Probably the operatic star for whom it was made would have wanted a light costume that would not drag her down nor impede her singing.

Célie was busy pinning up the skirt. "This is all it needs, Madame. This, and a little off the sleeve. Then it will be fine." She stood back when she had finished, and admired me.

"I don't feel particularly comfortable," I said. "It's hot."

Célie nodded. "It will be cool in the courts. But I do not understand the Chinese en fete," Célie continued. "They look at the moon and bang drums. Perhaps they make wishes."

I slid out of the costume. "My father told me that in olden days the Night of the Moon Festival was really fun. People ran around the streets giving each other mooncakes, letting off firecrackers and climbing the hills to look at the moon. They still do that, of course, but it isn't the festive occasion it used to be."

Célie said, "There was nearly much quarreling in the kitchen. Maurice refused to make mooncakes. So Ah Lin is making them—but not the Canton way."

"I know what she means. The Cantonese ones are rather stodgy; the North China ones are light and flaky, usually with almond and date filling."

"But if Ah Lin uses his kitchen, Maurice will sulk."

I said with amusement, "I'm sure he will."

"You will enjoy the party," Célie said. "Mr. Farache is coming."

I turned to her in surprise. "I don't quite get the connection."

"I'm sorry, madame. But My Lady says that he likes you very, very much. He is a charming man."

"No doubt," I said, but the coldness was only in my voice. I was glad Oliver liked me. Somewhere in the mêlée of suspicion and fear and threat, there must be something that was good and clear and un-complicated. But even as I thought that, I remembered Lilo's words.

Theodora had said, "Oliver has his use."

Oliver has his use—how? To pry me from any last hold I had on Marius? I had none, except a tie of the law which could so easily be broken. With that thought, guilt struck me. Should it be I who asked for my freedom? Had Marius been trying to make it clear to me here in Hong Kong that he was waiting for me to take the first step away? One thing I knew for certain: Theodora was doing her best to help our final break!

I tried three times that day to reach Father, but he was neither at his apartment nor at the Yacht Club. I knew, however, that I would see him on the night of the party, for Theodora had already told me he was coming. Somehow I would have to get him away from the crowds and take him to my room, the only place in the whole com-pound of pavilions where I could be certain of not being overheard. I would make him tell me what he knew.

The thought occurred to me again that if Theodora's name and her apparent integrity as a collector was in danger, she would sacrifice the jade girdle. She would tell the police, "Mrs. Brent advised me to buy this jade. I had no idea it was stolen property. As soon as I real-ized it, I came straight to you." And there would be no one to prove that, in all innocence, I had made a costly mistake.

XIX

THE MORNING OF THE Night of the Moon Festival was heavy and overcast, matching my mood. I dreaded the evening when Father would come and I would have to talk to him. It was obvious, if what Lilo had told me was correct, that my father was not coming in any spirit of festiveness. At the same time, whatever it was he and Theodora had planned to say to each other, I was the subject of it all —and I was certain that the object was another rare jade. It was possible that I was to be blackmailed into valuing it and Father was coming to stop that happening.

Somewhere in the distance, I could hear the drone of a plane's engine. I wished I were on it; I wished I were flying back to London; I wished I had never come to Hong Kong nor met Marius again; nor ever taken an interest in jade. I hated the day; I dreaded the night . . .

The Pavilion courts were full of activity. Flowers came by the load; luscious foods; lanterns; the musicians arrived to test their places for the best volume of sound in the little tea pavilion. Theodora directed everything from her room, sending Célie and Ah Lin and Lilo running to carry out directions. Sufficient lanterns had to be hung to illuminate the courts; there must be lights on the lotus pool, the cloisonné stork and the gilded Buddha in his garden niche. A sixfold screen had to be carried out by an army of workers to block off the servants' court, leaving sufficient room for them to move to and fro but making it obvious that guests were barred.

The simpler people of the Island always took to the hills in order to get the best view of the hare which generations of Chinese had believed sat in the moon pounding the elixir of life. I hoped for their sakes that the clouds would clear. Now that the moon had been conquered, I wondered how much their faith had been shaken. Perhaps a few children still looked for the hare as some Western children still looked for Santa Claus.

I spent some time in the small room where I had taken Theodora's collection of semiprecious stones. I wanted to sort them and catalog them because, although she was disinterested, I found them beautiful.

As I worked, my thoughts were on myself and Marius. Something had grown all too slowly out of my separation from him, shocking me into an awareness of lives beyond my own, ways of thinking that were not like mine and yet were as right and justified as mine. The mind veers from self-reproach, preferring not to see its own involvement in another's dilemma. But in that quiet room, moving amethysts and garnets into their right places like pawns on a chess board, I knew that I had been involved.

It was only a few days ago that Marius had said to me, as we sat on a hillside talking of ambition, ". . . *you* taught me." When we had lived together in London I had never pushed him to more success, I had not pressured him in any way. But I had, by my own actions, showed him that by supreme single-mindedness one could achieve success. And Marius had tasted the exciting possibilities, had overreacted and fallen into Theodora's golden hands.

I lost interest in the gems lying in the trays before me. I put them back in the lacquer cabinet and went to see if there was any way I could help for the party that night. Theodora didn't need me, so, restless and anxious, I went out and down to Central District.

For a while I wandered up and down the narrow stepped streets, jostled by shoulder poles, carts and shopping baskets, passing through wafts of cooking smells, of pork and curries. There was something almost therapeutic about the overcrowded streets and the cheerful poverty. I wasn't foolish or sentimental enough to believe that money was unimportant. But these people, with their ivory faces and their volatile manners, had the happiness of the Chinese character that Theodora would never know. There could be no other way in which Red China could have achieved the making of a nation without poverty and without inflation, but by the willing cheerfulness of her people. I had heard so much in Hong Kong of the pros and cons of the new China—and I had no strong personal feelings about their politics—but it seemed to me that whatever they were not, they were most certainly happy.

Full of rambling thoughts, I wandered until I was tired. Then I took a taxi to Hankow Road. I had called the London jeweler who had asked me to look at the turquoise and he had given me a reassuring reply. "I trust your judgment, Mrs. Brent. Even if my potential buyer won't pay the price for the stones, I am certain I can find someone who will. The money will be deposited in the Hong Kong and Shanghai Bank."

Although many shops were closed because of the Moon Festival, I was relieved that the ragged premises which housed the lovely stones were open and the men were working at their benches. After we had talked and I had checked the stones, I arranged for their transport to London. Then I left and immediately ran into some friends near the Mandarin Hotel and had drinks with them.

When I arrived back at the Pavilion someone with his back to me was stepping through the double doors. I heard Ah Baht's heavy keys rattling against the locks. At the same moment that I managed to avoid being hit by a basket of dried fish swinging from a shoulder pole, I walked full tilt into Marius.

His car was parked close to the wall and he leaned lightly against it as he greeted me. "Hello. Have you been out spending a lot of money?"

"Yes, but it wasn't mine."

His eyes were narrowed and amused. "You once told me that when you are buying, you pretend that you are buying for yourself, because that is the only way you can get really competitive about prices, especially when you are bidding at a sale."

"That was a long time ago, when I was raw to the game and I had to whip myself up to a kind of tough determination. Otherwise the experts would have scared the life out of me. Now, I'm impersonal."

"And no longer covetous."

I said angrily, "I was never that. If you are, then you don't take on a job dealing in valuable things for others to enjoy."

"Fair enough. Shakespeare had a phrase for you, didn't he, Sarah? 'Joy's soul lies in the doing.'"

I knew the rest of that quotation only too well. At the time of our parting two years ago, I had sat in a theater seat watching a production of *Troilus and Cressida* and hated it for those words. They had dug deep into my mind, bitter and cynical—and, where I was concerned, becoming true.

I turned on my heel and started to walk away, the hated words beating in my mind. "Things won are done; joy's soul lies in the doing. Men prize the thing ungained more than it is."

Marius called after me, "Odd! I thought you were arriving, not leaving. Or were you going to knock and run away?"

It was absurd to be hurt. My importance in his life was over and the sanest way for us to behave, since we had to meet, was as he was behaving to me, with flippancies and casual pleasantries.

"I've changed my mind." I almost walked into a weaving bicycle and immediately afterwards grazed my shin against a scarlet-lettered pillar that stood outside a restaurant. A kitchen god beamed at me from the corner near the window and the eternal mah-jongg pieces clicked somewhere inside the ramshackle building.

I didn't look back and Marius didn't come after me. That, I decided in my sudden emotional state, was symbolic. We went our ways. Out of the corner of my eye I saw his car pass by, and without looking at me, he raised his hand in a brief salute.

In my nervous and oversensitive state, I was haunted by painful pictures I had never seen . . . Marius sitting by the Lotus Pool with Theodora . . . Marius talking to her, laughing with her . . . touching her. I saw it all and could not face it, I walked back to the crowded streets, looking in shop windows for gifts to take back to friends in England. And all the time came the beat of the name Marius . . . Marius . . .

Pain, or jealousy, or both? I wanted some time to elapse before I would cross those lovely courts and see Theodora, seated in her chair under the acacia, smiling and silently purring like a splendid, contented cat.

When I eventually returned, she was already at her black lacquer dining table. She always ate lightly at lunch, and by the time I entered the room, had finished her first course of Maurice's excellent pâté. She wore very loose cream lounging pajamas which shimmered slightly as she twitched her fork at me in greeting.

"I'm sorry I'm late," I said.

She reached for her wine glass and said, without looking at me, "Marius told me a little while ago on the telephone that he saw you outside the doors here nearly an hour ago."

Her manner implied "So where have you been since then?"

"That's right, Marius and I did meet. I'd been to the bank to arrange for the transfer of the money for the turquoise."

"And arrived at the door here and then changed your mind?"

"Yes."

"How strange. Did you and he have an argument that upset you?"

"No. We hailed each other and . . . and then . . . well, just passed by."

Ah Lin entered with pâté for me on a lovely sage-green celadon plate.

"I'll have my salad now," Theodora said, "and then coffee in the tea pavilion. The sun is too bright to sit by the pool."

As she was speaking, I thought: Marius came here to see her this morning, then later telephoned her . . . like a lover, as if even that brief period from the Pavilion back to his apartment was too long a parting to bear. And spoke of me in passing . . . I had no taste for the pâté or the lobster salad that followed. Theodora left me, ordering newspapers to be brought to her with her coffee in the tea pavilion.

Later, as I left the dining room, Lilo stopped me. "Please, Mistress Lady wants you."

The scarlet and gold tea pavilion was at the far end of the Court of the Lotus. Theodora was seated in a yellow-cushioned chair and her coffee stood on a low carved plinth that always reminded me of a catafalque. It was possible that it had been built to bear a large Buddha or perhaps the symbol of the year when the palace was built —a dragon, a hare, or even the beloved Goddess of Mercy, Kuan Yin.

Later, at Theodora's party, the musicians would sit in the pavilion and play for the guests. For the time being, the chairs and music stands were discreetly piled some distance away near a hibiscus hedge.

Theodora put down her newspaper as I came up the three steps into the tea pavilion.

"You wanted to see me?"

"Yes." She waved me to the second chair. "I've been thinking. As in a way it concerns you, you should hear the news now." She was smiling. "Or did Marius tell you when you met at the door?"

"Tell me what?"

We watched one another, waiting. Still smiling, Theodora explained. "When he came to see me this morning we talked about his —well—his life and his plans for the future."

"I hope he has some," I retorted. "There's a splendid hospital back in London waiting for him."

"My dear Sarah, Marius knows what he is doing."

"Does he? I'm glad to hear it."

"You mustn't be cynical."

"I'm sorry if that's how it sounded. I wasn't taking it all personally, but Marius's London hospital needs good people like him."

"He is learning so many wonderful things out here."

"He *says* he is."

"And you don't believe him?"

I let the question go. "What did you want to tell me?"

She folded the newspaper on her lap and laid it on the stone slab by her side. The perfume she used was overwhelming that morning, as if by mistake she had used it twice. "I have decided to take an apartment up on the Peak."

"Leave *here*?" I stared at her in utter disbelief. "You'd risk the damp and the mists on those marvelous silk panels and the lacquer?"

"Of course I wouldn't give this up. I intend to take the apartment for Marius."

It was a purely reflex action: I laughed. But the stony expression in her eyes jerked me out of a sense of the absurd. Theodora was perfectly serious.

I said, "I gathered from him that he spent most of his time at Dr. Hai's Clinic and stayed at a hotel here just occasionally."

"Oh, he has almost finished his studies over in the New Territories. But he wants to remain here for a while."

"Well, I'm not his keeper. He must do as he likes."

"I'm glad you see it like that. I already have a place in mind. It has fine, high-ceilinged rooms and a large terrace. There are servants' quarters, so he would be well looked after."

"I'm sure he would, but it doesn't sound quite Marius's style."

"If you are implying that it is expensive, it is. As if that matters!" She leaned her head back against the yellow cushion and added dreamily, "I have no view here except my own garden. I love it, of course, but sometimes I long for the sight of space, of sea and sky." She darted a look at me. "The view from that Peak apartment is quite breathtaking. You look right out over the Island, and it's high enough to be above cloud level so that Marius wouldn't have to suffer the mists. To go there on a lovely sunny autumn day . . ." She stroked her left hand with an almost sensual movement.

I had a swift, irrelevant thought. *In the garden this morning, did Marius kiss her?* Then I thought again: *But that's not irrelevant.* A fine apartment, a rich patroness . . . Theodora herself had once said: "Men have their price."

I said, trying to keep the hardness out of my voice, "Am I mistaken? Is Marius to have the whole apartment or a room—like a lodger?"

She gave an exaggerated wince. "It will be his, of course. For as long as he wishes," she added. "And when he is at the apartment I shall go up there and it will be lovely to have a companion; to know that . . . well . . . that Marius will be waiting for me."

"I see."

"It's all rather wonderful, Sarah. Not only will Marius and I share that lovely place, but I'm going to help him with his clinic, be his partner because I shall give financial assistance to get it started."

"What you mean," I said, hurt and brutal, "is that you are buying him."

"My dear girl, you may put whatever context on it you like. The point is that both Marius and I agree on the plan."

"You are buying him." I took a deep breath, controlled my anger and said more quietly, "I thought you were returning to the States in a few weeks."

"I haven't finally decided." She gave me a long, smiling look. "It depends on developments here."

"And when you really do decide to leave here and return to America or Europe, is Marius going to tag along? And from there—where? And what is to happen to the great clinic dream? Will he create it by remote control, from your New York mansion or your Mediterranean villa?"

"Sarah!"

"Yes," I said impertinently, "I'm Sarah. And Marius is still my husband."

"And you can't accept your loss gracefully."

"I'm not asked to accept anything," I retorted. "It's Marius who is doing that. Well, since you've both decided on your future arrangements, there's nothing for me to say." I got up and walked away from her. Suddenly I swung around. "Oh, but there *is* something I have to say. What you have told me I want to hear from Marius himself."

"You are being very foolish. As if I would lay myself open to a lie!"

I had reached the spot where the evergreen bauhinias almost hid the ancient wall dividing the Court of the Lotus from the one that housed the guest pavilion. The footsteps behind me were swift and heavy.

"Sarah, please, just listen." Her hair was a little wild as if she had thrust her fingers through it. She caught my arm and her nails dug into my flesh. "Why hold on to someone you can't live with and who can't live with you?"

I looked at her, wondering. Either Theodora collected men for her vanity's sake or because there was a need, even in her, to belong to someone living and breathing. But she didn't know how to give back in love. Theodora was only generous when it was expedient.

"Why don't you say something?" She waited. Then, as I remained silent, she said, "Don't tell me you are still in love with Marius."

"In love? Or do I still love him? There's a vast difference. But it doesn't matter which way you ask the question, because I shan't answer you. How I feel is my affair."

"Don't you understand what I once said to you? You never really knew him, not the real Marius. You saw him as you wanted to see him. I'm older than you and I can read people. Marius is no god, my dear."

"I never wanted him to be." I leaned away from her and my fingers brushed the soft warm petals of a full-blown rose. "Now I want to go," I said.

"One has to learn to accept the inevitable."

"Oh, yes."

This time I escaped through the moon gate into the guest court. Theodora didn't follow me, and I crossed under the arch to a stone seat.

I stared without blinking into the blaze of scarlet salvias and fought an impulse to telephone Marius. I couldn't believe Theodora would lie to me, for she knew I could check with Marius. She had offered him a way to have his dream. The cost would be his freedom. It was incredible to me that even he, with his dedication to his work, was prepared to pay such a price. Theodora, a woman fifteen years older than he. But Theodora, a millionairess.

He'll hate the life. But then, it would *be* his life, too. That was part of the deal, that he would win his clinic. For that, he had trafficked in stolen jade; for that, he had sacrificed his freedom to Theodora.

I would have to divorce him. The thought was a relief and a despair—that paradox that I could no more understand than thousands of others before me. The powerful emotion that had enmeshed me when I first met Marius had turned out to be the prison gate through which I had entered—as so many had done—believing it to be the door to the enchanted garden. But an enchanted garden was a child's place. The adult's garden was what he or she made of it, an oasis or a desert.

If, in the end, Marius failed in his scientific experiment with Chinese medicine and clashed in his private life with Theodora, then his world would lie in ruins. He could of course go back to purely orthodox surgery. But the radiance that came with great faith in one's ability would be lost, and the contamination of wealth that was used only to buy would have destroyed him.

And I would care.

My eyes were tired. I let my lids fall so that I saw, with relief, only a kind of gilded blackness. Then, as if somewhere inside my mind was a stern, impartial observer, the summing-up came like a shock. "You want to be able to return to London despising Marius for what he is doing, telling yourself that you are glad to be free of him. *Be-*

cause you feel partly responsible for the break-up of your marriage, you want to lay a greater guilt on him. You are metaphorically tossing the coin, gambling on the bad coming face up more times than the good; wanting to destroy your blind and obstinate love once and for all."

XX

THE FIRST OF THE GUESTS arrived at half past seven. The Pavilion courts were set as for some glamorous musical. The lanterns hung steady, glowing all the richer because the moon was invisible, and throwing up delicate patterns on the leaves of acacia and frangipani.

The musicians were in place in the tea pavilion, playing on lutes and wind instruments—the five-tone Chinese music a soft background to the increasing sound of voices as more and more guests arrived. Delicate food was piled on the *famille verte* plates.

Ah Baht guarded the doors and Ah Lin was in charge of seeing that the dishes on the tables set against the bauhinias were kept well-piled with food. The mooncakes which Ah Lin had made were set proudly in the forefront of the tables on yellow Ming dishes. Lilo was in charge of women's wraps in the second guest pavilion next to mine.

Theodora must have decided to become royal for the occasion, for she wasn't present to receive her guests. Oliver arrived, elegant in white coat and black tie. He walked straight up to me, but we were immediately joined by two sisters whom I had known when we were schoolgirls. There was none of the lank hair and buck teeth about them now. They greeted me effusively and fastened their eyes on Oliver.

I edged away, looking for Father, but by the time I judged most of the guests to have arrived, I couldn't find him in the crush.

Some of the guests' costumes were lovely, some were very homemade, but even these scintillated. One woman guest carried a fan of kingfisher feathers, another wore an elaborate gilt headdress copied from a Chinese opera. But for one thing, they could have been women from centuries earlier met together in this future age. The ladies of the old dynastic courts had had their feet bound from babyhood and for all their lives were helped, or even carried, by their servants because they could not walk. Theodora's guests, in ample-sized slippers, trod her marble paths. One woman even came as a mandarin wearing a black cap on her bright head and a silk padded gown which must have been stiflingly hot. In her long left sleeve she carried, as the old mandarins used to do, a golden Pekingese dog. Even while she drank champagne and ate the rich food, the little dog remained cozy in her sleeve as his ancestors had done centuries ago.

Champagne in lovely chased crystal tulip glasses had been handed out before someone near me gave a slight gasp. Theodora stood in the lamplit doorway of the main pavilion like a raven among a great pride of peacocks. She was swathed in dead black, her hair hidden under a black turban, her coat and flared trousers of black silk. Only her lips were scarlet and her eyes brilliantly made up by Célie.

"My greetings to you all." She glanced upward. "Although the moon hasn't yet shown itself, let us drink to it all the same." She reached out and took a glass from a waiter by her side, lifting it high as if she were making a libation to the gods.

It was formal and entirely theatrical. And yet it was in keeping not only with the brilliance of her guests and the shattering contrast of Theodora's own appearance, but also with something that suddenly seemed to change the atmosphere. Behind the theatricality, Theodora was tense and on edge.

Against the playing of the musicians, people laughed and chatted and wandered through the courts. I knew many of the guests and whenever we met, their comments ran on very similar lines. "Sarah, what's happened to you? Or has living in a palace gone to your head? Well, then, prove that it hasn't and come and see us."

"Later," I would say, "when I am free."

We would talk a little and laugh and remember the fun we used to have. I would promise to let them know when I left the Pavilion to stay at the Mandarin Hotel, where I had booked for my holiday. We would move on to greet others.

Whenever I was near Theodora I would hear her voice, and her laughter came with a staccato impact, rising and then suddenly stopping as if a tap had turned it off.

We met once, both reaching for the same tray of champagne. It was my second glass and I felt as tense and yet as curiously flat as if I had been drinking water.

"I shall want you later on, Sarah, so please don't go off into some remote corner. It's very important."

A jumble of fears flashed into my mind. She was going to tell me that Marius wanted a divorce. She was going to tell me . . . Oh, God, what? I flung Marius out of my mind.

"I thought Father might be coming. I know he's been yachting, but he should be back by now."

"Oh, yes, your father will most certainly be here. Just wait."

The evening was well on, but still I couldn't find him. People were milling through every court and the effect was like a colorful and disorderly ballet.

Marius was also missing, but even when we were living in London, he had always been an uncertain guest at large parties. He didn't like crowds where everyone had to shout against a barrage of other voices in order to be heard. He liked his friends in small doses.

I didn't want him there. Cowardlike, I wanted to find Father and force him to tell me what he knew. But I couldn't bear to face Marius. Moving among Theodora's brightly costumed guests, I willed that he would not come.

An hour and a half later, there was still no moon and I felt sorry for the crowds waiting on the dark hills of Hong Kong. Considerable inroads had been made by Theodora's guests on the caviar and the smoked salmon and the marvelous mousse, of which Maurice was master. The third and fourth glasses of champagne had animated the guests so that most of them had probably forgotten the discomfort of their elaborate costumes.

I went looking for Mister Wu. He hated crowds because his nose was on a level with the feet of the guests. I found him near the gate, bunched up under a marble urn overflowing with heavy-headed yellow lilies imported from the south and brought to the Pavilion that morning by the flower boys.

From the court on the other side of the wall, a voice suddenly burst out, ". . . to destroy the bloody thing. Damn you and damn Marius."

For a moment I stood frozen into inactivity. Father's voice . . . Father's fury was just there. I only had to go through the arch into the next court to see him. In that moment of hesitation, there was a sound of heavy running footsteps. I darted through the opening in time to see Father disappearing swiftly in the direction of the outer doors. I didn't even look for Theodora. I dropped Mister Wu among the flowers and raced after Father.

He was already at the doors. Ah Baht was sitting there on guard and shot to his feet as Father came, leaped over the step and into the street. I, too, ran out, calling after him. As he passed under the lamplight I saw his hair standing up in a wild halo as if he had been clawing at it.

"Father . . . it's Sarah . . . *Father!*"

He wrenched open the door of his car, and before I could reach it, was away, scattering cyclists and children sleepily waving their little paper toys.

I swung round, looking at the long line of cars, knowing that I would have no hesitation in using one to follow him, but far too inexperienced to open locked car doors.

"Missy, will you come inside?" Ah Baht asked from the door.

Without realizing what I was doing, I had been backing away from Father's car and was almost at the archway where the gateman sat. At that moment Theodora dashed out, pushed Ah Baht aside, and leaped behind the wheel of her white Rolls-Royce. I watched it crash backward and forward into bumpers and fenders as she tried to get free of the guests' cars which hemmed it in.

As I dodged an oncoming bicycle to reach her, I thought: She must have guessed she would need her car tonight or it wouldn't be here. But Ah Lee-ming hadn't been waiting in the driver's seat, so her plans were a highly personal secret.

I reached the window of the Rolls and rapped on it. I had no idea whether Theodora saw me or not because, like a black witch bent over the steering wheel, she crashed into another bumper, backed again, swung the car free and drove off.

Behind me, Ah Baht stammered, "Mistress Lady does not drive her car, ever. There will be an accident."

My wrist was suddenly gripped from behind, and I was swung nearly off my balance. Marius said unceremoniously, "Come on."

He gave me no time to protest or resist, but bundled me into the small Triumph which was double-parked outside the Pavilion walls. He slammed the door on me and was round and behind the wheel before I had time to protest.

The car sprang to life with the first turn of the starter and we roared down the street with the harsh shriek that small and rather old cars make when pushed to excess.

"First Father, then Theodora. Now you," I shouted above the scream of the car. "Perhaps you'll tell me what it's all about."

"Someone," he said and missed by inches a cart full of happy Chinese, "is going to get badly hurt. I only hope to God it isn't your father. I wouldn't have wanted it this way, Sarah. Heaven help me, I wouldn't."

"If my father is hurt in any way, you will be partly responsible. I know that much . . . *Marius, be careful!*" I cried. "You can't catch Theodora, if that's what you're wanting to do. She has a faster car."

Through the windshield I could see, as a backdrop to my fear, people who had been sauntering over the roads leaping out of our way; bicycles and cars swerving. Marius hit nothing, but his speed broke all laws.

He said, "She can't drive all that well. She's too used to being driven."

"Marius, tell me. Do you hear? *Tell me.*" I was gripping his arm with my hand.

"I won't be able to tell you anything if you don't leave me free to drive."

We tore onto the Pokfulam Road, past a bus, past cars filled with families from outlying districts making for the Peak. I sat tense, one hand gripping the door handle, not because I wanted to await a chance of escape, but out of fear. Because I no longer seemed to know Marius.

"Is it Father or is it Theodora you're trying to save? And kill us in the attempt. Marius . . . *is it Theodora?*"

"Perhaps."

"You saw them both leave. You were there at the party. You came late."

"No. I was not there."

"Then how . . . ?"

"I was waiting outside, waiting for the party, Sarah—the other party—to begin."

I shivered. "I know so much," I said. "Some of it Lilo told me. She overheard Theodora and my father talking. And some Theodora herself told me and some . . . some I worked out for myself. It's jade, isn't it? I was to be asked to value another piece that was stolen, like the jade girdle. And Father found out and is trying to stop Theodora from having it. You know where that second jade is, too, don't you? That's why you're chasing after them. *Look out!*"

"If you shout at me like that again, you'll lose one of your nine lives—and I'll lose my one."

"I nearly lost one the night someone attacked me at the Pavilion. Or doesn't that count?"

"Ah, yes, that . . . But then, Lilo shouldn't have disobeyed Theodora again and left the doors open at night to sneak her relatives in. That was just the opportunity that was needed for an intruder to slip in."

"Someone hiding and waiting to attack me. Marius, who was it? The Avenger?"

"Good God, that's a fancy name for someone."

"I only know that a man has been watching me—or watching the

Pavilion—and he drives an Avenger car. *You* know what his real name is."

Marius remained silent. I turned and saw his profile harsh against the intermittent street lights as we passed.

"Suppose we stop the talk until we get to where we're going?" he suggested.

"Where *are* we going? You're not driving blind."

"Believe it or not, I am. But I shall have a sign somewhere along the road."

I thought of the dark hills and the thrashing sea beyond Deep Water Bay. How often I had water-skied there in the past and walked through the pines at Middle Bay and now and again heard the harsh cry of the tiny deer which lived in the woods. Good, sweet, far-off days . . . I wondered if we were going seaward to a dark boat or inland into the hills.

"You don't want to talk, but, Marius, I must know. Please, just tell me. Is this all because of Theodora? *Is* it that she intends to buy more stolen jades and Father is trying to stop her? And are you involved?"

"You ask three questions. I'll answer in three words. Yes. Yes. And yes."

"But why drag me along?"

He said, and his voice held harsh mockery, "Surely you couldn't resist seeing a very beautiful ancient jade? That would be quite out of character."

"So I'm being taken on this maniacal drive in order to value another damned jade. I won't, Marius. And no one can make me." A flash of suspicion made me add, "What has Theodora done? Promised that if you forced me to value it for her, she will give you the money for your clinic? Is that it?"

"Ah!" Marius said. "Thank God. There it is."

I saw it, too. It came from a little to our left—a flashing on and off of headlights. I could just see the dark shadow of a car turning off the main road and climbing a hill. Marius followed. The moon had disappeared again and it was very dark. All I knew was that we had driven on to a track that led over the hills, far beyond Deep Water Bay.

"Whose car is it that flashed at us?"

"The one that knows the way they went."

"They" . . . Father and then Theodora—the one to try to implicate me, the other to save me.

I had tried to stifle my fear by questioning. Now that fear had caught me by the throat and all I could do was sit coiled like a faulty spring that would break when released; every muscle aching with the effort, my mind not daring to penetrate beyond what I was quite certain I now knew.

Father's words, quoted by Lilo, burned in fiery letters in my mind. *I will not let you hurt my daughter.*

His daughter, Sarah Brent . . .

As soon as we turned off the main road we began to climb steeply. The track narrowed; bushes brushed the sides of the car, which dipped into potholes and rose again. Marius could no longer drive with speed. The moon came out fitfully to light up the wild, black country and then was swallowed up again by a cloud. In the moments when it was lost, the stars were clear and sharp, spangling the black sky. Away in the distance I could see the blaze of lights I took to be the offshore restaurant boats, and even further away, the glow of Hong Kong, where the neon lights must gleam without flickering so that they would not confuse the pilots landing their planes at Kai Tak airport.

Had it been daylight I might have recognized the hills over which we lurched and swayed. At night, the place had no identity. Once, when a front tire landed in a hole and Marius had to rev and coax the car out, we were stationary for a moment and I thought I heard the crash of sea waves, but it could have been the rustle of dry leaves against the side of the car. There had been a yellow fire warning recently because the Island's notorious humidity had dropped.

After what seemed an age of bumping over the stones and wiry grass, and all the while with a deliberate and keyed-up silence between us, I saw movement ahead and the outline of people and two cars. Marius stopped and I flung open the door of the Triumph. Our headlights shone on someone on the brow of the hill. The figure was crouched, arms pounding away at the earth and the stones. The people in the shadows seemed to be watching and waiting, but there was no sense of patience, of acceptance. The air was charged with a peculiar tension, a watching for some significant moment.

As Marius turned off the engine, the crouching man looked up. In the unnatural color of our headlights his face was greenish yellow as if a group of trees nearby found a leafy reflection in it. It was terrible and recognizable.

I cried, "Father!" and began to run toward him.

He saw me and shouted something. Someone held my arm. I wrenched myself free and stumbled on over the rough ground. A man's voice behind me said, "Leave it to us, please, Mrs. Brent."

I shook off the hand and raced on and my eyes didn't move from the figure ahead of us, etched against the black sky. Father straightened himself and began to run away from us, holding his elbows close to his sides as if he were carrying something.

"I asked you to leave this to us." The man was still close behind me. Without passing, I looked over my shoulder. I had been racing like a mad woman, but the Avenger, on my heels, wasn't even out of breath.

Seen from a distance, the brow of a hill is always deceptive. It took me a while to reach it, but my father outran me.

Then, quite suddenly, he turned.

And that was the moment for which those standing in the shadows some way behind me were waiting; powerful spotlights from cars swung into action.

"Go back, Sarah." It wasn't like Father's voice at all. It tore the air with desperation. "For God's sake, *go . . . back . . .*" He lifted his hands above his head and with a frantic swing hurled whatever it was he held away from him.

It fell without a sound onto the grass, and behind me a woman screamed. I didn't look to see who it was. I guessed, Theodora had to be there, but I didn't care. I shot forward as Father started to stagger down the hill. But before he was out of sight, he stumbled and fell. He lay still, and when I cried out, my voice seemed to echo round the hills.

As though his act was another signal, this time to people below, two men appeared from the other side of the hill and reached Father before I did.

"Leave him to me." I knelt by his side.

They pushed me away very firmly. "To *us*, if you please." They were very polite and very quiet as they knelt by his side. They carried blankets and a stretcher.

It was then that I saw an ambulance parked in the narrow road that snaked around the lower slope of the hill. It must have arrived in advance, waiting at the scene of some anticipated tragedy.

"Leave us. We must get him to hospital," one of the men said to me. Then I heard the word "oxygen." Arms lifted me to my feet and I fell shaking against whoever was behind me. Then, when I had the strength, I turned my head.

The Avenger said, "It's all right, Mrs. Brent. You can go to your father when he is safely in the hospital. But please, now, you must come with us. It is important."

"I don't care what you think is important. I have to go with my father. *What is wrong with him?*"

"I'm not a doctor," said the Avenger, "and for the time being, I think you had better leave him to the hospital authorities. He won't even know whether you are with him or not; he won't be asking for you . . . not yet."

I clung to a stunted tree near where my father had fallen until I saw the ambulance men carry him down and drive away.

Then the Avenger's hand became more firm on my arm, insisting. "The sooner all this is cleared up, the better. You must understand that and come with us."

I walked like someone in a nightmare back to the cars under the shadow of a line of camphor trees. Marius came and took my hand. I tried to break free, but he was too strong for me. As I looked back, I saw that the Avenger had gone to the place where Father had stood and picked something up. He joined us as Marius opened the car door.

"Look." The Avenger moved his hand so that a powerful light from one of the cars shone onto it. In his palm was part of a jade bar, badly broken and chipped, but with its tip ornamented in elaborately worked gold in the shape of a dragon's head. "This is what your father came to fetch."

I turned away from it.

"It is part of jade treasure taken from a newly excavated site in Shensi," he said.

"I don't care! *I don't care.* My father is ill and it could be that it's my fault. Because of that damned jade, because he wanted to save me. I am beginning to see. *I don't care about stolen treasure. My father . . .*" I broke off. The words that were alternately rushing and hiccuping out of me were lost as Marius shook me hard.

"Stop it, Sarah. You'll be taken to your father later. Now get in."

A sound almost obliterated his last words. I looked up. The white Rolls was lurching and racing away from us down the hill.

Marius pushed me unceremoniously into the car. "I'm sorry, but it's no use being gentle with someone on the verge of hysterics," he said.

"I'm not. But you talk of hysterics when my father has been taken ill and—"

"And it's your fault. All right. So you've said. Now stay where you are, because if you try to run away, I promise you, you won't get far."

Marius had closed the car door. It was immediately reopened. The Avenger was a bigger man than I thought, for as he leaned in to speak to me, he filled the space between me and the thick shadowy trees. "You may not know it, Mrs. Brent, but I owe you an apology. I thought that you had become caught up with the tomb robbers; I believed you were being used as a go-between. Your husband refused to accept that fact. It was his patient waiting and watching that exploded that part of my theory to pieces." Then he closed the door and turned away and I saw the trees again and the headlights of two cars parked to our right turning simultaneously and then speeding ahead of us down the track.

I said in a cracked voice to Marius, who had switched on the engine, "Who is . . . the Avenger?"

"I don't know. Who is he?"

"The man who just spoke to me."

"Oh, Robert Shui."

So now the Avenger had a name. The car jerked forward over a particularly large clump of stiff grass and I shot out of my seat. The sudden movement was like the opening of a valve. I began to cry quietly, without sobs. Tears poured out of my eyes, and the car's headlights took on all the colors of the rainbow.

XXI

I HAD NO IDEA of time or distance. I could no longer think straight, although I was faintly aware that Marius was driving very slowly. Presently, I took my hands away from my streaming face.

"That's better," he said and handed me his handkerchief. "Now wipe your face and we can talk."

I wiped my face and felt no better.

"You know now, don't you, that what your father did tonight was in order to save you from being forced to assess the value of that jade Robert showed you."

"Yes. My father must have found out about the robbery."

"Oh, no. He knew from the beginning." Marius was maneuvering the car over the dips and rises of the track.

"You mean he was watching out for stolen art treasures?"

"You could put it that way."

"I *do* put it that way. Marius, Father didn't just save me tonight. He saved you too. You and Theodora—"

"Your *father* and Theodora," Marius corrected and brushed against a hedge of gordonias, their leaves shining in the headlights.

"Why link them? I don't understand."

"How could you? People seldom suspect those they care for."

I swung round on him, accidentally jerking his arm. The car rolled slightly at the swing of the wheel. Theodora's voice was still in my mind asking how far I would go to protect someone I loved. "What are you trying to say?" My voice was a whisper, but Marius heard.

"Something," he said gently, "that might come more easily from me than from a stranger."

I was staring ahead of me again and the moonlight made me blink.

"Ch'i stole," Marius said, "but your father was the middleman, the contact between Ch'i and Theodora."

"I don't believe it."

"Of course you do, because you know I wouldn't lie about a thing like that."

"Then you don't know my father. He was never avaricious. He never envied those with more than he had."

"Oh, no. But he could resent and he could seize on a chance of revenge."

"Father—vengeful?"

"Yes. You always knew, Sarah, how he admired the formality and the culture of the China that is now gone. You were probably away when he was retired from government service."

"I was in England but I knew, of course, that Taiwan was to him the real China. I told you that, didn't I?"

"And since I've been here," Marius said, "I've learned more. Your father was becoming an embarrassment to the Hong Kong government. He wouldn't cooperate with any efforts at a fair relationship with Red China. In fact, he meddled; he made things difficult. In the end, the government had to let him go. He was made redundant."

"But he always seemed so happy yachting with his friends. Oh, no, this is crazy! There must be some other explanation. Marius, there *must* be."

"He made the best of it in front of you because he loved you. But Ch'i was one of a small gang of tomb robbers. He was traced from Shensi, where the looting took place, to Peking. Then the police lost the trail. They were certain, however, that Ch'i would find his way to Hong Kong, where the big buyers are—and Robert Shui was sent to look for him."

"From China?"

"Yes. Robert is a high-ranking police officer in Peking. He was concerned with the bribery racket that went on at one time among Chinese provincial authorities issuing visas to migrants. He decided that Ch'i could have got to Hong Kong by that method. When he first arrived, Ch'i probably lay low. Then when he thought it safe, he looked for someone who would help him sell the jades. Someone with rich connections who could put him in touch with a collector. He found such a person."

"Father?" I asked weakly.

"Yes. The underground world always has an ear and an eye open for illegal opportunities. The fact is that Ch'i heard that your father had lost his government job through his resentment of the new regime in China. Your father knew Theodora, and that is how it came about."

Half of my reeling thoughts were on Father. I wondered what they were doing to him; whether he had regained consciousness; whether he was asking for me . . .

"Do you realize, Sarah, that you were instrumental in the police finding Ch'i? Robert and his assistant were looking for him and guessed that he would be in hiding somewhere in the hills. Then while he was cruising along Wong Chuk Hang Road, Robert saw you. It struck him as odd that a well-dressed girl should be walking with a uniformed chauffeur down a rough track on an isolated hill-side. He watched you get into the Rolls. And you were carrying a parcel. He followed you back to Theodora's, and he added up the salient facts of what he had seen. A girl coming from a seemingly uninhabited hillside carrying a small parcel; a chauffeur and Rolls; the home of a very rich woman collector. After he had seen you enter the Pavilion he went back to the hill track. He climbed up and found the shack. There was a wheelchair, but no crippled user; there was also, in a drawer of a cabinet, a tiny chip of something which, when tested at police headquarters here, proved to be jade. Robert knew then that the trail had been found again."

I had missed seeing a chip somewhere on the belt. Jade broke easily . . .

"It was too dangerous for Ch'i to sell direct, for he must have known a search was on for him. There had to be someone to bridge the gap between the seller and the buyer. But having seen you carry-ing a small parcel from the hut to the car, Robert decided that you were the go-between. You worked for a very rich woman, you were ambitious—"

"You make it sound like an offense." For the moment I was jerked out of my stunned misery by indignation. "And how did this man, Robert Shui, know anything about my character?"

"I suppose I must have talked to him about you. In fact, I know I did."

"You—and the policeman?"

"We met through Dr. Hai at the Clinic. They were good friends. And so when Robert suspected you, he naturally came to me and told me. I knew, Sarah, that you would never cheat. But Robert believed he had the whole story neatly tied up. A valuable jade pass-ing from Ch'i to a rich and greedy collector. You, Sarah, bang in the middle, the connecting link. From that moment, you were watched."

"Who . . . killed . . . Ch'i?"

"We don't know yet. It could have been an accident. Ch'i had a great deal of money which he should have shared with the tomb rob-bers. When he decided to break away from the gang, he must have known that he was being watched on both sides, by the police and by the thieves, and he lost his head. In order to cut the land trail, he could have tried to swim to some isolated place, failed and drowned. But that's just my surmise, and it no longer really matters."

"Tonight," I said, "Theodora thought she was going to receive another stolen jade. And I was to be forced to value it. I know this because Lilo heard her quarreling with my father over me. He . . . was daring her to use me again. Marius, what he did tonight, in racing to destroy the jade before she could get it, was for my sake. He is in the hospital because he tried to stop Theodora from using me."

"Yes. But face facts, Sarah. He was part of the cause of the whole damn thing."

"The other jade, or jades, were hidden up there in the hills?"

"With Ch'i or your father always on guard near the spot. After all, they didn't have to hang around long. Theodora was only too avid to buy anything they could get hold of."

Father wandering the hills with his camera—a cover-up for watching that particular place. Father seeing the man, whom Ch'i could have warned him was a policeman, standing with someone else. Then taking a photograph of them with his telescopic lens fixed, finding that the other man was Marius. Nam Tsao telling me that Father was ill and he laughing her words away . . .

"Marius, did you know that Father was a sick man?"

"He didn't want anyone to tell you. But if you're living in fear of being caught trafficking in another country's stolen treasure, the penalty is grave. And suffering from very high blood pressure is one of the worst illnesses when you are under emotional strain."

"If I'd known, I'd have come out here and taken a job in Hong Kong to be near him. Oh, God—and now it's all too late." I sat quietly through the next few minutes of our journey. Then I asked, "How did Robert Shui know that tonight would be the time when Theodora had planned to buy another jade?"

"Because I told him."

"You?"

"Theodora telephoned me this morning. She was in a very excitable state, and I was certain that that was nothing to do with the party —she has been a hostess at too many to be tense about them. She told me that she would have to leave her party for some time on a piece of sudden and important business and asked me if I would act as host while she was away. I told her that her guests would probably want to know where she was. She said she couldn't tell me, and anyway, this was wholly her business. As it happened, I didn't act as host. I was waiting outside. But events moved too swiftly. She couldn't wait to look for me."

"She was going to fetch the jade? But why not have . . . have Father . . . bring it to her?"

"That's what she had planned. But your father obviously refused to do this because she had implicated you. And she anticipated trouble. But she must have been determined to get her treasure. Your father came to the Pavilion tonight without it, saw Theodora and threatened to go to where the jade was hidden and destroy it. That's when she went tearing after him and Robert and his men followed them."

"Why was the ambulance waiting there?"

"A precautionary measure. We were afraid someone was going to get hurt."

And it was Father.

I could think only of him nursing his grievances through all those years, and I ached with pity and love. My mother must have known of his resentment against the new China, but she had been loyal; whatever he had said to her, however deeply he felt, both she and he had kept it from me. I was their child, their "jeweled daughter," and a parent's bitterness must not mar my career.

Vignettes came to me out of the long past: myself, as a very small child, and Father sitting beside me on the night of the Chinese New Year watching the fireworks and saying, "You know, Sarah my darling, the story of Cinderella actually originated in China eighteen hundred years ago." Saying, "I want you to love the sea, as I do," and ducking me in the water and I, the child, shrieking with joy, pleasing him that I loved the warm China seas. He must often have been a happy man. He *had* to have been happy. The snake of revenge that was coiled inside must often have been overcome by his pleasure in his friends and his life. I wanted desperately to believe that; I wanted desperately to think of him as happy.

I was weeping again quietly—loud sobbings are for stormy emotions. Mine were deeper. Someone I loved had been involved in the thefts. Theodora was right. Only I had guessed the wrong person. Theodora had hoped that I would suspect Marius in order to bring about our final break. She must have known that I would never have suspected my own kindly, easygoing father.

"Your friend Robert Shui," I said, with as much indignation as I could produce through my stark misery, "your noble detective, or whatever you like to call him, tried to kill me. Was that an accepted part of having me watched?"

"Of course it wasn't."

"But he threw the knife at me when I disturbed him."

"Robert—an assassin?" We were driving so slowly that it was as if Marius dreaded to arrive. "Oh, no. You'll have to know him better than that before we leave Hong Kong."

"Then, if he didn't . . . ?"

"He couldn't be everywhere, watching every suspected person. He had two men assigned to help him, and the man who broke into the compound was overzealous. He thought he might be able to identify some of the stolen jades. But he entered the wrong pavilion, found you and threw the knife—not to kill you, but to scare you into not coming out of your hiding place and turning on the light and identifying him. He was taken off the case when he confessed to that bit of activity."

I remembered something else in that moment—the walk down the hillside with Father after we had discovered that Ch'i had fled. The light that had flashed momentarily in my eyes could have been, as I had thought at the time, from a car's windshield or a pair of field glasses . . . the Avenger pointing me out to a colleague. *"That is the woman. Take note of her."*

I had not been mistaken in my sense of having been watched, but it no longer mattered. My father would soon arrive at the hospital and I must be there.

The car had stopped. As if Marius knew my thoughts, he said, "I'll take you to see your father later. But this is one ordeal I'm afraid you'll have to go through."

Ah Baht, puzzled and inarticulate, opened the door for us. "Missy . . . Master . . . there are men with Mistress Lady. There is much trouble."

"It's all right, Ah Baht," Marius said and guided me along the dark paths.

When I had left, there was a party in full swing. I returned to blackness and emptiness under a temperamental moon which came and went with the onslaught of the rapid clouds.

Robert Shui or the police before him must have cleared the courts of guests, turned off the lights as if to turn the page on a festivity, silenced the musicians, dismissed the temporary staff.

Theodora sat quite still, in dead black among the glorious colors of her drawing room. Behind her the little pearl faces of the Chinese men on the great screen glinted in the lights; the scarlet lacquer cabinet and the golden Buddha seemed to defy her chosen mourning.

Three men stood near the door, and one was the Avenger. I realized then why Marius had driven so slowly. He had wanted the police to arrive first, and while we had cruised along Pokfulam Road and I had been blind with tears and despair, the police cars had raced on.

"Ah, so you're here at last." Theodora looked at me with burning eyes. "*Now*, you can tell these—gentlemen—that I have no intention of having my name as a collector disgraced. Tell them that your father was the one who sold me the jades and that *you* were involved. Tell them that he was too much of a coward to sell them direct to me and so called you in. Tell them how you valued the jade you knew was stolen and how you were preparing to value others."

Before I could speak, Marius, standing behind me, said, "It isn't any use, Theodora. You went after Sarah's father tonight because you knew he was going for the jade to change the hiding place or to destroy it—God knows which—because you had involved Sarah, and that was something he could not allow. But you went after him to get what you had to have—more possessions."

She sat upright, straight and defiant. "You know it all."

"Yes, I think I do."

His hand on my shoulder gave me confidence. I said to Theodora, "You spoke of someone I loved being involved with the jade. You didn't dare mention a name, but you knew that I would never suspect my father. How *could* I? He had lived here almost all his life; he was respected and . . . and . . . I thought, happy." My voice shook for a moment, then steadied again. "So that left Marius, which was exactly what you intended, wasn't it?"

She sat very still, her eyes blazing.

"You took a chance," I rushed on, "that I might go to Marius and make him tell me everything."

"Oh, no, you wouldn't have done that." She gave me a curious bitter half-smile. "You were too afraid it was true, Sarah. And when people are ridiculously in love, they don't want to hear the truth."

"So you lied," I cried to her. "Oh, how you lied—"

Suddenly she sprang alive. Her whole body quivered with the flame of her fury. "Did you think I wanted Marius as some temporary amusement? Another experience in life? Don't you know? I loved him. I . . . loved . . . him."

I laughed at her.

"I trusted you," she raged on, "and now you are trying to place the burden of guilt on me. And these, these men from China, believe you. Oh, God, are you all insane? But I'll win. I'll win, because I'll take you to court. You, who call yourselves the police, and Sarah, and—"

"You've lost." Marius's quiet voice stemmed the storm of her words. "Face it, Theodora. Just for once, you've lost."

She turned her hate onto him. "You came here and played a game with me. You pretended."

"Oh, yes, I pretended a certain friendship, but a remote one."

"Remote!" She spat the word at him. "You call it remote friendship when you let me plan to finance your clinic?"

Marius interrupted her again. "I wanted you to talk on and on. There was a chance that you might be too confident and too confiding. So I let you tell me about your impossible dreams."

"You gave me to understand—"

"I gave you to understand nothing. You persuaded yourself that what you wanted you only had to say, and you could have it. But I'm no woman's purchase, Theodora." I turned and met Marius's eyes. "You should have known that, too," he said to me.

"I should have, but I was frightened for you and for myself. Fear often makes one lose perspective."

Marius had moved a little away from me. "I came here in order to clear Sarah's name," he said. "It took time, but it happened tonight."

Theodora passed a hand over her forehead. Then she ripped off the black turban. Her hair fell loose about her shoulders, but it did not lessen the hard white shock of defeat. She thrust out a hand and her rings glittered. "Oh, go . . . just go . . . all of you."

Robert Shui said, "I am afraid I have a search warrant, Madame." He broke off as a man's voice cut through his words.

"What the hell is going on here?" Oliver strode into the room. "Why was everyone thrown out? Some of us have been waiting at the Mandarin for news of what's happening, and no one has let us know anything. I've come to see for myself."

The Avenger said, "This is a private matter, Mr. . . ."

"Farache. Oliver Farache."

"Ah, yes, of course. Lady Paradine's last husband," the Avenger said pleasantly. "Please, would you leave us?"

"What are we supposed to have done?" Oliver demanded. "Been drunk and disorderly? Well, we weren't."

Theodora said, "Oh, for God's sake, Oliver, shut up. The detective has told you. This is a private matter. Now go." She paused, turned and gave him a long, slow look. "But before you do, tell me. Why did you come to Hong Kong?"

"I'd been thinking about you again, Theo. Not that I had ever quite forgotten. There was always a chance that I could charm you back to me." His eyes narrowed with amusement. He seemed not to be aware of the silent solemnity and the tension around him. "Did you really think I was too proud to take your money? Dear Theo, I was after far more than you had placed in the bank for me."

"Remarriage?" she snapped at him. "As if I would!"

"Oh, it happens."

I looked at the Avenger and his two men standing by the door. There was no hustle. They were letting Theodora and Oliver have their moment of face-to-face conversation. After all, it was obvious that they were satisfied they had their quarry; the jade was some-where quite close and it would be in their hands soon.

Still, with supreme disregard of the police, Oliver said, "These weeks out here have proved that remarriage is impossible between us. In spite of your money, my dear, you are no man's catch. So thank you very much. I'll take the next best thing. I'll use that lump sum you paid into my banking account to restore Cadence Manor."

I stepped back, trying to find something to lean against, and felt Marius's arm like a prop against my shoulders.

Theodora saw my movement and turned hating eyes on me. "Did you have to have everything . . . *everything*?" She hammered her fists on her knees. "Youth—and Marius."

Robert Shui stepped into the middle of the room. "We are wasting time, Madame. The jade . . ."

"*No!*" But she knew she had lost.

Marius said, "Come, Sarah. We'll go to the hospital now."

Behind us, as we went through the door, I heard the rustle of Theodora's wide black silk trousers and I knew that she was moving to unlock the door of the strongroom and that the jade would return to China.

Oliver caught up with us in the hall. "We had a few good times to-gether, didn't we, Sarah? You must come to Cadence Manor after its restoration—with Theo's money."

It was Marius who said quietly, "Fine. We'll both come."

I never saw my father alive again. By the time we reached the hos-pital, he was dead. They told me what I knew to be the truth, that it had been speedy and merciful.

As we drove back down the avenue of camphor trees and past the doctors' cars, I seemed to be reeling in a kind of dark dream. When we reached the hills, I got out of the car and sat down by Marius's side on the moonlit grass. Dry-eyed and stunned, I felt like stone.

It was Marius who stirred me out of the shock. "We each worked
25 for the other, Sarah."

"*I* did. I love you." It was a stark explanation and it had to be said that way.

"You wouldn't have done what you did unless there was feeling. You'd have gone to the police with your suspicions, thinking, as you did, that you would be involving me and not caring. We were each other's defenders."

From below us, the junks were like huddled shadows on the satin water. Distance merged the illuminations of the crowded streets, making of the neon signs necklaces of gold and rings of emerald.

"There has been such emptiness," Marius said. "Oh, not in the work sense. In that, I've learned so much. I know now that everything useful has to be incorporated to reach nearer to perfection. What I studied in England must be merged with what I've learned here. And yet what I looked for was evading me. Until now."

I asked, with my face turned away from him, "And now?"

"I think we both made the same mistake. We are individuals, Sarah. For my part, I wanted to fit you into a pattern I had pre-made for you. And you didn't fit, as I didn't fit into your pattern."

"We should have been intelligent enough to have known all this while we were together."

"Oh, no. You see, it's very difficult to receive a truth about oneself. Only very rare people learn it in one moment of enlightenment. We aren't rare people. We had to learn piece by piece, painfully. I discovered how I felt about you only when you were suspected of something I knew you could never have done."

"If we start again, there's still a risk," I said.

"Of course. But there's no other way because we know we are important to one another."

We sat very quietly, close together, hands and shoulders touching. So we might fall and rise again, fall and rise. But we would do what we had to do to achieve the closeness we wanted. We would "learn" each other as one learns a strange language or a poem or the words of a song. Nothing was easy, even having to live with someone you loved.